I0536170

LEE PIPER

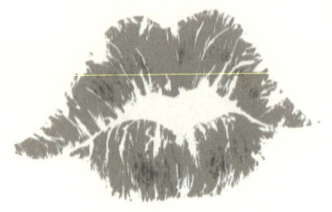

EVERNIGHT PUBLISHING ®

www.evernightpublishing.com

LEE PIPER

DEDICATION

This book is dedicated to my babies, all of them. Wherever you are, you're my world.

ACKNOWLEDGEMENTS

Rock My World could not have been possible without the support of the best husband a girl could ask for. Thank you for always turning the TV off when I wanted to read you the next section, for putting up with my non-stop dinner table chatter about fictional characters, and for living out your wedding vows every single day. I love you for it.

Thank you to my beautiful baby girls. You two are the reason why I get out of bed in the morning and have a smile on my face when I shut my eyes at night—regardless of how little sleep I get. I can only hope that your life ahead is full of the joy which unbridled imagination and creativity brings.

Chantal, I am forever grateful you always answered your phone, offered super helpful feedback and continuously reminded me to believe in myself. Mum, thank you for reading every word, for not washing my mouth out with soap and for still being able to look me in the eye afterwards.

A huge shout out to Cass and Tarina, your support, advice and (at times) inspiration was instrumental in the creation of this book—you girls rock. Rosie, arguably the hardest wording SSO in the southern hemisphere, you somehow managed to squeeze in time to read my manuscript so thank you, over and over again.

To Stephanie, my awesome editor. You taught me about the power of a well-positioned comma rather than semicolon and answered my myriad of questions with humor and grace. Apologies for the hundreds upon hundreds of 'ly' words, I'll try to cut down in future

In the months it took me to write this novel, not a day went by when I didn't blast Cog's kickass album, The New Normal. I have no doubt you boys would be shocked to hear it inspired a contemporary romance, but I can't thank you enough because whenever I listened to your music, I imagined it was Mondez playing.

There is no way in hell I'm going to forget about you, dear reader. Without your support, this would still be a pipe dream. If I was the hugging type, I would draw in each and every one of you for the biggest bear-hug in the history of the universe. Sadly, I'm not. But I hope the following words will suffice:

Together, we have created something beautiful. Thank you.

ROCK MY WORLD

A Mondez Novel, 1

Lee Piper

Copyright © 2017

Chapter One

Her new music was broken, loud and stern.
She was a shadow, both dark and light,
But she didn't give a fuck either way.
-MONDEZ, "Backbone"

I didn't want to be here.

Seriously.

I mean, if I made it through the night without catching an STD from standing in this godforsaken shit hole, it would be a miracle.

"Just come out for a couple of drinks," my best friend and housemate, Riley, had said. "It's Mondez's last live show for months. You'll have the time of your life, I promise," she'd declared. "I'll even introduce you to some of the guys in the band. Levi and Dominic are awesome, you'll love them."

I'd grimaced, but she chose to ignore me.

"C'mon, Grace, I'm sick of your excuses," she continued. "You never leave the house on weekends anymore. Living off a diet of whiskey, spite and Conan Doyle novels isn't healthy. We *have* to go."

So I gave in to her, just like always.

But, like everything else I'd tried since Dad's death, soon wished I hadn't.

"Hey, Dad." I stared down at the glossy gray slab of marble. A month had done little to dull the polished finish despite it being the middle of winter and drizzly as fuck.

Shivering, I wrapped my jacket tighter around my small frame, cursing the woolen beanie pulled low over my ears, which would no doubt start reeking of cat piss soon enough. Wool and water—what a crap combination. I shook my head.

"I brought you something." Holding the whiskey bottle high, I blatantly ignored the questioning glances of mourners walking past. "Knew you'd hate flowers so..." My voice trailed away. I miraculously unscrewed the bottle top despite numb fingers and poured a healthy amount over the young blades of grass already making their way through the sodden soil. To be honest, I half-wished the alcohol would burn them to a crisp before my eyes. Bastards. Didn't they know life had officially stopped four weeks ago? I sure as hell did.

After taking a healthy swallow, I put the whiskey lid back on and placed the bottle at my feet. Then, stepping forward, I brushed away a stray leaf from the top of the headstone, my fingers lingering on the cold surface.

"It's all gone to shit, Dad," I murmured. "Everything. Dylan's gone." I gave a wry smile. "Bet you're not surprised. You never did like him, did you?"

Silence.

"Yeah, well. Turns out, I've got rubbish taste in men." Taking a deep breath, I blurted, "Mum won't answer my calls." I paused. "Probably because I called her a selfish whore when she said she wouldn't come to

the funeral."

Silence.

"No great loss, I suppose. God knows she was a terrible mother to us growing up, so why the heck would she be any different fifteen years later?" Gritting my teeth, I continued. "And don't even get me started on that sister of mine. Even I didn't think she was capable of—"

I stopped. After clenching my hands into tight fists, it took several minutes of reciting every expletive known to mankind—in three languages—to finally relax them again.

When I finally had my emotions back under control, I tenderly traced the gold lettering of my father's name. "I need you, Dad." To my utter horror, my voice broke. I scrunched my eyes tightly closed demanding the tears to stop, the pain to stop, everything to just fucking stop. I was over it.

They didn't.

"I need you here, with me. Nothing makes sense anymore and I just ... I can't ... I hate it, Dad. Hate everything." Tears clouded my vision and streamed unchecked down my cheeks. "I'm angry all the time and I don't even know why. It's like I'm broken or something. I feel completely fucking broken."

Silence.

"Dad?"

Nothing.

"Daddy?"

Silence.

Hanging my head, I wept.

Since then, I'd developed this slight problem. It essentially stopped me from going out, socializing, and meeting new people. Hell, it basically prevented me from acting like a well-adjusted member of Australian society.

I called it Smart Mouth. Those on the receiving end of it, however, called it much, much worse. Let's just say, my head to mouth filter was defective. It always got me into trouble.

And I wanted a refund.

I wasn't always like this. I used to be nice, naïve, gullible. Whatever. I used to laugh until my belly ached and tears rolled down my cheeks. I would smile at strangers and hug those I cared about. I even loved with an open and trusting heart. But not anymore. Oh no, Dylan put a stop to that when he left me for she-who-must-not-be-named just after my father's death, one year ago. His timing was impeccable. And the betrayal hurt so much that I kinda shut down after that. Emotionally, I mean. It was just easier that way. Well, except when I was with Riley, of course. She was definitely an exception. Needless to say, everyone else I came into contact with considered me a … bitch. Let's be honest, there was really no other word to describe me.

When we first stepped inside the music venue—aptly named The Hole—I had to stop and allow my eyes to adjust to the darkness. I tried not to make a face at the combined smells of sweat, beer, and vomit, but failed miserably. Despite this, the heavy guitar riffs blasting through the speakers washed over me. They reverberated through my chest and down through my body. It wasn't unpleasant. But I made damn sure not to show this realization to Riley or I'd never hear the end of it. And I'd never have a Friday night to myself ever again.

To my far left, a mass of heaving and sweaty bodies, mostly males, swarmed the tiny raised stage where the lead vocalist of a rock band took up the mic and started belting out a song about love. Or was it treachery? It was hard to tell the difference when it sounded like he'd just had a fingernail removed with pliers. I shook my head, suddenly angry. Strands of raven black hair fell chaotically about my face from the impulsive movement.

What was I doing here? Why did I always let Riley talk me into things like this? I was going to sit on the couch at home in my pajamas and drink a really full glass of the best whiskey my teacher's wage could afford, or two, while reading *A Study in Scarlet* for God's sake. I hadn't read it in ages.

Riley noticed the irritation on my face and stopped for a moment, carefully considering me. She seemed to be weighing something important because her perfectly sculptured eyebrows drew together in deep concentration. It was probably relating to the likelihood of me inflicting bodily harm on someone in my current mood. Her face cleared, seeming confident in her decision. "You need a drink."

There was no way on God's green earth I was going to argue with that logic. So we pushed our way through the throng of people and managed to reach the bar relatively unscathed.

"Riley, you made it." A petite dark-haired bombshell working behind the bar beamed up at us when she recognized my friend. She reminded me of a pin-up girl from the forties, with vintage black eyeliner, porcelain skin and bright red lipstick.

"Wouldn't miss this one for the world, Brea." Riley smiled mischievously and gave her a quick wink.

I shook my head at Riley, bemused. "Now, I know this is all a ruse. You dragged me out tonight because you're interested in a guy."

"He's not just *some* guy," Riley gushed.

Oh God. I took a step back in bewilderment. She had it *bad*. Once I recovered my equilibrium, I replied sarcastically, "Really? How is this one any different to all

11

the rest, Riley? Does he have a chocolate flavored dick or something?"

"He's amazing, G," Riley responded, completely ignoring my wit. "He's talented and funny and clever and—"

"Sexy as hell, or so I've been told."

I spun around at the sound of a deep voice chuckling behind me and was greeted with a wall of muscle. I mean, the gray t-shirt barely contained the bulging broad chest. In all the right places.

I gulped.

My eyes instinctively traveled upwards. In front of me were wide shoulders, which looked like they could hold the weight of the world without breaking a sweat. There was a strong neck with a large, detailed hawk or some other bird of prey tattooed all over it. I could spy a chiseled jaw with sand colored stubble peeking through, straight white teeth peering out from behind a lopsided grin, and quite possibly the most kissable lips I'd ever seen.

Sweet God.

I inhaled sharply, immediately disturbed by my reaction.

My eyes, intent on making a fool out of me, continued upwards. Next was an aquiline nose and penetrating sky blue eyes that were openly laughing at what must have been my stellar impersonation of a stunned mullet. I didn't even get around to ogling his hair (short, light brown and tousled) because my intellect packed her bags and left the building. Clearly, I had no more need for her when this man was in my general vicinity because I literally lost the power of speech. There were no words.

Nope, none.

And I hated myself for it.

I'd never been one of those girls who fell apart at the sight of an attractive guy and I wasn't about to start now. *Get a freakin' grip, woman.*

"Like what you see?" The beautiful stranger lowered his voice so only I could hear it.

Thankfully, his arrogance helped kick start my Smart Mouth. "I've seen better."

Lie.

"No, you haven't."

Damn it.

He grinned.

"*Levi*," Riley shrieked, before rushing forward and throwing her arms around his neck. Her five-foot-nine frame seemed dwarfed in his embrace and I couldn't help but wonder what it would be like to be wrapped in those arms myself. Naked.

Once Riley disentangled herself and I shamefully recovered from my wayward thoughts, I muttered to her under my breath, "Why don't you just shove your tongue down his throat and get it over with?"

Riley turned, confused, and then stuck her tongue out at me instead.

Levi raised an eyebrow in surprise, his eyes darting between our muted exchange.

"Levi, this is Grace. Grace, Levi."

"*Drink*." I spun on my heel and leaned on the bar, desperately trying to make eye contact with the forties pin-up girl.

"Two beers and a whiskey. Thanks, Brea."

I jumped at Levi's unexpected voice, turned, and then scowled up at him.

"Who says I like beer?"

He lazily looked me up and down. I'm embarrassed to say my body loved every second of it. From my small tingling feet encased in black flats and

13

possibly standing in the contents of someone's stomach, to the tips of my chaotic hair, no doubt unruly from the heat generated by too many pressing bodies in this confined space—yeah, every part of me relished his gaze drinking me in. Damn it.

"Who says it's for you?" he countered, smirking at my flushed face.

"Jerk," I muttered, turning my back on his mocking gaze and conveniently becoming enthralled in the vocalist's rendition of a deflating bagpipe.

Brea appeared as though from nowhere. She expertly flicked the bottle tops off two beers, poured a healthy amount of whiskey into a short glass with ice, plonked them all on the bar, winked at Levi and said, "Here you are, hon, they're on the house," before moving to the far side of the bar to serve someone else.

Growling, I gave up on the drink idea and returned to Riley who had moved to a booth in a darkened alcove. She raised her eyebrows, questioningly.

"Don't even start." Grumpily, I slipped across the cracked leather seat, empty-handed. I even slammed my clutch down on the oaken table for dramatic effect. God, I hated how I reacted to Levi. I mean, I'd only just met the guy minutes before, and yes, he was ridiculously attractive. Absurdly so. But it was clear he was the man Riley was interested in *and* he was already grating on my very sober nerves.

"Here you are, ladies." Levi barely contained a laugh while handing a bottle of beer to Riley, who simpered before taking it. I rolled my eyes in exasperation at her antics. Seriously, could the woman be any more obvious? He then turned, and with a mischievous glint in his eyes, offered me the glass of whiskey. "Here kitten, you look like you need something stronger."

What did he just call me? But more importantly, how did he know I loved whiskey? Did I have '*Give me the strong stuff*' tattooed on my forehead or something? I gritted my teeth, annoyed at his accurate impertinence and his stupid, gorgeous smile, before snatching the glass from his outstretched hand.

And that's when it happened.

Our fingers accidentally touched. I kid you not, it was as if a thousand volt charge of electricity shot from the tips of his fingers, through my hand and up my arm. I froze. My eyes instinctively widened, my mouth popped open, and I stared at him in shock.

What. The. Fuck. Was. That?

Levi's gaze faltered briefly. A slight frown crossed his face before he smoothed his features, and sat next to Riley. "So, are you looking forward to seeing Mondez play?"

I honestly had no idea what her reply was. Instead, I sat dazed, staring down at my left hand after shakily unclasping it from the frosted glass and forcing it into my lap. *Strange*, I mused, slowly turning it over and discretely inspecting it like it was up for forensic testing. It still looked the same. My pale fingers and short, unpolished nails stared back at me, refusing to give an answer to my mother of all questions.

"Isn't that right, Grace?" Riley turned to me, her clear eyes expectant.

Shit.

I quickly tried to mask my confusion by noncommittally murmuring, "Mmm hmm."

"So you're looking forward to seeing Mondez too then, huh?" Levi's blue eyes taunted my clear lack of understanding.

Get it together, girl, I internally scolded myself. *So you touched fingers and felt something. Big freakin'*

15

deal. He probably feels that shit every day. I mean look at him, he's a walking Men's Health model for God's sake.

In a bid to recover what self-possession I had left, I decided on a forthright response to his question. To be fair it wasn't a far stretch for me. But if it meant I could wipe that smirk off his face, the one I was so not interested in kissing senseless despite what my racing heartbeat had to say, then so be it.

"No," I replied, glaring back at him.

Riley nudged me under the table with her knee but I ignored her.

"Have you heard any of their music?" he asked, his eyes now alight with laughter.

Snicker at me will you? Asshole.

"Nope."

"But you don't like them."

"Got it in one."

Suck on that.

"Um, G—" Riley began. But Levi cut her off with a quick wave of his hand.

"How would you know if you've never heard them play?" He smiled and leaned forward in his chair. "I bet when you see their lead singer up on stage, you'll want him to fuck you straight after the show."

I shifted in my seat, at once shamefully aware of my clenched thighs, yet unbelievably annoyed at the direction this conversation was heading. I didn't get dragged away from my favorite book to be set up as a fool by some conceited, rock-loving aficionado, sex god or not.

So, I pointedly looked from him to the lead vocalist currently on stage. The performer was looking and sounding remarkably similar to a donkey in heat, and I should know because I saw a documentary on them once. Freakin' hilarious. My eyes once again met Levi's and I flatly stated, "Let's just say I don't have high hopes if this lead singer is anything to go by."

Levi's gaze never left my face and his lips quirked up even higher, clearly enjoying some personal joke that I neither knew or cared about.

Okay. This was getting old and very, very annoying.

"Not every band is the same, kitten," he began.

I saw red.

"Don't fucking patronize me, Levi," I spat. "I know not every band is the same. I would just rather be at home doing what *I* want on a Friday night. In fact, I'd rather be doing *anything* else right now. So no, being forced to listen to some egotistical narcissist with a hard-on for the groupies in the front row is not at the top of my bucket list, okay?" I was almost panting with rage by the time I'd finished my tirade and had to take a long drink to calm down.

Crazy Grace needed to get back into her straight jacket.

Pronto.

Levi's eyes widened and his smile wavered slightly. But then he schooled his features and they turned into something different entirely. Dark, dangerous, sexy as hell. "That's quite a mouth you've got there, kitten."

Well. Maybe now he would leave me the hell alone and go torment some other sexually frustrated female. To my right, Riley held her head in her hands and I instantly wished those words back. However, before I could apologize to her, Levi leaned forward and rested his elbows on the table. He lowered his voice and murmured, "I like it."

I narrowed my eyes and was about to tell him where he could shove his uninvited innuendo, when I remembered Riley. I looked across at her. Jesus Christ,

I'd done it again. I really should trade in my Biggest Bitch Ever nomination for a Worst Best Friend of All Time award. I shifted closer to Riley's bent frame and hesitantly placed my hand on her back. "I'm so sorry—"

"C'mon, dickwad, we're on in five," boomed a loud voice directly in front of our booth. Riley and I instinctively looked up at the sound and I swore I heard a sharp intake of her breath. Standing at our table was a carbon copy of Levi. My eyes quickly moved from one to the other, making sure in my overly aroused state I wasn't seeing a mirage. Nope, he was real all right. Though on closer inspection, this new version was slightly shorter and if it was at all possible, stronger. My eyes flicked back to the original, confusion written all over my face.

"No worries, Dom." Levi's bottomless eyes never left mine. "Think I'm done here anyway." He tipped his head back and swallowed the rest of his beer before gracefully standing up. How a man of that height wasn't all awkward limbs and movements I'd never know. Giraffes would hide their head in shame. Levi placed the bottle on the table and smiled at Riley before turning to leave.

It wasn't until the two of them sauntered off in the general direction of the stage, at least a foot taller and half a person wider than everyone they passed, that I realized I had been holding my breath too. It escaped from my chest with a hiss and I was left feeling oddly deflated.

Shaking the sensation off, I turned to my best friend. She was currently hurting because of me and I felt awful. "Riley, I'm so sorry." My eyes were beseeching and my hand rubbed the small of her back, trying to soothe away the angst I caused her.

Again.

"I knew he was baiting me and I should have just left it. I'm a horrible, horrible friend. Please say you'll forgive me. I hate upsetting you."

She turned to face me, blue eyes serious. "Just once, *once,* G, I would like you not to insult someone I'd just introduced you to."

I nodded my head, emphatically agreeing with her. In all honesty, I hated the person I'd become. But it was like I couldn't turn my damn Bitch O' Meter off. If I knew where that pesky button was located, believe me, I would have used it.

My eyes clouded over and I looked down at my lap, blinking vigorously. I wasn't going to cry. I was not. Especially with the final sounds of an equine mating ritual in the background, courtesy of the vocalist still on stage. It was simply too ridiculous.

"Oh, G," Riley put her arm around me and squeezed tightly, "let's just both forget about it, okay? I know you have … issues. I know you can't always help being a complete cow to … well, anyone with a pulse really. But especially sexy guys."

I snorted.

"Come on," she chided playfully, "even you can't deny the fact that he's smokin' hot."

I shrugged my shoulders. "The whole Spanish Inquisition wasn't exactly a turn-on, Riley," I lied.

"No, I meant—" But her next words were drowned out because it was as if we were both body-slammed with a wall of sound.

Boom.

I had to shut my eyes in an attempt to take it all in. Whoa. The tight drums and dirty guitar riffs ricocheted off the walls and surrounded me with an all-encompassing sensation of sound.

I think my soul just wept.

Yes. This is what I need to hear, to feel, to help keep the anger at bay.

And then the vocals started.

I shuddered, and was pretty sure my panties went up in a ball of flames. It was as if the voice, which was simultaneously guttural yet beautiful, resonated with a secret need buried somewhere deep inside me. So deep, I didn't even know it existed until now. I opened my eyes, desperately searching for the stage. I needed to see the man responsible for this epiphany. And there he was.

Levi.

Fuck me. He was glorious.

I stopped breathing. It was overrated anyway. And after my verbal spat not ten minutes ago at the man currently servicing me with an aural orgasm, dying of shame suddenly felt like a viable option.

"Let's move closer." Riley dragged my dazed ass out of the booth and towards the stage where everyone in the place, excluding the bar staff, had migrated. We stood just behind the mosh pit, thankfully out of harm's way from flailing limbs and random head-butts, though still had an awesome view of the phenomenon currently on stage.

For the next hour, I stood as though in a trance. Levi's vocal range was out of this world. At times he was melodic and sweet, while at others he unleashed a verbal attack on my eardrums. Oh, and he played guitar. Holy mother of God, the combination was such a turn on. Hell, I bet if I handed him a sudoku right now, he'd have it done by the end of the chorus. He was that damn good.

I couldn't get enough of it.

Or of him.

His band consisted of Dom playing lead guitar, a stocky tattooed guy with an eyebrow ring on bass, and a mass of long brown hair with thrashing arms covered in ink worked the drums. All of them were equally talented. Freaks of nature, really. I mean, the music they created, a sensory smorgasbord of delectable individual parts, was a true credit to their distinctive abilities. Yet, when my eyes sought Levi again—and they always did—I felt lost and found in that same instant.

This wasn't good.

Chapter Two

It's my adversary,
I won't let it be,
'Cos this life's just ordinary.
-MONDEZ, "Nemesis"

The final bars of Mondez's closing song slowly faded into nothingness. There was complete and utter silence throughout The Hole for at least a minute. It was surreal. Guess I wasn't the only one struggling to come down from that experience after all.

And then it began.

The noise spread slowly at first, through the diehards in the front row, where it gradually gained momentum via the disheveled fans in the mosh pit, and finally reached a resounding peak when it hit us in the 'standing room only' section at the back. There was a deafening roar of screams, applause, whistles, stomping feet and, "Fuck yeahs". Despite the cacophony of blatant admiration generated by the crowd completely losing their minds, it just didn't seem enough to me. It almost felt like a token gesture, rather than what Mondez really deserved. But to be honest, even if the Rod Laver Arena was full to the brim with frenzied devotees shrieking earsplitting accolades, I still don't think that would have cut it either.

The band must have thought it was ample praise, however, because they self-consciously waved to the crowd. It seemed as though the experience of people enjoying their music was still new to them. It was kinda cute really. And, similar to a porcelain unicorn figurine being received as Christmas gift, they didn't quite know what to do with it. But, once their equipment was righted and safely stored in the greenroom just off stage, they slowly made their way through the crowd, being fist bumped and shoulder slapped by the guys and ravenously felt up by the girls. Bitches. Who did they think they were? Surely a handshake was ample acknowledgment of a job well done. Or even a nod in the band's general direction. Yeah, that would be way more appropriate.

Brea suddenly popped up next to Riley, interrupting my inner rant. She'd just finished her shift and was now officially ready to party. "Weren't they *amazing*?" Her dark eyes danced and she clapped her hands together in barely contained excitement. "They make me wild every damn time. What did you think, Riley?"

Riley shook her head. I don't think the power of speech or logical thought had returned to her just yet. It wouldn't be long though, and she'd be back to her usual communicative self. Of that, I was certain.

Brea continued, "They're gonna be *huge* one of these days and then watch out everyone, they'll take over."

The aforementioned conquerors of the world were making their way towards us, probably because we were standing in between them and the bar. Regardless, I stood like a deer in headlights, with eyes as big as saucepans, unable to move a muscle and absolutely terrified because of it. What I was scared of exactly, I couldn't say. The aftereffects of my embarrassing tongue-lashing towards Levi before the set perhaps? Or was it my panty-exploding epiphany during? It was hard to tell.

I was so fucking confused.

So I made the same decision that any other self-respecting woman would in this situation. I was going to hightail it the hell out of there and hide in the bathroom for a good twenty minutes. Okay, maybe thirty-five.

Forty minutes, tops.

"Riley, you'll be all right with Brea if I go grab some air outside, won't you?" I asked, before attempting to head in the opposite direction and giving the current track world record a red-hot go.

Before I could begin my athletic campaign though, Brea threw her tattooed arm around Riley. Because of their height difference, it landed somewhere in Riley's midsection, but the gesture of sisterly solidarity was duly noted and appreciated. "You betcha she will, won't you, lovely?" Brea turned to Riley. "In fact, you're looking mighty thirsty there, girl. Let's go get us some drinks, on the house of course. God, I love my job." And with surprising strength for someone so little, she dragged Riley away without a backward glance. Brea was like a barely contained wildfire, she engulfed those around her in a ball of pure energy. That much vitality in pint-sized form was simply too exhausting to watch.

I turned and ran.

Once safely inside the confines of the toilet cubicle—thankfully clean—I took a deep, steadying breath. And then unleashed Teacher Grace on my ass as though I was a Year Nine student with behavioral issues. My inner dialogue went something like this:

"*Right, Grace, here's what you're going to do. One: you are going to chill the fuck out, especially when it comes to biting the ridiculously sexy heads off certain band members.*"

"Whatever," I mumbled under my breath to my inner lecturer, pretending not to be completely petrified. "After tonight I'll probably never see him again anyway." Well, unless Riley managed to get his number. In which case, I would be in serious trouble because the thought of him with her, or any other woman for that matter, made my insides clench to the point of agony.

Teacher Grace snapped her fictitious fingers in front of my face, and my errant thoughts immediately stilled. She was a real badass. "*Two*," she said, while still glaring at me, "*stop lusting after the guy your best friend likes.*"

"Shit," I muttered angrily. It didn't matter how much Levi affected me, either on or off the stage. It didn't matter that since first meeting him, I had experienced a whirlwind of emotions completely foreign to me since Dylan left. Or during the twelve months we were together.

I simply would not hurt anyone like that.

"*After all*," Teacher Grace continued, her eyes narrowing, "*there was one person and one person only who stood by you through a very dark time, remember? She cooked your meals to make sure you still ate. She marked your essay drafts so you'd be up to date with your programming. She even bought you endless boxes of tissues, and not the inexpensive kind either. They were the ones with aloe vera in them so your skin wouldn't chafe.*"

"Riley," I breathed.

"*Exactly. Which brings me to point number three. Prioritize your friendship with that woman over your shrieking girly bits.*"

I slowly nodded my head as realization finally hit home. I knew what I had to do. Teacher Grace made a hell of a lot of sense despite being a complete ball breaker. Thankfully, she disappeared after her verbal reprimand and before I was diagnosed with multiple personality disorder.

Okay. I could do this. I was a strong, independent young woman who had complete control over my emotions, actions and Smart Mouth from here on in.

Yay me.

I slowly unlocked the cubicle door. Mercifully, the poster-clad bathroom was devoid of gossiping girls applying eye makeup even heavier than necessary, so I made my way over to the mirror. Intense green eyes, which looked far too big for the heart-shaped face and freckled nose, stared back at me. The usually pale skin was flushed about the cheeks and the black hair, which had long since given up on adhering to any fashionable style, hung in loose waves to her shoulders.

She looked completely overwhelmed.

I quickly washed my hands and face, trying to find some semblance of normality in doing such a mundane task, and felt slightly calmer. Once finished, I looked at the girl in the mirror again and attempted a smile. "You've got this," I said out loud. The unexpected noise echoed in the dark room, amplifying the emptiness of the space. With newfound resolve courtesy of Teacher Grace, I pushed my shoulders back, tipped my chin up and strode towards the exit.

It didn't take long to locate Riley again. She was in the same booth as before, sandwiched between Dom and Brea and they were all laughing hysterically at something on her phone. Riley looked drunk and I marveled at the vast array of shot glasses in front of them. For a moment, I began to wonder where the other band members were, but then stopped myself short. Surely being faced with just one of them was more than enough for my frayed temper right now. I sighed. Great, it looked like I was designated driver then. This night was just getting better and better. Now how was I supposed to ignore my screaming hormones and maintain silence on all things frustrating, when I couldn't even drown in the blessed relief of a drunken stupor?

Head down and feeling mighty sorry for myself, I turned and walked towards the bar. Riley was going to need a liter of water if I had any chance of moving her from that booth to the passenger seat of her car. Which was why I didn't notice Levi until I literally walked into him, spilling the jug of water he held in his hands. It dripped all down the front of his t-shirt, completely saturating him. *Shit fuck shit.* I looked up at him, my mouth a perfect O.

"Guess I'll be needing another pitcher then." He looked somewhat annoyed at my clumsiness.

"Here…" I grabbed a pile of napkins off a table nearby. The people sitting there were smirking behind their light beers and I bit my tongue to hold back what I really thought of their pathetic choice in alcoholic beverages. Amateurs. After turning back to Levi, I proceeded to pat him dry, my tongue poking out the corner of my mouth. It was a habit I'd developed in primary school which reared its ugly head whenever I concentrated ridiculously hard on something. Embarrassingly, I hadn't yet managed to break it.

My hands surreptitiously moved over his well-formed pecs. Honestly, the man was soaked.

"Um, Grace?"

And down over his tightly sculptured abs. Poor guy, he was completely drenched.

"Grace."

Until I reached the hallowed V that led tantalizingly downwards to the top button of his black jeans. I mean, I didn't want the guy to catch a cold after all.

"*Grace.*" Levi placed his fingers under my chin, which gave me yet another electric shock, but this time in the nether regions. I almost groaned out loud on the spot. He lifted my face to meet his hooded expression. "If you're going any lower, kitten, we're gonna need a private room." There was a wicked glint in his eyes.

I stepped back, horrified at my actions. God, I was no better than one of his female fans giving him a congratulatory groping session after the show. *Bad hands*, I scolded myself. *Bad, bad, hands. What were you thinking?* Guess that was the problem really. Where Levi was concerned, I wasn't.

Stifled laughter erupted from the nearby table and it took all of my newfound self-control not to grab the now empty jug out of Levi's hands and hurl it at their heads. My face flushed. Soon I'd be a walking stoplight. Hell, I'd already managed to halt traffic.

Levi didn't seem at all affected by our sniggering audience or the beads of water still cascading down his front, creating a pool at his feet. Instead, he jerked his head in the direction of the bar before walking away. "C'mon."

I trailed after him, dragging my feet like I was on my way to detention or something. How was I ever going to ignore my raging hormones and prioritize Riley's friendship when I was forced into a situation where it was just him and me? Well him, me, and the remaining hundred or so patrons of The Hole, but you get my point. Once again, I took a deep breath—I'd be a freakin' meditation expert by the time this night was through—and reminded myself of what I had to lose if I ever again acted on my rampaging impulses. Riley was my best friend. Levi was the guy she was interested in.

End of story.

"So, are you having a good night?" Levi asked, once I reached the bar.

"Really? That's the best you can do?" I rolled my eyes. "All the ladies must flock to your bed with that one-liner."

"I don't need pickup lines to fuck women, kitten."

"You really believe that, don't you?" I retorted,

before internally kicking myself. *No insults, Grace, you promised.*

Levi smiled down at me, no doubt amused at my internal struggle. Yep, there was no doubt about it. The man was gorgeous. Not that I cared, of course.

"You look like you need a drink."

"Funnily enough, you're not the first person to make that observation tonight."

"So what'll you have? Another whiskey?" He smiled again and even though my knees felt slightly shaky, I also managed to wince at the memory of my verbal diarrhea.

"Water."

"Water?"

"Water. I am officially the designated driver." I let out a deep sigh.

Levi nodded his head sympathetically. His eyes softened as he looked down at me and I could almost see myself in their reflection. This whole turning over a new leaf thing was fucking marvelous.

I blinked and looked away.

"Water it is then." He grabbed another full pitcher from the smiling barman who tactfully chose to ignore the sopping wet t-shirt situation proudly on display in front of him, while I collected enough glasses for everyone at our table. A dark part of me desperately wished it was somehow full to the brim with vodka.

Straight vodka.

When we reached the booth again, Levi dumped the jug in the center of the table and sat down opposite his brother. He gracefully scooted along the leather seat, leaving space next to him free for me.

I must not jump his bones.

I must not jump his bones.

This became my new meditative mantra as I

29

awkwardly settled in next to him, trying to keep as much space as possible between his muscular thigh and my somewhat trembling one.

"What happened to you?" Dom asked Levi, pointedly staring at the damp t-shirt that was slicked against his sculpted chest and rock hard stomach. I tore my eyes away and prayed fervently to the gods of chastity belts and all things celibate to get me through tonight without being arrested for indecent exposure.

In order to distract myself, I instead focused on Dom. Even with the slightly drunken slur, he was no doubt a very attractive man. His hair was the same sandy brown as Levi's. His eyes were a similar shade of blue, though slightly out of focus. However, he was built more strongly, with rippled muscles growing in places I didn't even know existed and bulging agreeably in places I did. Though when I looked at him, and I mean *really* looked at him, I didn't get the same electric shocks, currents or any other power-driven experiences that I did when I was with Levi.

Interesting.

Levi caught my eye and smiled down at me. Once again, I felt the beginnings of another electrical phenomenon coming on. It was exhausting. If he kept this up for the rest of the night, I'd be able to power the entire west coast for a whole month. And then some.

He then looked back across to his brother. "Grace happened. That's what."

I shrank down in my seat, beyond embarrassed, as three pairs of eyes turned to me in collective astonishment. Okay, so two pairs were astonished. One pair was more resigned than anything else.

"Grace, you didn't," Riley began. She was swaying slightly.

"What?"

"You were going to be good, remember?" she continued, swaying even farther to one side. Dom would have to prop her up soon if she wasn't careful.

"Oh, she was good," Levi murmured. "She was very, very good. One might even say, thorough."

"Did you guys fuck or something?"

Four pairs of eyes simultaneously turned to Brea. She simply threw back another shot and slammed the empty glass back down onto the table as though discussing the weather.

I choked back a laugh. I was aiming for cool and dismissive but it came off as manic and hysterical instead. Though I had to give it to Brea, the girl was forward and mighty perceptive too if my intentions at the time were anything to go by.

"Not exactly."

What?

I turned and glared at Levi but his smile just grew wider. Right, so I was on my own with this one then. "For Christ's sake, of course we didn't fuck, Brea. Jesus," I spat out, way more incoherently than I had originally intended.

"Pity, looks like you could both use a decent lay. I'm getting another round. Be back in a bit." She shrugged her shoulders and bounded out of the booth.

We were all silent for a minute.

Awkward.

"So, it was an accident then? I mean, with the water and everything," Riley continued.

"Of course it was an accident, Riley. What do you take me for? Some kind of psycho who loiters around full pitchers of water ready to drench unsuspecting passersby?"

Levi chuckled at my ill-timed wit and I had to sit on my hands. Suddenly, the temptation to throttle him

31

proved all-consuming. Maybe I wouldn't get hauled in for indecent exposure tonight, maybe it would be first-degree murder instead.

Riley slowly nodded, though it came off a bit wishy-washy and she ended up tilting to an alarming degree until she landed, cushioned against Dom's monstrous shoulder. I could have sworn a small sigh escaped her.

I quickly peeked at Levi, interested to see what his reaction would be. After all, my best friend was virtually comatose against his brother and she'd been as subtle as a mallet to the face with her intentions towards Levi before the set. But his expression remained serene as he poured everyone a glass of water. Dom looked dubiously down at his cup, as though it were going to sprout legs and walk straight off the table, taking his drunken night along with it. But Riley simply smiled and took a sip. Good, just four more glasses like it and we might actually manage to get the hell out of here—away from the man seated next to me who was doing my head in. My heart suddenly lurched at the thought of no longer seeing Levi. Traitor. Who needed a heart anyway? I mean, all they did was expose themselves and get trampled on in the process.

Levi suddenly turned and caught me looking at him. I flushed, wanting to shift my gaze away but something in his penetrating eyes held me in place. Whoa. And he just kept staring.

And staring.

And staring.

The room around me and all of the people in it slowly receded into nothingness. We were the only two people left in existence. My breath caught as his eyes then leisurely traveled over my face, my hair, and slid down to my emerald green silk top. They took in my small breasts and then unhurriedly moved back up again before finally resting on my exposed shoulder. I suppressed a shudder. Just.

If he didn't say something soon, and preferably about something as inane as the tax laws in Berlin, my new meditative mantra of *I must not jump his bones* would fly right out the window. Who was I kidding? I'd hurl the fucker out and then gleefully bolt the window shut so he could never get back in again. There might even be a happy dance thrown in for good measure.

I cleared my throat, and with the intelligence of a highly observant toddler, said the first thing that came into my head. "So what's with the bird?"

Levi kept staring at my shoulder. His pupils had dilated slightly and I was reigning in every ounce of my self-control so as not to react to that mouthwatering fact.

"The bird on your neck. The tattoo."

His eyes flicked back to my face but he said nothing and I *so* didn't notice that his breathing was heavier than it was five minutes ago.

"Well?" So help me God, if the man didn't say something in the next five seconds, I'd take him right here in this booth.

He smiled dangerously, plainly sensing my desperation for a distraction and drawled, "It's a raven, kitten."

Right. Some material to work with. Thank fuck. "So you're an Edgar Allen Poe fan then?"

Levi raised his eyebrows in surprise and I gritted my teeth. Did he really think I was that stupid? I grew up on the classics. Of course, I'd read *The Raven*, it was one of Poe's most famous poems.

"You know of him?"

"Uh, yeah. I teach a gothic poetry unit to my Year Tens every year." Okay, so I may have only been out of

33

university for *one* year and the term 'teaching' could be loosely interpreted as showing my students an episode from *The Simpsons* which featured a nifty version of the poem. But he didn't need to know that.

He looked even more surprised at my last statement and if he wasn't careful, those sexy eyebrows of his would disappear right off his heavenly face. "So you're a teacher then." It was more of a statement than a question.

"Yep."

"Huh."

What the hell was that supposed to mean? Contrary to popular belief, I was actually really good at my job. I knew the content well, didn't baby my students, and I pushed them beyond their capabilities. Granted, I might have momentarily 'broken' a few in the process, but they were the spoon fed asswipes who needed to stand up on their own for once. So I decided, and not unexpectedly, that the best form of defense to his monosyllabic inference was offense. "So what do you do then, Raven Boy?"

Smooth.

"I play music. And study."

"Study what?"

"Education. Secondary education."

"Huh."

I had nothing. Not for that unforeseen development anyway.

"*Shots*," Brea shouted before ceremoniously plonking five small glasses down in the middle of the table.

The spell was broken. Right. Of course. Other people existed too. Once again I leaned back in my chair. I'd like to say that it was with relief, but I'd be lying. I didn't even realize until then that my body had instinctively gravitated towards Levi's while we were talking. And while he was virtually eye-fucking me. I quickly pushed back the memory with a barely repressed moan.

"Shhh," Dom stage whispered. We all glanced over at him and there was Riley, passed out on his shoulder. She had one mighty contented smile plastered all over her face.

Maybe she got so drunk that she mistook one brother for the other? Alcohol did strange things to people. Hell, with the amount she'd ingested, in the right light and from a certain angle, even Brea could be mistaken for one of them. But more importantly, how the hell had I managed to get so engrossed in a conversation with Levi that I didn't even realize my best friend had lost consciousness right in front of me? I really needed to work on my acceptance speech for the Worst Best Friend of All Time award, I had so much damn material.

"I think that's our cue to leave," I said. "Somehow…" My voice trailed away as I was suddenly perplexed by how I was going to get her from the booth to the car without inflicting grievous bodily harm on either one of us. Not that I didn't deserve it of course. Maybe a bit of self-mortification, Benedictine monk style, was exactly what I needed to get my head out of my own ass. I scooted out of the booth as gracefully as my skinny black jeans would allow and Levi followed, standing up next to me.

"I've got it." In one fluid motion, he slid Riley out the booth and scooped her up into his arms. Fucking hell, it felt like I'd walked in on him carrying her over the threshold or something. Bile suddenly rose in my throat.

"But the *shots*…" Brea shrugged her shoulders and turned to Dom. "Fuck it. More for us then."

Dom's face brightened considerably at that. He

mumbled a distracted, "Later," before downing a shot.

I rolled my eyes. Honestly, the guy could be bought easier than a whore with a crack addiction.

"Let's get this girl home," Levi said, turning and heading towards the exit with Riley nestled comfortably in his arms. *I'm totally okay with this*, I told myself, following their retreating forms.

Really I am.

Once standing in front of Riley's car, with the cool sea breeze from the Indian Ocean washing over my heated skin, I encountered my first problem. "Um, the keys," I mumbled. It was now Levi's turn to roll his eyes as I fished around in my clutch for what felt like an eternity. Riley had driven her brand new cobalt something or other to The Hole, which meant that I carried her keys. It was a ritual we had started years ago. If she provided transportation, I was the handbag. Literally. Finally, I fished them out, dangling the ring triumphantly on my index finger.

But when I looked up, Levi had already opened the passenger door and was in the process of gently placing Riley on the seat.

"Wha—How?" I stammered, before narrowing my eyes at him. I was about to unleash Teacher Grace on his fine ass with a serious lecture about breaking and entering.

Levi clicked the seatbelt in place and straightened up, laughing at me over the hood. "Grace, this car was built after 2014, it has keyless entry."

"I knew that." Even mumbling, I was a terrible liar.

Levi leisurely made his way around the boot of the car and stood not even a foot away from me.

My breath hitched. Despite the mild night, goose bumps appeared and I subconsciously rubbed my arms with my hands to warm them.

"I'll follow you home."

Like hell you will, my inner voice retorted. But I remained mute. I blamed the whole warm/cold phenomenon my body was currently trying to rectify. The aftereffects seemed to have turned my vocal responses to mush.

Levi continued, "Since you didn't know how to get into the car, I'm guessing it's Riley's. In which case you've probably never driven it either and that could be dangerous."

"I know how to drive."

He just raised an eyebrow. The bastard. Levi slowly stepped towards me with that mocking look in his eyes. Seriously, I didn't know whether to punch the guy or kiss him. At this point, punching him would be way more satisfying.

When our toes were almost touching, he leaned down and murmured in my ear, before pulling back slightly. "Really?"

I tilted my chin up at him in defiance—Christ he was tall—and glared into his absurdly attractive face. "I know how to drive," I repeated, ignoring the warmth gradually spreading through my body from the heat generated from his eyes.

He leaned infinitely closer, his lips hovering just above mine. I could smell his minty breath, the remnants of his spicy cologne, and a stronger, muskier scent which must have been pure Levi. I needed to bottle and sell that shit—people would go nuts for it.

My mouth was suddenly parched, where was a pitcher of water when I needed one? Maybe I could suck on his t-shirt for a while to rehydrate. God knows I had to do something other than stare nonsensically up at the guy. *C'mon Grace, think. Do something. Anything.* I swallowed with some effort—okay, it was a start at least—before licking my lips. Levi's gaze dropped to my mouth and I had to do everything in my power not to reach out, pull his face to mine, and kiss him until he forgot his own name.

He moved his left hand towards me and it skimmed across my hip before reaching around behind my ass. "Prove it," he murmured.

I gasped out loud because in one fluid movement he flicked open the door handle and I shot forward into his chest. Levi wrapped his right arm around my waist, taking me with him when he stepped back. He pulled me to his side and held me against his body, opening the car door with his left hand.

"*What the fuck?*"

I could hear Levi chuckling softly at my startled expletive.

It took me a moment or two, or ten, to get my head together. And then I got angry. *What the hell am I doing?* Time and time again this guy had played me for a fool tonight and I was making it so goddamn easy for him. What the hell happened to the impenetrable exterior I carefully built around myself after Dylan left? The one that held me together, defended my hollow insides and barricaded me from these egotistical jerks. Especially the ones who loved watching women fall to pieces in front of them, just so they could laugh at the disintegrated parts which were then draped at their feet. There was no way I was going to let any man effect me like that. Not Levi—not ever again.

No. Fucking. Way.

So I stomped to the car, threw my purse down by Riley's feet and dumped myself onto the plush leather seat. Granted, it wasn't my most graceful of moments but it was the best I could do under the circumstances. I had to get away from him, *now*. Which was when I encountered problem number two.

How to start the flippin' car.

I groaned inwardly. In front of me were countless lights, switches, knobs and screens. *Surely you'd need a pilot's license for this thing?* I searched endlessly for somewhere to insert the key but couldn't find a spot that even vaguely resembled the ignition. So, I resorted to imagining Levi's face was the steering wheel and repeatedly pummeled my fist into it instead.

Next to me, Riley shifted in her seat and then began to snore. I glanced over at her and was pretty sure I could see drool dribbling out the corner of her mouth, so there was no chance of any help from that quarter.

Fuck my life.

"Need a hand, kitten?" Levi crouched next to me and I internally bitch slapped myself for not slamming the door shut once I sat down. And for not locking it too, if I only knew where the damned locks were in this thing.

"I don't need anything from you, Levi," I spat.

"C'mon, don't be like that." He leaned across me intending to point something out, "Look, here's where you—"

But I didn't let him finish. Instead, I turned, glared at him and growled out, "If you put your hand anywhere near me again, with God as my witness, I will rip that arm out your socket and stab you in the balls with it. Understood?"

Levi rocked back on his heels, surprised by my vehemence and regarded me for a moment before murmuring, "Who did this to you, Grace?"

I faltered at his swift change in subject and looked away before hastily trying to shove the key into any empty orifice I could find. There was no way I was going to have that conversation with him. Well, sure as hell not sober anyway. "Just leave me alone," I muttered. Thankfully, the key suddenly fit, kind of, in one of the slots I had just jammed it into.

In my elation, I almost missed him mumble, "Wish I could."

But of course my raging hormones seemed to have supersonic hearing and my eyes flew to his unreadable expression "Don't mess with me, Levi. I meant what I said—leave me alone." I pushed the key in deeper, ecstatic at the thought of finally getting away from him and all this confusion.

"Kitten?"

"For fuck's sake, *what*?"

"You've put the key in the cigarette lighter."

My eyes snapped to the key that was currently on the verge of being roasted alive, and I yelped before snatching it out. Levi's now familiar, but still freakin' annoying, chuckle echoed next to me and I seriously considered ramming the molten piece of metal deep into his eye socket.

He ignored my protestations and leaned across me, pushing a button situated just behind the left-hand side of the steering wheel. At once, the car purred to life. "Push button start," he deadpanned.

I narrowed my eyes at him.

"Now, just give me a minute while I go get my car and then I'll follow you home. Not that I think you don't know what you're doing or anything." He winked, stood up, and carefully closed the door before striding off.

For as long as I could draw breath, there was no damn way I'd let him do that. So before Levi could get too far, I threw the car into reverse and pumped the accelerator, almost colliding with him on the way. Smiling gleefully, I then slammed the car into drive and rocketed out of the car park, gravel flying in all directions from beneath the vehicle's screeching tires. As I glanced in the review mirror, I caught sight of Levi's astonished expression. It was pure bliss. I couldn't help myself, I laughed the whole way home.

Chapter Three

Sick of these games we're playing,
Pretending that you don't know.
Confusion's around me,
Hold on tight and then let go.
-MONDEZ, "Pretenses"

Several hours later, I finally flopped down onto my bed, spread eagle style. Completely exhausted. My euphoric high after leaving Levi in a cloud of dust was sadly short lived. Once I pulled into Riley's parking bay at the base of our small apartment block, I realized that I had to carry her up two flights of stairs all on my own. Transferring a comatose woman from her car to her bed took mammoth effort and I was pretty sure my back and I were no longer on speaking terms. Don't even get me started on my calves and thighs—let's just say we had words.

Once I managed to plop Riley onto her bed, I removed her shoes and clothes before wrangling on some of her exorbitantly overpriced-for-the-amount-of-material-given-in-return silk pajamas. I then threw her sea green Egyptian cotton sheet over her and returned a couple of minutes later with the largest glass of water I could find and some aspirin.

She'd feel like crap in the morning.

After that I had a quick shower to scrub off the many layers of blood, sweat, and tears caused by lugging her drunk ass upstairs. I then shrugged on my own PJs before collapsing into bed. Throughout it all, I didn't once think about a pair of mocking blue eyes. Honest to God, I didn't.

I sighed and checked the time on my phone. It was past two in the morning. I slammed it back onto the bedside table in disgust. Despite my limbs feeling like dead weights and my back hurling abuse at me, I was too wired to sleep. So instead, I let the events of the night tick over in my head. Over and over again.

And that's when the guilt kicked in.

It was strange, because not only did I obviously feel guilty for being shamefully attracted to Levi, but I also felt guilty for acting like a complete and utter bitch around him too. I mean, first, there was my insulting rant where I pretty much called him an arrogant prick to his face. Then, there was the embarrassing groping session after spilling that jug of water on him, and finally, was my blatant refusal of his help in getting Riley safely home.

I sighed.

Even worse, was that during Mondez's set I'd never felt so—completely clichéd I know, but true nonetheless—*alive*. It was as though all of the anger I had been carrying around within me, safely stored in my biting comments and snide wit, dissipated completely. For the short time he was on stage I felt … centered. Whole even. Obviously, it wasn't his intent when performing to make me feel these things, I wasn't that much of a deluded fool. But the fact remained—he did. Levi was the one person who reminded me of what it was like to be content. And this emotion had long been alien to me since Dylan walked out.

It was official. I was a horrible person.

Suddenly, the notification screen on my phone lit up.

Levi: **Hey it's Levi. U make it home okay?**

Me: **How'd you get my number?**

Levi: **Riley left her phone behind. She needs a stronger password, even Dom figured it out**

Me: **You stalk people now? Is that because**

your pick up lines are so shit?

Levi: **Can't figure out if ur a kitten or a wildcat**

Me: **I'm not your concern either way.**

Levi: **Right. Seeya round then**

Me: **Look, I'm sorry.**

Levi: **For what?**

Me: **Everything. My Smart Mouth mostly.**

Levi: **Can't get enough of ur smart mouth. It's driving me crazy**

Me: **Don't say that.**

Levi: **I'm an egotistical narcissist remember? I can say whatever the hell I want**

Me: **Goodnight.**

Levi: **Was it?**

Me: **?**

Levi: **A good night?**

Me: **Verbal abuse, pitchers of water & exhaust fumes to the face aside … Yeah, I guess it was.**

Levi: ☺

My groggy mind slowly registered the sounds of thunder outside. Strange, I thought to myself amidst a sleepy haze, I could have sworn it was going to be fine all weekend. The thunder clapped again and my eyes popped open. Unless the storm was centered directly over our front door, then someone was no doubt pissing the neighbors off something terrible with all of that banging. I fought off the covers and padded quickly towards the door. As I moved past Riley's bedroom, I could hear her faint snores, so thankfully she hadn't been disturbed by the noise. I decided to find out what the hell they wanted and then send them on their merry way. But as I opened the door a fraction and peeked through the gap, my breath suddenly caught.

Holy shit.

It was Levi.

"Um…" I didn't think it was possible, but in the light of day he was even more beautiful than I remembered.

"Afternoon, kitten."

"Afternoon? How'd…" My train of thought faded into nothingness at the sight of his lopsided grin. *Get it together, girl.* I internally shook myself. Hopefully, my mental scolding would help me put more than two words together into some semblance of a normal conversation with the man.

"Well, after Brea told me where you guys lived, I drove on over and then bumped into this really nice old lady downstairs."

"Mrs. Jenkinson."

"Yeah, that's the one. She let me know which apartment was yours, but man, can she talk."

I was going to kill her.

"You gonna let me in?"

"Oh, right. Sure." My ability to function as a rational human being hadn't quite kicked in yet despite my firm talking-to just moments before. I blamed the red t-shirt hugging his colossal chest in a way that made my eyes water, and the ripped black jeans hanging delectably off his hips. As I opened the door and he stepped past me, I *so* didn't breathe in the scent of him.

That'd just be weird.

"Nice place." He slowly took in our cramped living room. There was a black leather three-seater couch, with a matching coffee table and TV unit that belonged to Riley. The walls displayed various pieces of designer artwork, which discretely matched the throw cushions on said couch. Let's be honest, there was no way in hell they were mine either. Needless to say, she owned everything in our communal living spaces.

Levi turned around. "It's a bit warm though." He

stopped abruptly, his eyes raking my body from head to toe.

I shifted uncomfortably beneath his gaze and futilely ran fingers through my no doubt unruly hair, which hung loose to my shoulders. I really hoped I wasn't impersonating a mad scientist here.

"You're a Hitchcock fan, huh?"

I peered down at my faded black t-shirt with a white cartoon profile of the man himself printed on the front. When I'd ordered it online I was sure I'd asked for a small, but when the shirt arrived it was most definitely a large. I honestly couldn't be bothered returning the damn thing, so it was relegated to the sleeping attire department of my lackluster wardrobe instead. The material was ridiculously soft and comfortable, despite the fact the hem only just covered my...

And that's when the panic set in.

"I'll just go grab some shorts."

"Please, not on my account."

I could hear his chuckle follow me as I raced down the hallway.

Once in my room I quickly scanned its contents, desperately hoping that somewhere in this mess I had some clean clothes to throw on. Both bedside tables were covered in books, while the floor was awash with yoga pants, tank tops and shorts. Ironically, there was also a vast array of empty coat hangers in the wooden wardrobe pushed up against the western wall. I raced around the other side of my queen-sized bed, begging for a miracle and *hallelujah*. A small pile of clean clothes was waiting, no doubt lovingly put there by Riley last weekend. So I shimmied into some old cutoff denim shorts, popped a strapless bra on and pulled a light blue tank over my head. To be frank, I really didn't need the bra. My small breasts were the bane of my existence in high school but now I was glad for them because they didn't encourage any unwanted attention and would be one less body part to droop and wrinkle as I aged. I didn't bother with my hair—like a temperamental teenager, it had a mind of its own anyway.

Upon reentering the lounge room, I swear to God, it looked like I had opened the page of an interior design magazine. My breath stopped. Literally. If I wasn't careful my face would soon match the color of my top. Levi was sprawled out on the couch, one arm lazily resting on the leather armrest, the other casually thrown over the back of the sofa with fingers tapping against the seams in time to a beat in his head. The ankle of one of his legs rested across the knee of the other. It was simply absurd how mouthwatering this guy was. Surely, he was an occupational health and safety hazard and needed to come with some form of signage? A high visibility vest was needed at the very least.

I forced my lungs back into action. The sound of my ragged breaths must have caught his attention because he turned his head and smiled up at me. It was an openly appreciative grin, though of what I couldn't say. Maybe it was the fact that I had put some clothes on? Or it could have been my comical dumbstruck expression. Who knew? Either way my heart, seemingly grateful for the oxygen kick, did a flamboyant celebratory flip inside my chest.

"Um, can I get you anything?" I awkwardly mumbled, trying to avoid letting on exactly how much he was affecting me by being there, all model-like in my apartment.

"Is Riley home? I've got her phone."

It felt like my stomach plummeted to the cement slab at the base of the building. Stupid stomach. Stupid fluttering heart. What was the point of internal organs anyway, except to remind us of how much we desperately wanted what we couldn't have?

"She's asleep."

"Still?"

"Yeah, she's not much of a drinker. It hits her pretty hard."

"Not like you, huh?" He smiled. "Now, how does a girl such as yourself start drinking whiskey anyway?"

I shrugged my shoulders in feigned boredom before turning for the kitchen. I wasn't about to tell him that I learned to drink from my father. He started drinking most nights after Mum left him for another man. It was strange what some people put up with because the dozen or so affairs she'd had before that never seemed to affect him. Even though I was only six I still clearly remembered that day, it was forever etched in my mind.

The front door slammed and not long afterward I could hear the smash of china as it hit the wall in the kitchen. My sister and I stared at each other, frozen and in shock.

Earlier, Daddy had told us to go play in my bedroom because he and Mum were going to have a 'grown-up conversation' by themselves. We'd been playing school. I'd only started at the local primary school the year before and loved to line up my toys and pretend to be their teacher when Ballerina refused to join in. Which was pretty much always. But today she'd let me have my way so I'd been nice back and let her have some arts and crafts time.

My sister stood and grabbed my hand. She threw the bedroom door open and ran, dragging me behind her towards the source of the noise. Daddy was in the kitchen pouring himself one of those Special Occasion drinks, the ones with ice in them and not much else. I was confused because he looked too sad to be celebrating anything.

"Don't come in here, girls. I don't want either of you getting hurt."

Ballerina led me to the dining table and pulled out a chair for me to sit down on. She gracefully settled in next to me, not saying a word while Daddy swallowed what was in his glass and then poured himself another. Slowly, he moved his way towards us. After sitting at the head of the table, he rolled the glass between his fingers, silent.

"Daddy?"

Red-rimmed eyes glanced up at me.

"Daddy, where's Mum?"

Ballerina glared at me as though I had said something terrible and I suddenly felt embarrassed by my question, though wasn't sure why.

"Your mother's ... gone away for a while. I'm not sure when she'll be back."

My eyes immediately welled up with tears. "Does that mean you're going away too?"

Dad carefully put his drink back down on the table and placed a warm hand over mine, squeezing it. He then gave me a small, warm smile.

"Grace, my love, you're stuck with me forever."

I grinned back up at him.

I shook my head.

"I'm gonna make a coffee. Want one?"

"Sure."

I tried to make myself busy with the cups, milk and sugar but could feel Levi's eyes following me. His physical presence simply hoarded up the small space. The realtor had described the kitchen as *cozy* before I moved in two years ago at the age of twenty, all fresh faced and full of naive delusion. But now the adjective was a freakin' joke because it implied that the inhabitants of the space were comfortable with each other. I sure as hell wasn't at the moment.

To describe what it felt like being this close to Levi in my own home eluded me, especially knowing that I couldn't do anything about my rampant need for him. It was probably similar to a caged animal—all nervous tension and repetitive pacing. Which explained why I kept taking single items out of the cupboards and drawers rather than collecting them all in one go.

Open. Take one cup. Close. Open. Take another cup. Close.

Surely, I'd be committed soon. Being this receptive to the presence of another wasn't a good sign for my ongoing mental stability.

"You're doing it again."

My head shot up and Levi was leaning over the kitchen counter, staring at my mouth with a half smile on his face.

"That thing with your tongue. You did it last night after almost drowning me too."

Thing? What thing? I frantically racked my brain for what he could possibly be talking about but came up blank.

"You must do it when you're thinking."

Ah. *The whole poking-my-tongue-out-the-corner-of-my-mouth-like-an-overheated-cocker-spaniel thing.* Yeah, that's one of my quirks I really wanted to draw his attention to. Fucking attractive with a capital A.

"It's sweet."

I gaped at him.

"You're sweet. Definitely a kitten."

I snorted, effectively ruling out his last observation. "I've been called many things, Levi, and *sweet* definitely hasn't been one of them."

"Yeah? What are you normally called?"

"Heinous bitch, mostly."

He chuckled softly and I couldn't help but smile in return.

"You don't scare me, Grace." His blue eyes were clear and it was as though he could see straight through me. It was odd really, I'd spent the last year honestly not giving a shit about what other people thought of me. But with Levi looking at me like that, I suddenly worried that what he found was lacking somehow. I was broken, definitely. But deficient? Strangely, I hoped not.

"Fuck, you're beautiful."

My heart stopped as he reached out his hand and trailed the backs of his fingers down the side of my face, leaving tingles in their wake. His calloused thumb lightly skimmed over my bottom lip. Thankfully, it was devoid of any lolling cocker spaniel tongue. His hand then moved to the back of my head, instantly losing itself in the tangle of my hair.

I gave myself exactly three seconds to shut my eyes and bask in the afterglow of Levi's completely unexpected utterance. And another two to enjoy the feel of his fingers against my scalp. He was the first lick of caramel ice cream at low tide during summer holidays— pure heaven. However, Teacher Grace was about to lose her shit at my *blatantly wanton behavior*—her words—so I opened my eyes again and gently removed his hand from my hair before placing it on the countertop between us.

"You've got the wrong woman, Levi," I murmured.

Since when did I have a husky voice?

"Really? Because I'm pretty sure it was you I was calling fucking beautiful. Do you see any other heinous bitches around?'

51

"No, I ... It's just—Look, I'm not Riley, okay?"

"Riley? What's she got to do with it?"

"You're kidding me, right?"

He stared at me, incomprehension written all over his flawless face.

Please, God. Don't let him be stupid. I could never fall for someone who couldn't tell the difference between his ass and his elbow. Fuck, what am I thinking? I could never fall for him period.

"Are you seriously telling me that you guys don't like each other?"

"I don't want Riley."

"Maybe not, but she definitely wants you."

He smiled at me like I was a student with severe auditory processing issues and I had to take a deep breath not to wipe it off his face. With a crowbar.

"Look, kitten, if there's one thing I know, it's how to read women. Trust me on this, I've had years of experience."

I rolled my eyes.

He regarded me for a moment before continuing. "She's not interested."

It was now my turn to sport the latest rage in facial expressions. Complete incomprehension didn't suit my skin tone but it sure as hell brought out the disbelief in my eyes. Not only was he acting like an arrogant jerk, but he was entirely wrong when it came to Riley's interest in him. Surely, her thesis length recount of all his positive attributes last night was an obvious sign. I mean, the girl practically launched herself at him when he interrupted her rant too.

"Then why are you here?" I asked.

"I told you, to return Riley's phone."

"Bullshit."

He cursed under his breath.

"Why are you here, Levi?"

"Fine. Because of *you*, Grace."

"What?"

"Your body is fucking sensational and that smart mouth makes me want to do dirty things to it. Is that so hard to believe?"

I paused for a second, trying to take it all in. But then I exclaimed, "*Hell yes*, and saying all this shit just proves you've got horrible taste in women."

"I've got excellent taste."

His eyes were smiling but I continued on regardless. This was going to be like ripping off a Band-Aid—fucking painful but necessary.

"It doesn't matter what you think, Levi." Hear that? That was the sound of my stupid heart weeping pitifully into a Kleenex. What a pathetic organ. It would be wallowing in cookie dough and then complaining about the size of its hips soon enough.

"The fact is, Riley likes you and I'm her best friend, so I think I'd know. Plus, I would never do anything to hurt her."

"She's not interested, kitten."

"Are you fucking blind as well as deaf?" I almost shouted at him. Levi's obstinacy was really starting to piss me off. But instead of getting angry in return, an emotion I could easily deal with, he smiled. It was that slow, panty-sizzling, and quite frankly, infuriating one of his that I desperately wanted to both pummel and kiss, though not necessarily in that order.

"Look, the fact remains. Riley *does* like you," I glared him into silence, "and I don't."

"Really?"

I tipped my chin up defiantly. "Really."

"You haven't once imagined me naked?"

I glared at him.

53

"It hasn't crossed you mind how amazing my cock would feel inside you?"

"No."

"Because I could pick you up by that sexy ass of yours and fuck you against the wall if you wanna find out?"

"*Levi.*"

"Bullshit." He grinned wider, and then indicated downwards.

My eyes followed the direction of his gaze and to my utter horror, our fingers were still entwined. On closer inspection mine seemed to be frantically clinging to him, almost like his hand was my life raft and this conversation was the fucking Titanic.

I groaned.

"Levi, hey. I thought I heard voices."

I quickly tore my hand away as Riley strolled into the kitchen, wrapping a pale silk robe around her lithe waist. Her blonde hair was disheveled and her face devoid of any makeup, but the genuine smile that lit up her eyes made her instantly gorgeous.

Riley continued, "In fact, I could have sworn I heard *raised* voices." She looked pointedly in my direction and I feigned innocence in return. "So I figured that G had a visitor who needed rescuing."

"Hey, Riley. Thanks but Grace here is nothing I can't handle." As he said this, Levi even had the audacity to turn and wink at me. I narrowed my eyes at him.

Riley quickly glanced from Levi's humorous expression to my thunderous one and smiled. "Glad to hear it. Now, who wants a smoothie?"

"Christ." I dropped my head into my arms on the countertop. Riley was what some might call a health and fitness enthusiast but I thought the term *freak* was much more apt. She was forever making bizarre food and beverage concoctions, jam packed full of ingredients with names I'd never even heard of. I mean, what the hell was Slippery Elm powder anyway? Apparently, it was an absolute dream for the digestion, but slippery anything couldn't be trusted as far as I was concerned.

Levi laughed at my morose reaction while Riley simply ignored me. She was well aware of my thoughts on the subject.

"Levi, can I tempt you?" Riley asked.

I peeked my head up at those words and raised a mocking eyebrow at the man in question. "Yeah, Levi, are you *tempted?*"

Levi looked at me for a second but I couldn't read his expression. He then turned to Riley. "Nah, thanks anyway. Grace was gonna make me a coffee." He stared at me again. "That's what I want."

"Coffee? But it's boiling in here. And that stuff is seriously dehydrating." Riley leaned across the countertop, her blue eyes coy and her smile beguiling. "C'mon, Levi, let me make you something. It'll be delicious, I promise. Won't it, G?"

But I was beyond listening. Riley's last action spoke volumes of her interest in the man and I was in the process of trying to negotiate my suicidal heart into not jumping off a rooftop. Glancing to my bereft fingers which only moments ago had been interwoven with Levi's, they somehow looked pitiful on their own now.

God, this was an absolute joke. I had to stop feeling sorry for myself. Riley's happiness was much more important than my own desolate body parts. If I wasn't careful, I'd make my feelings known to all and sundry which would essentially ruin everything.

So I put on the bravest face I had and said, "You know what guys? I'm not really that thirsty after all. In fact, I'm more tired than anything, so might just head on back to bed. Riley, you make Levi a smoothie, he won't regret it. And Levi…" My gaze shifted to his fathomless eyes. If I didn't stay strong now I'd lose myself in them right in front of my best friend. "See you around."

I gave him the ghost of a smile as my heart plummeted down multiple stories to meet its grizzly death. Then I turned and slowly headed back to my bedroom where I could bawl my eyes out in peace.

Upon reentering my room, I immediately flopped face-first down onto my bed and prepared for the torrent of tears to come. Only they didn't. So instead, I rolled over and stared up at the off-white ceiling plaster, which was in the process of slowly decaying before my very eyes.

I could still hear the faint murmur of voices coming from the kitchen—one was soft and melodic while the other was deep and somehow resonated directly with my groin. Ignoring this insatiable and quite frankly freakin' annoying need within me, I instead decided to look at my current situation in an objective manner. Teacher Grace would be so proud.

So. Here I was again.

To be honest, I didn't know which was worse. Waking up to a text message from Dylan, kindly stating that he was leaving for a shot at a relationship with Satan's asshole or voluntarily foregoing the man I desperately wanted and instead handing him right on over to Riley. Either way, I was pretty sure my heart was beyond repair after all that stampeding.

I groaned.

This was completely fucked.

But then I sat up, cross-legged on my bed. *Right, I can either sit here and host a one-woman pity party or I can do something productive with my self-enforced banishment.* Option one sucked, hardcore, so option two it was. I had a shitload of papers to correct anyway.

I hopped off my bed and rummaged around under it for my laptop and headphones. Once successful, I jumped back into place, leaning back against the dark timber headboard with my laptop resting in front of me. I needed to get some essay drafts edited and back to my Year Tens by Monday and online submissions made life a heck of a lot easier. So with the sound of heavy guitar riffs blaring in my ears, which conveniently muffled out any external voices and consequently put a halt to any subsequent physical urges, I made a start on them.

After what felt like a couple of minutes I looked up to see Riley's head poking through my partially open bedroom door and immediately took out my headphones.

"Hey."

"Hey." I gave her a small smile. "What's up?"

"Am I interrupting?"

"Has that ever stopped you before?"

She grinned and opened the door wider before walking into my room and plopping herself down on the corner of my bed.

I shut my laptop but not before noticing that I had been drafting for over two hours. I wasn't sure whether to be pleased with my successful distraction method or embarrassed by the fact that I actually enjoyed reading the essays. The kids had done an awesome job and it only took the very real threat of them never experiencing a lunchtime outside of detention again, to do it.

Riley's fingers played with the frayed corner of my dark blue bedcover, pulling at the loose threads of the worn fabric. "You really need a decent coverlet, this one is beyond disgusting."

"It's all right." I shrugged my shoulders dispassionately. Shopping wasn't exactly my favorite pastime.

"It's really not."

I sighed. "As much as I love discussing the intricacies of bedding with you Riley, is there a point to this conversation?"

"You're right." She turned and faced me squarely, her eyes staring into mine.

I gulped, this wasn't going to be pretty.

"What have you got against Levi, G?"

"What?"

"Levi. Why don't you like him?"

I desperately tried to remain nonchalant. Though the cogs in my brain were whirling at the speed of light, trying to figure out where this was all heading. They were also frantically trying to camouflage the intense heat about to flush my cheeks at any given moment. It seemed to be an unfortunate side effect of the medical condition that was anyone mentioning the name *Levi* in my presence.

God, I really didn't want to talk about him with Riley. After all, she knew me better than anyone and would instantly pick up on my true feelings for the brash Adonis if I wasn't careful.

So I resorted back to meditation and took a deep breath before saying, "I've got nothing against him."

"Well, it's just that you were heaps rude to him last night at The Hole and this morning I'm pretty sure I could hear you yelling at him. Not to mention the fact that you completely bailed on him in the kitchen earlier. I mean, the guy wanted a cup of coffee and you didn't even make him one."

I looked down at my laptop, wishing that it would miraculously come up with a method of teleporting me the hell out of there so I didn't have to listen to all of my terrible social failings. I truly hated the person I had become in the last few years. It was like Dylan sucked all of the life out of me and left only the dregs behind. What happened to the woman who was able to hold open conversations with very attractive men? The one who rarely, if ever, verbally abused them multiple times within a twenty-four hour period?

I let out a long sigh.

"I know he might come off as a bit … self-assured."

"That's putting it mildly."

"But he's a great guy, G." Riley's eyes were sincere and I felt even worse for it. "Can you please make an effort to be nicer to him? For me?"

This was going to tear me in two. How was I going to sit back and watch Riley grow close to the man I was harboring feelings for? I mean, granted they were under a ton of spite and aggression but were still there nonetheless. And how the hell was I going to do this with a fake smile plastered all over my face? Pretending I wasn't slowly disintegrating from within was surely going to kill me.

I looked up in time to see a slither of paint flake away from the ceiling and slowly float down to the faded beige carpet in the corner of my room.

"Sure, Riley," I murmured, mesmerized by the symbolism behind an otherwise mundane event. "I'll make an effort if it means that much to you."

Riley's smile was wide as she launched herself at me, enveloping me in a bear hug of mammoth proportions. "Thanks, G," she squealed, as I oomphed in return. "You're the best."

Odd, I thought to myself. *Despite being smothered by the affections of my best friend, right now I just feel like a hypocrite instead.*

Chapter Four

I don't know what you're meaning,
Can't deal, you and me every day.
Don't want this healing,
Cast off, dragging my heart away.
-MONDEZ, "Leaving"

When I raced into my office on Monday morning, a whirl of disorganization and flapping limbs, Carli was already seated. Hell, she even looked as calm and self-possessed as the Dalai Lama himself. You see, our desks were pushed against two of the four walls and Carli's was always immaculately ordered, even down to color-coded Post-it notes and correlating paper clips. I honestly didn't know how she did it. She was a freak of nature.

Mine on the other hand, looked like a teacher had wheeled in a cannon, stuffed it to the brim with random stationery and paper paraphernalia and then fired it in the general direction of my workspace.

It was a mountain of chaos.

Carli looked up and smiled. The highlights in her auburn curls looked glossy with the movement even under the artificial light. I had no idea how she got it that shiny, and if I ever decided to give a shit about my own tangled mess, I really should remember to ask her.

Shaking my head, I searched the confined space, frantically trying to find somewhere to put my laptop bag, subject folder, diary and pencil case. Cluttered bookshelves lined the two remaining walls, overflowing with textbooks and dusty resource folders from the last decade. Lame posters took up space on the walls with images of people on bikes reaching the top of a mountain and the word, *Success* written underneath, and the god-awful cat hanging by its claws and the phrase, *Hang in There* stamped across it. Previous teachers must have put them up. Probably in a deluded bid to distract themselves from the fact that there were no windows and the only light source was a moody iridescent globe that occasionally chose not to work.

I swear it had PMS.

Or was just some sort of electrified bitch.

I gave up trying to find an empty space on my desk. After all, there was something to be said for swiping a heap of crap onto the floor in one fluid arm motion. It was strangely satisfying. Once done, I dumped my laptop and other materials on top, and then began the arduous task of locating my Year Nine's English folder.

Again.

I sighed. It'd be so much easier if all my stuff had GPS tracking devices installed on them. Luckily, I had the first lesson period free so wasn't yet in full-blown panic mode.

"You're looking even more frazzled than normal for a Monday morning, Grace. Everything okay?"

What could I say? That I was currently in the process of falling for the guy who my best friend fancied? That despite having yelled abuse at him, dousing him in fluids, groping him senseless *and* standing in front of him partially naked before refusing to make him a coffee, he still thought that I was sweet and beautiful? It was simply too ludicrous for words.

So instead I mumbled something entirely incomprehensible and hoped it passed off as being, "Yep, I'm fine."

"Don't tell me Riley talked you into a caffeine-free diet again. You know that experience didn't end well last time and I'm pretty sure Lucas's balls will never be the same again."

I grimaced at the memory. Releasing a week's worth of pent-up caffeine-free aggression on the now ex-history teacher who deemed it appropriate to grope me at the staff dinner six months ago wasn't one of my finest moments.

"I'm okay, it's just been a strange weekend."

"Yeah?" Carli turned and looked quizzically up at me from her office chair. That girl looked *hot*. She seriously rocked fitted sports pants. I stopped, looked down and then realized I was completely lost in a sea of stationery.

It was lucky she could find me at all.

I shook my head again, I really needed to focus. After all, I had a heap of work to do today. There was new content I needed to deliver to the students and exams to prepare them for. I was even going to *encourage* our current English coordinator to actually do her damn job for once and allocate sufficient funding to cover our textbooks for next year. Hell, while I was at it, I might even prove to everyone that I could do a much better job of it than her.

After taking a deep breath, I crouched down and began piling random pieces of paper into towering mounds at my feet. Well, that's what people who had their shit together did, right? They organized their surroundings and this had a knock-on effect to their headspace and therefore their life in general. They *so* didn't spend the entire weekend fantasizing about the touch of a musician's fingers against their skin or replaying certain panty-scorching conversations over and over again in their heads until they knew the words by heart. Right?

Right?

I needed to change the topic of conversation to something less humiliating.

"So, how was your date with Pete? Get any action?" I wiggled my eyebrows and she laughed.

Phew, crisis averted.

"Grace, I had such an incredible time. He took me to this new restaurant that just opened up on the foreshore of Meelup Beach and we sat and talked for hours. It was perfect."

I nodded my head enthusiastically but felt a stab of jealousy to the heart just the same. It must be awesome spending time with someone you either didn't have to continuously run away from or want to kill.

She continued, "So when the place closed we both went back to his place and ... hung out some more."

"I bet you did."

Carli smiled again and I could see how genuinely delighted she was with Pete. I was pleased for her, she truly deserved to be happy after the horrendous time she'd had on the dating scene. Let's just say, profile pictures from online dating websites didn't mean shit. But I couldn't help feeling sorry for myself too. The situation I currently found myself in was well and truly a pain in the ass.

"*Crap*, I almost forgot." I looked up at Carli as she continued, "Serena dropped by before."

"*Serena?*" I was pretty sure all dogs within a five-mile radius had just cocked their heads from my high-pitched shriek.

"Don't worry, I said you were doing preparation stuff in the library."

I sagged with relief, but only slightly.

"But she wants to see you in her office though, like *now*."

I groaned.

It was no secret I wasn't enraptured with the newly appointed principal of Geographe High. Serena had been preparing me for upcoming *leadership opportunities* by riding my back ever since her damn arrival. Well, that's what she chose to call her overbearing interference anyway. I just called it fucking annoying. Which left me in the precarious position of wanting to prove myself to her, but hating having to do it in the first place. Surely my class results were enough evidence? But no, sadly not.

"What's the bet Dean Thornton is in her office right now demanding my immediate resignation?"

Dean Thornton was one of Geographe Bay's wealthiest businessmen and he made sure the entire universe knew all about it. Daily. His son, Mark, was in one of my classes, and was also the bane of my existence. Seriously, the kid was an absolute dick. He was a walking advertisement for contraception. Don't get me wrong, on the whole I genuinely loved working with students. I mean, that's why I chose to become a teacher in the first place. But there was something about this teenager that rubbed me up the wrong way.

Big time.

Just picture the most stuck-up, insolent, disrespectful adolescent you can think of. Then add a heap of pimples plastered all over a lanky frame and spiky dark hair. That was him—a fucking waste of space. Anyway, in class last Friday, I dared to offer him some *constructive* feedback on his recount draft. He hadn't taken the criticism well.

Or at all.

"I'd lay twenty bucks on it."

I smiled darkly. "Shall we make it a fifty to see if he gets out of there alive?"

"Done."

A couple of minutes later I was seated on some ridiculously uncomfortable utilitarian-looking couches in the main foyer of the administration building. Serena was making me wait. She always made me wait. I wasn't sure if it was a personal thing, where she was trying to stamp her authority over my time, or if she was legitimately in the process of trying to placate a very pissed off parent. Regardless, I still felt pretty freakin' annoyed at having to be here at all, and my current frustration didn't bode well for this meeting.

Martha, Serena's PA, put down her phone receiver and gave me a well-practiced smile. It was no doubt designed to instill confidence into the hearts of the soon-to-be lion fodder but such niceties were wasted on me for two reasons. One, Serena didn't in the least bit intimidate me. And two, I had no heart left to instill any confidence in.

"She's ready for you now."

I nodded my head and gave Martha a grim smile before standing and wrestling some stray strands of hair back into my messy bun. I quickly straightened out my black pencil skirt, checked to make sure my red fitted blouse was still tucked in at the waistband and was glad for the extra inch of height from my patent leather pumps. Believe me, with Serena, I needed all the help I could get. Once satisfied that I looked less disheveled than I felt, I marched on into her office.

And then stopped dead in my tracks.

What the hell?

"I'm so glad you could make it, Grace," Serena said coldly, "finally." Her green eyes assessed me, no doubt waiting for some form of weakness to show so she could pounce on it with unabashed glee.

When she wasn't being a complete and utter bitch, Serena might be what some would call attractive. Beautiful even. She was about thirty years of age, with long bleached blonde hair that was always pulled back in a sophisticated knot. This highlighted her open face that was sun-kissed and sprinkled with freckles, though her skin showed a hint of aging through slight wrinkles that appeared around the edges of her eyes when she smiled or scowled. The latter was much more frequent where I was concerned.

I didn't say anything in return to her greeting which, let's be honest, was really an insult in disguise. I couldn't. I just frantically tried to maintain the illusion of outward calm while my internal workings were in the process of dealing with an all-encompassing meltdown.

Levi was here.

In Serena's office.

He was actually *here*.

Holy fuck.

When Levi looked up to find me gawking at him, he at least had the courtesy to look as equally bewildered as I felt. His blue eyes immediately widened, registering genuine shock. But as his gaze fluttered over my outfit it grew dark. Was it with lust? Desire? *God, I hope so. I mean, God, I hope not.*

Shit.

And of course my traitorous body responded shamelessly to say the least by hardening and moistening in the appropriately designated areas. *Christ.* In order to distract myself, I turned back to Serena, confused.

"Grace, I'd like you to meet your new student teacher, Levi Mondez. He will be working with you for the next six weeks while he's on his final placement from Greater Western University." Serena glowered up at me as she clipped out her final words of warning. "I'm sure you'll make him feel very welcome."

My confusion transformed into outright anger, and I gave her my famous glare of epic proportions. There was no way in hell this was happening. Seriously.

"No."

"No? This isn't a request, Grace. In order to continuously improve your teacher ranking you need to demonstrate an ability to mentor others within a structured educational setting."

I raised my eyebrows and was about to say exactly where she could shove her structured educational settings, but she continued.

"This will also look favorably on your application for the role of English coordinator next year."

Crap. She had me there, and by the satisfied look on her face, she knew it too. I really wanted that role and would do a much better job of it than Spread-Her-Legs Sophie, the school's current and shall we say, *promiscuous* English coordinator. Sophie's sexual exploits were legendary around campus. Rumor had it that she'd already made her way through the science department, well, all the men under fifty anyway, and was currently in the process of shacking up with a different environmental studies teacher each week. Married ones included. The girl was ruthless but I had to admire her dedication and drive. It was just a pain in the ass that after all the effort she spent servicing her vagina, very little was left for the improvement of our English department.

"Fine," I bit out, "I'll do it."

"Of course you will. Now, this week Levi is only to observe and note your teaching practices. However, next week he will be required to take over some of your classes. It's up to you to determine which ones, though I don't want your Year Twelves to be disrupted. They need continuity during this crucial stage of their studies."

I tried so hard not to roll my eyes at her condescending manner. Of course I wouldn't set a university student free on my unsuspecting Year

Twelves, particularly one this damn fine. The girls, and to be fair some of the boys too, wouldn't be able to string more than a sentence together for the entire six weeks, let alone pass the freakin' course. Did she honestly think I was that deranged?

So instead I pasted on my most disdainful smile and asked pointedly, "Are we done?"

Her jaw clenched as she spat, "Yes."

I inwardly fist pumped the air, thrilled that I'd riled her. This morning was looking up after all.

Serena then turned to smile across at Levi. "Welcome to Geographe High School. I'm sure you'll enjoy your time here."

"Thanks."

And with that one word, I was completely undone. Levi's voice was even more sensual than I'd remembered. As he stood and towered over me, with those intense blue eyes and that lopsided cajoling smile of his, I had to do everything in my power not to climb the man like a tree and shamelessly rub myself all over him.

School principal be damned.

So as a distraction, I chose not to look at his face at all. Which of course was a huge mistake because it meant my eyes hypnotically trailed down his white business shirt. It did little to disguise the delectable raven tattooed on his neck and even less to contain his broad chest and protruding biceps. I swallowed. There was no way I was going to let my eyes travel any farther south because I honestly didn't trust myself with what would happen next if I did. So they just had to make do with his shirt buttons.

How the fuck could Levi's shirt buttons be sexy?

This was nonsensical.

Lord in heaven, how are me and my saturated

panties ever going to survive the next six weeks?

In order to refocus, I inwardly punched myself in the boob. It happened once when I was younger. My older sister and I were fighting in the backyard over … God knows what really, but at the time it seemed pretty important. Anyway, it hurt like hell and certainly got my attention then, so it couldn't hurt now. Figuratively speaking.

"Come on," I muttered to Levi's mouthwatering shirt buttons, before leading him out of the lion's den and towards the relative safety of my microscopic office.

As we crossed the quad it felt like all the staff and students we passed stopped dead in their tracks and unashamedly ogled the man just behind me. There was going to be news of a delicious new student teacher spread throughout the school by the start of lunch. I'd bet my sweatbox of an apartment on it.

When we finally entered the office and I shut the door behind me, I was grateful Carli was blessedly absent. That way she wouldn't have to witness my gradual demise from sanity into madness. I stepped towards my workspace and couldn't help it, I face-palmed my forehead while letting out a muttered oath. My half of the office literally looked like the aftereffects of an earthquake. One that had reached 8.4 on the Richter scale at the very least. My continued embarrassment was seemingly endless where this guy was concerned.

Behind me, Levi chuckled and I instinctively curled my hands into fists. Surely my reactions to him weren't healthy. I mean, the guy made me feel like I was bipolar. Well, this time would be different because he was on my turf now and I wouldn't let him get to me. After all, this was my place of work. This was where my intellect was respected by all and my Smart Mouth feared by many. I wasn't going to let any man, especially Levi, rile or turn me into a quivering mess. We weren't at The Hole for God's sake, I had a job to do.

Man. The. Fuck. Up. Grace.

I took a deep, steadying breath and squared my shoulders before turning around to face him. Surprisingly, being armored with a professionalism and cutthroat efficiency I didn't entirely feel made the whole situation I suddenly found myself in appear slightly less insane.

"Right. This is my office." I spread my arms wide in case he was a visual learner and needed the gesture to aid in his understanding of the freakin' obvious. "So this is where you'll be based," I swallowed, "for the next six weeks."

Levi took a step towards me, gently murmuring, "Grace—"

"As you can see, there's not much room. But I can move some of my stuff so you've got somewhere to work when you're not in class—"

"Grace—" He took another step forward and was now a hairbreadth away from me. But I still didn't stop babbling, or meet his eyes.

"Though, we'll have to find you a chair from somewhere. I'm sure one of the classes nearby will have a spare one you can use—"

"Grace, *stop*." He cupped my chin in his warm hand and I breathed in sharply at the contact as my eyes flew to his, startled. "I just want you to know that I didn't set this whole thing up on purpose, I swear." His expression looked genuine.

I nodded and said softly, "So this is why your band's taking a break for a couple of months, because of your placement here."

It was his turn to nod.

"Let go of me."

Levi slowly unclasped my chin and withdrew his hand, though his heated gaze told me exactly what he thought about the loss of contact. Mine must have said exactly the same.

The two-faced bastards.

"This is my place of work, Levi. You can't play me here like I'm your guitar or something."

"Play you?"

"I won't let you."

"I'm not trying to play you, kitten. I thought I made it pretty clear what my intentions were on Saturday."

I shook my head. "I told you, I won't hurt Riley like that."

"And I keep telling *you*, she's not int—"

The bell rang for class. Fortunately, it stopped that agonizing conversation dead in its tracks and I quickly turned around to scan the floor for my teaching folder. When my gaze finally came across it, hidden beneath a curriculum binder from 2007, I shook my head. I honestly didn't even know what that binder was doing there.

I grabbed the remainder of my gear before stating, "Let's go." After that, I strode out of the office and towards class.

I could do this.

I had to.

Nearly all of my Year Tens were seated and ready to go as I entered the classroom, no doubt reeking of my pent-up sexual tension. The kids and I previously had the whole I'll-lock-you-out-of-the-room-if-you-don't-arrive-to-class-on-time-and-try-explaining-*that*-to-Mrs. Nebril-when-one-of-her-cronies-spots-you-skullking-in-the-corridor-during-lesson-time conversation earlier in the year. It only took Mark's attempt at testing that theory to prove to the rest of the little treasures exactly how serious I was in my threat. I received a very firm talking-to from Serena about failing to provide learning opportunities for all students in my care blah, blah, blah. But I honestly thought the experience was well worth it. And after watching Mark try not to cry once he punched the locked classroom door with his fist, the whole class agreed with me on that one too.

As Levi strolled in after me, a collective gasp burst from the girls and the boys suddenly sat up a hell of a lot straighter in their chairs. Poor things. They looked like constipated meerkats. To place such a godlike man within the midst of so much pubescent insecurity was really unfair on them all.

"All right everyone, listen up." I glanced around at the sea of hair flicking and intense scrutiny, trying to mask a smile. "This," I gestured to Levi who thankfully stood at a professional distance, "is Mr. Mondez. He will be working with us for the next six weeks." I swallowed again. "So make sure you give him the same respect you would give any other teacher." I narrowed my eyes at them. "Got it?"

A mumbled *yeah* sporadically rippled throughout the classroom.

I smiled sweetly. "Now, I emailed back your edited recount drafts yesterday so I want you to work on the good copy which is due by the end of today." With that, the students opened up their laptops and grumbled under their breaths about the relevancy of creative writing for their future career prospects. I graciously ignored their complaints as they eventually got to work.

"So where do you want me?"

Many x-rated images immediately sprang to mind but I quickly shook my head to clear them all. I opened my mouth to reply, only no words came.

Not a single one.

Christ, this was awkward.

So I cleared my throat and searched the room, hoping for inspiration to thwack my momentarily nonexistent vocal chords upside the head.

The class was a typical rectangular shape, with a bi-folding wall at the far end covered in posters from the latest feature films currently out in cinemas. Student work, mainly posters on classical texts, took up all the space on the left wall which faced another of windows. They showed the crystal clear sky, meticulously tended school oval lawn, and far off in the gleaming distance, the beach.

I *loved* the beach.

And more than anything in the world, I wished I was there right now. My dad and I always used to spend time together at a secluded cove only us locals know about. It was a place where we would sit, talk, be. My mind cast back one year ago.

"Here you are, one caramel ice cream."

I rolled my eyes, though still accepted the offered confection. He knew I would, I always did. "Dad, one of these days, you're going to realize that I'm actually an adult now."

"Impossible," he huffed, "through my eyes, you're always my cheeky little monkey."

"I'm never going to live that one down, am I?"

"Nope. But if it makes you feel any better, I still call your sister Ballerina."

"So do I." I smirked. Fawn colored droplets dribbled down the waffle cone and then onto my fingers. I quickly licked them clean. "So good." It didn't matter how many times a week he bought me this particular flavor, I never got sick of it. It was quite simply the

73

tastiest damn ice cream on the planet.

Dad chuckled softly at my obvious enjoyment and then groaned dramatically as he sat down next to me.

"Getting old, Dad?" I joked.

He shook his head, bemused, while taking off his leather shoes, gray socks and rolling his suit pants midway up his calves. "Ah, that's better," he sighed, wiggling his toes in the cool sand.

We both sat there quietly, taking in the clear azure sky and the sound of the waves as they crashed and rolled towards the shore. However, something in Dad's silence felt off. Usually we could sit like this for hours and it felt so comfortable, but today I could feel something else, trepidation crawled up my spine like an unwelcome spider. I turned to look at him then and instinctively noticed that my mind wasn't playing me for a fool. Dad had dark rings under his eyes that weren't there on Wednesday and his skin was looking ... oddly sallow. "You all right?"

It took him a while to respond. Though when he finally did, like always, he told me exactly what I needed to hear. "I am now, love."

"Grace?"

I sighed, then turned my attention back to the present. Right. The conundrum of where to seat Levi. He was staring at me with a puzzled look on his face and I gave him a weak smile. I then turned back to the class. The students were all doing an amazing job of maintaining the facade of actually doing their work when in reality they were probably playing *Grand Theft Auto* or watching a downloaded TV show. It was my fault. I shouldn't have let my mind wander.

I glanced behind me. The white teacher's desk, covered in crap and for once not all mine, was stationed close to the entrance on the left-hand side of the room. An extremely uncomfortable teal colored plastic chair was tucked beneath it. This looked like as good a place as any to seat the guy. At least now I could move amongst the students, both distracting myself from his lip-smacking presence and the kids from their off-task behavior.

Perfect.

"Take a seat at the teacher's desk." Thank God, some words at last. "That way you'll get to observe everything from there."

"No problem." He moved behind the desk and sat down, retrieving his own notebook and pen from a distressed brown leather satchel. I honestly didn't know how I missed him carrying that. But I was willing to blame those stimulating shirt buttons that completely distracted me from this tidbit of crucial information. When Levi opened the notebook and started writing, I swear to God, it looked like the latest edition of *Education Monthly* had just got a hell of a lot sexier.

Before I could do anything that I would no doubt regret in front of my students, like straddle Levi's lap and turn *Education Monthly* into a porn magazine, I quickly moved away. This caused a wave of fear to flow throughout the class as the kids frantically exited out of their games or TV shows and opened up their recount drafts before I reached them. Bless them.

Mercifully, I was able to ignore my raging female parts for the remainder of the lesson. Don't get me wrong—they never once ceased shrieking at me like the harpy they were, but I found turning my back on Levi really helped. It seemed the only way I could actually get some work done was if I pretended he didn't exist. So I sat with each of my students in turn, explaining to them in detail the comments I'd made on their drafts and the expectations I had for their final copies. Mark was absent which was probably why the class felt a hell of a lot nicer. At least I didn't have to contend with his dickweed attitude the entire time.

Man, he was a jerk.

So when the bell rang, I was genuinely surprised at how well I'd dealt with the whole I-want-the-same-guy-that-my-more-deserving-best-friend-did-as-well thing. Sweet.

"Good work today everyone. I expect your final copies emailed to me by the end of the day." I narrowed my eyes in warning at them. "Do not miss that deadline." After letting the threat hang in the air for a moment, I then put them out of their misery by declaring, "Class dismissed."

There was a mass thumping of chairs as they were hurriedly pushed back and then unceremoniously dumped behind the desks. The students then sauntered out of the room before swarming into the hall, no doubt eager to spread news of the magnificent Mr. Mondez. At last, the door swung closed behind them.

We were alone.

Guess it had to happen sooner or later.

I took a deep breath and turned to face Levi. He hadn't moved from behind the desk and was watching me closely with an unreadable expression on his face. Once again, I lost the power of speech. This was going to become a real problem over the next six weeks if I didn't get a handle on it soon and I desperately hoped I wouldn't have to resort to communicating with him in other ways … like through interpretive dance.

Levi slowly stood, never once breaking eye contact with me. He put his notebook and pen away in the leather satchel before swinging it over his shoulder and slowly making his way towards me.

I gulped.

This man held me completely spellbound by the intensity in his gaze. And if I didn't do something in the next few seconds to break the magnetic pull between us, I would either internally combust or beg him to put me out of my misery.

"We, ah, should really be heading back."

Genius. Pure genius, Grace.

He completely ignored me and stopped a few inches away before slowly leaning down to murmur in my ear. "You were amazing."

My brow furrowed and I stepped back, staring squarely up at him. "I was helping students draft their work, Levi, not solving the world hunger crisis."

"When are you going to learn to take a compliment, kitten?"

"At about the same time you stop giving them."

He smiled down at me and a small grin played about the corner of my lips. Parrying with him was growing dangerously enjoyable. I quickly turned and grabbed my belongings from the spare desk I'd dumped them on at the start of the lesson.

"We should really be going. I've got a double free period next but we'll probably need that time to clear out some desk space in my office and find you a chair."

"Yeah, that might take a while."

"*Look...*" For some reason I felt the need to grow defensive over my non-existent organizational habits. Don't ask me why. "I wasn't exactly expecting to have a student teacher when I first arrived at school today, okay? And I sure as hell wasn't ready for it to be *you,* so just—" I paused mid-sentence. Levi's face broke into a grin of swoon-worthy proportions and I was having a hard time remembering where I was going with my rant.

He stepped towards me again and this time I

didn't move back. I mean, I honestly didn't trust my legs with any given movement. So I also didn't stop Levi as he gently brushed the backs of his fingers down the side of my face before tucking a stray strand of hair behind my ear. "Relax, kitten," he all but purred.

Easy for him to say, he wasn't the one currently fighting a losing battle against gravity.

"We'll get it sorted out. There's no need to get your panties in a twist."

My eyes popped open in shock. "Don't think for *one* second that you're having any effect whatsoever on my panties," I growled out.

Liar.

He just grinned wider and brushed his thumb across my bottom lip.

I couldn't help myself. I opened my mouth and bit down on it.

Levi inhaled sharply from my involuntary assault and his pupils dilated to an alarming degree.

Fuck.

What was I doing?

So, before Teacher Grace could appear and cane my sordid ass, I released his thumb from between my teeth, spun on my heel and wrenched the door open. To say I essentially bolted back to my office would not have been an understatement. And to be blunt, I honestly didn't give a shit if Levi followed me or if he got lost along the way.

Chapter Five

Trapped in bright lights, it's all right,
Moving forward to this side.
-MONDEZ, "Echo"

When I stepped through the open doorway, swaying slightly and looking like I'd all but inhaled a bottle of whiskey on an empty stomach, Carli immediately rushed over to me.

"Grace, are you all right? What happened?" Her hands gripped my shoulders and she shook me gently, searching my face for clues as to why I'd turned into crazy cat lady minus the cats.

My mass feelings of self-loathing must have culminated into one hell of a distraught facial expression because the girl looked seriously worried.

"I'm … I'm okay." I bit back a hysterical laugh. "It's just been a weird couple of days, that's all."

The bell rang for the next lesson but Carli didn't move. "You sure you're okay, babe? You look … terrible."

I nodded my head, trying to appear more self-possessed than I felt and something in the gesture must have reassured her because she let go of me. Grudgingly.

"Right, we're going out for a drink tonight and you're not leaving until you've told me *everything*. Got it?"

I nodded again and the continuing irony surrounding my Smart Mouth not being able to formulate any words, biting or otherwise, was not entirely lost on me.

Carli's eyes widened as she stared over my shoulder.

Christ.

"Carli, meet Levi. My new student teacher."

She mumbled something vaguely comparable to a greeting and he muttered *hey* in return. Our students had no hope of expanding their vocabulary beyond grunts and monosyllabic utterances if this mode of communication was to continue for much longer.

Carli's hazel eyes then returned to mine. She whispered pointedly, "We'll talk later." However, her gaze softened as she murmured, "Love you."

A minute later, she was gone.

The door closed quietly behind her and the only remaining sounds were my labored breaths and erratic heartbeat. To be honest, I was pretty sure both could be heard from the performing arts building across the quad.

I'd seriously messed up with Levi back in the classroom. I mean, I'd stupidly dug a gargantuan hole and then carelessly hurled myself into it.

Teeth first.

Fortunately, I didn't have to worry. Levi moved to stand beside me, and staring at the disarray in front of us, threw me a lifeline by asking, "Where do we start?"

I gazed up at him, gratitude etched all over my face. "We need a bin. A fucking big one."

He looked down at me and smiled, his blue eyes clear. If only the world hadn't conspired against me and I could let myself get lost in them. In another lifetime, I'd crawl right on in there, set up camp and never want to leave.

Levi's eyes narrowed slightly. "Well, what are you waiting for, kitten? I'm getting old here."

Outwardly, I huffed as I turned and ventured into the corridor, dragging back the largest dustbin I could find. But inwardly, I was attempting to fight off the warm fuzzies. They were threatening to seep through my extremities and thaw the coldest parts of me that had been numb for a solid year.

"Let's just keep this as simple as possible and make two piles," I said, standing next to Levi once again with the wastepaper basket to our far right. "Anything English-related, we'll put there." I pointed to a miraculously empty corner of the office. "Everything else we'll put here." I indicated to the bin.

Levi nodded, knelt down on the paper-strewn floor and began rummaging through the mountains of crap I'd managed to assemble throughout my one year at Geographe High. I followed suit, though somewhat restricted by my heels. Thankfully, my pencil skirt had some give in the material so it accommodated the movement a heck of a lot easier than I expected. After a couple of minutes, I gave up on any pretense of propriety and discarded the leather pumps. It was heaven. Though sadly, nothing could be done about the skirt. Levi also stopped, undid his cuffs and rolled up his shirtsleeves as far as his muscular forearms would permit.

I tore my eyes away from that G-rated, though no-less-captivating strip tease and practiced some deep breathing exercises. I'd all but nailed the whole meditation thing ever since meeting the man on Friday night. But being this close to him was agony. Pure and simple. Riley had better hurry on up and marry the damn guy before my raging hormones mutinied against common sense and made a spectacular mess of my waning self-control.

I sighed.

Levi's eyes shifted to my bent frame but he said nothing. He then returned his attention back to shifting the countless folders, binders and loose-leaf papers strewn all over the floor.

After what felt like an eternity, I decided I had to

say something. We couldn't just remain there, kneeling next to one another and rifling through piles of shit in complete silence until the lunch bell sounded.

It was beyond lame.

I cleared my throat. "So, what made you want to study teaching?"

He smiled at my pathetic attempt at a conversation icebreaker. "For the paid holidays, kitten. Why else?"

"You've got to be kidding me."

He smirked.

"No one in their right mind would become a teacher for the fucking holidays, Levi. For one, they're few and far between and two, there's way too much crap in the meantime to make the holidays alone worth it."

"Relax, kitten, it was a joke."

"Freakin' hilarious," I muttered under my breath. Though my grip on what appeared to be a first-aid certificate loosened and I vainly tried to flatten out the creases.

"It's really a backup plan."

"For what?"

"Well, if Mondez doesn't end up kicking ass, at least I've got a real job qualification to fall back on."

It was actually a really sound plan and I grudgingly mumbled, "Good idea."

"I thought so."

I narrowed my eyes at his arrogance but for once remained silent. The certificate would survive another day and I threw it onto the pile of English-related stuff.

"What about you, why'd you become a teacher? And an English one at that?"

"Because of my dad."

Fuck.

I'd said too much.

"Your dad? Was he a teacher?"

I shook my head, pissed at being on the verge of opening Pandora's box if this conversation continued any further. My family wasn't something I liked talking about. Ever. It brought back way too many painful memories.

But I had to say something. I mean, the guy was staring expectantly at me. I took a deep breath. "He used to read a lot to me as a kid. The classics mostly. Poe, Conan Doyle, anything with a brooding subtext really. I guess they probably weren't the most appropriate choices, but I really liked them." I shrugged my shoulders. "Anyway, reading was something we'd both do together. When I was younger we'd share a book as soon as he got home from work and once I moved out, we'd meet at the beach to talk about the latest novel we were making our way through. Or other stuff. Either way, it was my favorite thing to do."

I paused, my mind instinctively drifting back to just over a year ago.

The late afternoon sun was fierce and perspiration gathered on my top lip. I wiped it away with the back of my hand and then took a long sip of water. "Hey, Dad?"

"Hmm?" He was digging a shallow hole in the sand with a stray twig. He always did that when he was deep in thought.

"I was reading A Scandal in Bohemia *last night—"*

"Ah," he interrupted, waving the stick around in the air like an orchestra conductor, "'To Sherlock Holmes she is always the *woman. I have seldom heard him mention her under any other name.'"*

"You seriously know them all off by heart, don't

83

you?"

"Don't you?"

I shrugged one shoulder. "That's beside the point. Anyway, as I was saying, I was reading the forward notes and apparently this professor guy from Oxford reckons Watson was a total player."

"A what?"

"A player. You know, like a womanizer."

Dad went back to digging his hole again. "Well, I guess there are passing references to his ... conquests in some of the other short stories."

"Only in one of them."

"You don't agree then?"

I shook my head, "Nope. Just because the character mentions the desirability of others, doesn't mean he's off screwing everything that walks. It wasn't like he was totally miserable with his lot and trying to find happiness everywhere else. I mean, he wasn't anything at all like—" I paused, horrified at what I'd almost said out loud.

Dad snapped the stick in half and threw it in a graceful arc towards the ocean.

"Sorry," I mumbled.

He wrapped an arm around my shoulder, squeezing me gently before letting go. "Don't worry about it, love. It was a long time ago."

I jumped with a start.

Levi quickly removed his hand from my shoulder and watched me closely, his blue eyes impenetrable. "You okay?"

I nodded but he refused to look away. "What?"

"Your dad must be some guy."

"He was," I murmured, looking down at my hands. This growing melancholy had to stop. Like, *now*. I wasn't going to feel sorry for myself. Not in front of Levi and definitely not while kneeling on the floor, holding onto a damn leaflet. It contained the image of a leering, bald old man who was apparently a professor on cognitive learning theories. But he looked more like a sexual predator to me.

"I'm sorry."

I stared up at Levi and blinked. The genuine empathy in his eyes made me feel like I'd just been kicked in the ribs by someone wearing five-inch stilettos.

"Thank you." I cleared my throat loudly, uncomfortably awkward, and looked away again.

This was simply too much.

He was too much.

And once again I was lost for words.

"How old were you when your father died?"

"Twenty-one. It happened last year."

"What about your mother?"

"What about her?" I gave a bitter laugh. "She was gone a long time ago, Levi. Last I heard, she was on to husband number four and living somewhere on the Ivory Coast. Didn't even make it to Dad's damn funeral."

He let out a muttered oath under his breath. "Do you have any other family?"

"Riley's my family."

"No, I meant do you have any brothers or sisters?"

My voice hardened. "I've got a sister." And it was either the way I bit out those four innocent words, or the way I was transforming Professor Sexual Predator into tiny pieces of confetti that made Levi stop his line of questioning.

Thank fuck.

I hadn't spoken that much about myself to anyone in a long time and was more than willing to forego the experience for as long as possible in future.

"We've done a pretty decent job of it, don't you think?" Levi asked. He was clearly feeling pretty damn proud of what we'd just accomplished.

I sat back and surveyed the scene. It was as though I were suddenly seeing my half of the office for the first time. The floor space was mostly clear, except for the tottering tower of English-related stuff. We were able to fit another chair in there and I decided to sort out the remainder of the pile another time. My eyes drifted to the bin, it was overflowing.

I gazed across at Levi who was still crouched down next to me. Turned out, he was seriously lacking in egotistical narcissism.

Damn it.

This made my burgeoning feelings for the guy even more unwelcome. But I decided to allow myself this one small moment to take something back for myself, especially now he knew me almost as well as Riley did. So I harmlessly, yet ravenously, consumed each delectable feature on his handsome face. Like a starved animal. My gaze traveled from his chiseled jaw, to his full lips, to his nose. When I finally reached them, those piercing blue eyes of his looked at me as though I was truly worthy. Worthy of more than I ever deserved.

Wow.

It was a revelation, despite being a sobering one. "Not bad at all," I murmured, a small smile played on my lips.

A slow grin spread across his face. "Damn right."

Grace, that's enough.

I broke eye contact, stood and stretched out the kinks in my legs. Levi followed suit. However, while attempting to slip my heels back on, I completely lost my balance and would have fallen straight onto my ass if it hadn't been for him. He grabbed me by the waist, holding me firm. My hands instinctively clasped his arms for support and the feel of his strong biceps beneath my grappling fingers almost made me want to cry afresh. Life well and truly sucked when the one muscular thing you wanted, was the one muscular thing you couldn't have.

"Thanks," I muttered, self-consciously glancing up at Levi before letting go of him. Somehow, I managed to put my pumps back on without further incident— miracle amongst miracles. Once finished, Levi unclasped his hands from my waist and smiled wryly down at me. He hadn't said a word, and for once I wished for a joking comment. Hell, I didn't even care if it was at my expense. I just wanted to break the sultry mood.

When I'd managed to scrape together the remains of my diminishing self-command, I looked up at him again. "Let's go, you look hungry."

"I sure am."

"I meant for food."

"That too."

I narrowed my eyes and Levi chuckled. So I huffed, turned on my heels and stalked my way towards the cafeteria.

The cafeteria sat snuggly in between the technology building and the library. At the far end were panoramic windows looking out onto the staff car park which was bordered by tall gum trees. This was probably so the teachers could make sure their vehicles weren't being broken into during the students' free time. But the other three remaining walls of the cafeteria were enclosed and littered with posters about upcoming events, food hygiene and advertisements for local sporting teams. As we walked through the swinging doors of the room, I threw over my shoulder, "It's best to get here early. That way you're not stuck with the leftovers."

Levi was directly behind me, probably to ensure I didn't make a spectacular entrance by falling flat on my face or something. I tried to stop the tingles from breaking out all over my skin at the thought of how amazing his hands felt wrapped around my waist, but failed dismally. Distraction was definitely going to be the order of the day.

"Trust me, Levi," I continued, "even leftover Bean Surprise isn't something I'd wish upon my worst enemy." I stopped short, tilted my head to one side and thought for a second. "No wait. I'd definitely give it to Serena."

Levi stood, facing me, his expression serious. "Yeah, I noticed a bit of tension there this morning. What's that all about?"

"Should I answer that alphabetically or chronologically?"

He shrugged his shoulders.

"She's a bitch, Levi."

"Seemed nice enough to me."

I was suddenly furious. "Well, you don't know *shit.*"

Who the hell does he think he is? Just because I didn't share every damn scrap of information about my entire existence, didn't mean my arguments weren't justified. Much.

Stomping towards the long row of heated cafeteria food on the left-hand side of the room, I ignored the grease-congealed unmentionables in varying stages of decomposition at the beginning and headed straight for the suspicious-looking sandwiches at the end. One could only pray they were made sometime in the last fortnight but I wasn't going to hold my breath for that miracle.

Levi caught up with me as I wrestled a tray from

the top of its stack with much more vehemence than necessary. Hell, I would have brought the entire pile down on myself if he hadn't steadied it with his hand. He stared down at my livid expression, no doubt a very becoming, blotchy red color.

"What the fuck was that all about?"

I didn't answer and instead thumped a rock hard sandwich down onto my tray.

"Grace?"

I stopped, but refused to meet his eyes. "Just leave it, okay?"

There wasn't enough alcohol in the entire world for that conversation. So I paid for whatever the sandwich was pretending to be before moving to one of the empty tables designated for teachers. It was situated in the far corner of the empty room and was entirely concealed by a colossal cement pillar with a vast array of penises sporadically etched all over it. Our students' artistic talents never ceased to amaze me.

I plonked down on the hard plastic chair like a truant teenager who was about to get ripped into by a teacher. Sulkily, I looked to Ellen—the lunch lady—for moral support, only she'd already left.

Shit.

Levi sat down opposite, regarding me thoughtfully. He held an equally dubious-looking sandwich, only didn't seem to question its origin or use by date because he bit into it. With relish.

"You know," he began, after swallowing a mouthful. "I couldn't help but notice that Serena—"

"Finish that sentence and it'll be the last one you ever say, Levi."

He nodded his head as realization slowly dawned. "I knew it."

I shoved a large mouthful of the rock-like

substance into my mouth in a desperate bid to quell my rising panic. *Damn it, why can't he be stupid?* A less perceptive person wouldn't have seen what I'd been trying so hard to conceal for the last few months.

I swallowed, though with effort.

"Hey, gorgeous girl. Here you are, hiding away. I've been looking for you everywhere."

I cringed at the shrill voice and forced familiarity from one of my least favorite people. Sophie stood before us. Her fake smile, tan and hair color perfectly matched her obscenely perky breasts. To be honest, I was surprised it took her this long to scope out the fresh meat on campus. Usually, her conquests weren't of much interest to me. Well, except when they screwed with our English department. Literally. But there was something in the way she was undressing Levi with her eyes that really aggravated the heck out of me.

"Sophie, to what do I owe this pleasure?" I gave her a false smile. "Have you come to tell me that my Year Twelves are actually going to get their *own* copy of *A Doll's House*? Because, it's been super fun having them share one text between three students and all." My barely masked sarcasm forced her eyes away from Levi.

"Oh, well no. That's not why I'm here. You see, as *English coordinator*—" I didn't even pretend not to roll my eyes. At every opportunity she would name drop her job description and it was beyond fucking annoying. "I just wanted to introduce myself to your new student teacher here." And with that she turned her back on me, completely ostracizing any future input I might have made to the conversation.

Sophie thrust out her perfectly manicured hand, complete with claw-shaped talons, at Levi. "Hi," she breathed, "I'm Sophie DiAngelo." She plastered on her most pant-destroying smile and I slammed the sandwich

I'd been holding onto my tray in disgust.

I'd suddenly lost my appetite.

Levi's eyes flicked to my thunderous expression, amused, and then moved back to Sophie.

"I'm Levi, it's a pleasure to meet you." He took her outstretched hand and shook it while I stared at their entwined fingers, pleading with my lunch to remain in my stomach.

Sophie simpered, leaned forward and thrust her ample breasts in Levi's face. His eyes automatically took them in. I would like to say it was because they were virtually pressed into his eye cavities, but honestly couldn't be sure. All I could be certain of, however, was my rising blind fury.

"Well, it's a *pleasure* to meet you, Levi." Finally, Sophie retrieved her hand. "Now if you need anything at all…" She smiled at him, while slowly tracing her fingers from the top of her V-neck down to her bounteous cleavage. "My office is just next to the administration building. You're welcome to drop by at any time."

Levi smiled. "Thanks, I'll keep that in mind."

I gaped at him.

What the fuck?

She was mutton dressed as lamb for God's sake. No man in their right mind went close to the woman unless they wanted a comprehensive lesson on syphilis.

"You do that," Sophie murmured, while I struggled to pick my bottom jaw up off the food-splattered floor. And reign in my barely contained wrath.

"I'll see you later." With that sleazy farewell, she gave Levi what must have been her most winning smile before sauntering out of the room, her tight black dress leaving little to the imagination.

I willed him dead with my eyes, extremely glad that we were the only two occupants left in the place. At least no one could pin his murder on me.

Levi met my lethal expression. "What?"

"Don't you fucking *what* me, Levi. I can't believe you fell for that shit, she's Spread-Her-Legs Sophie for Christ's sake."

He rolled his eyes. "What's the real problem here, kitten? The fact that she's putting it all out there or the fact that you won't? Because from where I'm sitting, you've got nothing to be pissed about. After all, you're not interested in me, remember?"

"I know that."

He grinned.

"Fuck off."

Levi laughed and I couldn't help it, I threw the discarded remains of my lunch in his face.

"You did not just do that."

I laughed long and loud at his shocked expression. I laughed until my sides ached, tears streamed down my face and I felt at least a ton lighter. As he peeled the remains of butter-slicked lettuce off his cheek and I eventually calmed down enough to breathe, it suddenly dawned on me that I hadn't felt this emotionally liberated in a long, long time.

It felt incredible.

"Sorry." I suppressed a giggle. *Since when did I giggle?* "But you deserved it."

"No you're not. And no, I didn't," he replied in mock anger. Though the corners of his mouth were twitching and there was a definite glint in his eyes. "Why do I always end up covered in shit when you're around?"

I quickly retrieved some napkins from a nearby dispenser and stood in front of him. Levi swiveled around to face me, still covered in my lunch.

"Don't worry," I purred sweetly, dabbing his face with a napkin. "You're still smokin' hot even with egg mayonnaise in your eyebrows."

"So I'm smokin' hot, am I?"

I shut my mouth with a snap. A tooth may or may not have been chipped in my haste.

"That's the nicest thing I've heard come out of your smart mouth, kitten."

"Don't get used to it. It won't happen again."

Our eyes stared into the others' and that warmth he first elicited from me on Friday night slowly uncoiled again. It began in my stomach and spread rapidly throughout my body. Humming. Each of my limbs prickled with that now familiar surging current and I was left feeling completely disorientated. By these feelings. By this man.

By everything.

Levi always made me lose my way, no matter how much I tried not to. Life was simply one cruel joke after another when he was in my orbit.

"What are you doing to me, kitten?" he murmured.

I leaned forward and gently rested my forehead against his, shaking my head slightly. "I could ask you the same thing."

"Fuck it."

Oh. My. Freakin'. God.

It was official. My world was never going to be the same again. I mean, when his lips touched mine— gently at first, searching, seeking, tasting—it somehow felt like I'd been there before. Seriously. It felt as though I was re-familiarizing myself with this beautiful sensation I had once cherished but then stupidly disregarded.

I honestly didn't know what to do with that terrifying realization. However, it was at around the time when his hands slowly, tantalizingly trailed up my outer thighs, pulling up my skirt and any traces of remaining self-control along with it, that I decided not to do anything about it at all.

Except drink the man in of course.

I was going to drown myself in this incredible experience so I would never forget how for one moment in my angry, empty existence, I felt entirely soothed.

My mouth instinctively opened in response to his wandering hands, and his tongue darted inside. It sampled, teased, and challenged my own as he sealed his lips to mine. Never one to shy away from a provocation, I then deepened the kiss. I matched him stroke for stroke, massaging his tongue with my own before surreptitiously running it over his front teeth. My hands, completely discarding the used napkin and finally free to explore, ravaged his hair, tugging and drawing his head back for greater access. A deep groan reverberated in his throat at the pressure I applied to his scalp and my lips quirked up in response. I loved that I could make him feel a hungry, all-consuming need which perfectly matched my own.

It felt incredible.

Levi's hands then traveled to my ass, rhythmically kneading each cheek through the lace of my panties. They weren't exactly my favorite pair but would have to do because I sure as hell didn't envisage *this* happening when I got dressed in the morning. I moaned into his open mouth, those strong, practiced fingers felt so damn phenomenal that I almost lost all sense of reason. As my legs buckled beneath me, he held me tighter and I could feel him smile against my mouth at the obvious struggle I had to remain standing.

To add fuel to the fire, one of Levi's hands then traveled to the front of my panties and those expert fingers of his started to massage my clit in slow, circular motions. I honestly couldn't do anything except clutch on to him for dear life. In the name of all things holy, I actually thought I was going to die. *Is there such a thing as an acute arousal-induced fatality?*

I'd have to check it out.

"Kitten, you're so damn beautiful," Levi groaned against my lips. "I've been wanting to do this since we first met."

I nipped his bottom lip in reply. He had to shut the hell up because if he kept talking to me like this, I would start to believe him. And I couldn't afford to combine the physical pleasure he was eliciting from me with any form of emotional connection.

I simply couldn't.

Wouldn't.

So, to distract us both from that potential landmine, I straddled Levi's lap. I gently pressed myself down onto the prominent bulge in his suit pants, essentially forcing those mischievous fingers of his out the way. And with any luck, any rational thought still lingering in his head.

Lord Almighty.

If there was ever a man to feel this good between my legs, it was Levi. Of course it was fucking Levi. I knew from the moment I first stared into those laughing blue eyes of his that there was something between us neither one could deny. I knew then that he wasn't only trouble, but would one day be the cause of my complete undoing if I truly let him.

For real this time.

"Grace," Levi moaned into my open mouth. I gently rotated my hips forward and back, essentially pumping him with the most intimate part of myself, as his hand moved back to cup my ass again. The way he groaned my name, as though I truly meant something to him, was honestly the best freakin' sound I'd ever heard in my life. So I tenderly wrapped the memory up and

tucked it deep inside that hollow shell of mine.

I would need it for later.

In the meantime, this hunger was nowhere near sated. I pressed closer again and picked up the pace. I then slid my arms down to his shoulders and wrapped them around his neck, nails digging into his skin.

Branding him.

And of course Levi responded with a growl. He gnashed his teeth and sunk them into my soft flesh, imprinting himself on my lower lip. Then he grasped my rocking hips and rhythmically moved me at the pace he craved until I could feel bruises forming from the pressure of his fingers.

It was fucking awesome.

If this was what Heaven felt like, then sweet baby Jesus, I was ready. Never in my life had I felt as turned on and desperately needed by another human being as I was at that moment, clutched in Levi's arms and hidden from view in the empty school cafeteria.

The school cafeteria.

Goddamn it.

Chapter Six

Every morning,
I dream it's all gonna change.
But every evening,
My heart still beats the same.
-MONDEZ, "Nemesis"

I tore my lips away from Levi's. We were both panting and I could taste the metallic tang of my blood. It took him a few seconds to regain focus and then a couple more to register the sheer panic stamped across my face.

"Grace, *don't*," Levi ground out, his grip tightening on me even more. The man had boa constrictor hands that five seconds ago I truly craved but now freaked me the hell out.

Despite our intimate proximity, I was already beyond his reach and he knew it. My shutters had swiftly descended, while the rest of me futilely attempted to grapple with the fact that I'd moved so far beyond wrong, I barely recognized what was right anymore.

I tried pulling away.

"No, Grace—"

"Let go of me, Levi."

A gust of wind escaped him as he dropped his arms, releasing me from his hold. Levi raked both hands exasperatedly through his hair. Hair, that only moments ago, I was unashamedly tugging, while eliciting groans from him that would undoubtedly haunt my sexually frustrated dreams for the rest of my days.

I quickly stood on obscenely wobbly legs and attempted to right myself. Without Levi's hands around me, the sheer magnitude of what just happened between us hit me with full force. It felt as though I was deserted in an oasis of guilt and surrounded by a sea of shame. Somewhere, far off in the distance and flickering away like a warning beacon, was my burning need for him. I chose to ignore it.

Levi stared at me, still breathing heavily, his eyes bright and pleading.

But I turned and ran.

****

"You *what?*" Carli shrieked, six hours later.

We were seated on the terrace of a Mediterranean restaurant and bar overlooking the ocean. God almighty Himself was in the process of dazzling us with one of the most exquisite sunsets Western Australia had to offer. Only I was completely oblivious to it all. Instead, my eyes were trained on the fifth whiskey neat I held cradled in my hands. Normally, the alcohol would have dulled the burgeoning panic which had been bubbling up inside me since first running out on Levi, but this evening it did nothing except amplify how much I craved the damn guy. And it made me irritable.

"Jesus, woman, my ears," I complained, my head still throbbing from the residual ringing.

"Please tell me I misheard you. Please tell me you didn't kiss your student teacher."

I stared down at my drink, my face perfectly matching the red cushion on the wicker seat.

"Oh my God, there's more isn't there?"

I took a deep drink, continuing to avoid her questions.

"Okay," she said the word slowly, stressing the two syllables. "Was there groping? Moaning? Dry humping? *Penetration?*"

"No."

"Phew."

"To the last part."

"*Grace.*"

I dropped my head into my hands and let out a groan. "That's not even the worst of it, Carli," I mumbled into the linen tablecloth.

"Come on then, let's hear it."

So I told her. Everything. From first meeting Levi on Friday night and feeling that instant spark, right through to taking the remainder of the day off on sick leave to get away from it. I even told her about Riley liking the damn guy. Saying those words out loud made me feel like I had anaphylaxis.

Anyway, I'd spent the afternoon down at my favorite secluded beach with my feet anchored in the sand and my hands over my eyes, willing that last broken look from Levi to disappear.

It didn't.

"Oh, babe. I don't know about you but I need another drink. Fuck the carbs."

I nodded and Carli went back inside to order another round. As I sat and stared at the now empty glass in my hands, my mind cast back to when I first met Riley—the best friend I'd just betrayed.

"What's your name?"

I looked up from the primary school sandpit, a bucket in one hand and a spade in the other. A lanky, tan-skinned girl with a blonde side ponytail stood before me. She wore a bright pink dress with purple butterflies on it and I noticed that she didn't have dark smudges of dirt all over her legs like I did.

After blowing ragged black bangs out of my eyes, I stated flatly, "Grace."

"My name's Riley." She stretched out a clean hand and I stared up at it, uncertain.

"Mummy always says it's polite to shake hands

when you first introduce yourself."

"Oh, okay." I put down the bucket and brushed some sand off my hand with my blue t-shirt before grasping her fingers.

Riley shook my hand vigorously before letting go. "What are you doing?" She pointed down at my spade which I still held clutched in my other hand.

"I'm going to build a castle. It's going to have a moat, lookout towers, a secret underground chamber for the princess and everything."

Her eyes widened in awe. "I'm really good at building sandcastles. Can I help too?"

"Sure. Do you want to fill up the bucket with sand or dig out the moat?"

"The moat." She smiled at me, her freckles catching in the sunlight, "We're going to make the bestest sandcastle ever."

Carli returned a few minutes later with two fresh glasses. She handed me one and then slid into her seat. Her eyes were empathetic yet firm. "You know what you have to do, right?"

I nodded and looked down at my drink, wondering how many more I would need before plucking up the courage to tell my best friend what I'd done with her almost-boyfriend. Not to mention my growing feelings for the guy.

Two and a half dekaliters at the very least.

My phone's notification screen lit up. After picking it up off the table and inspecting it, I frowned.

"Levi?"

"Riley. She's staying at her parent's place for the rest of the week. Her mum's sick."

"Is she all right?"

"Who? Riley?"

"No, her mum. It must be pretty serious if she's staying up there for a while."

I snorted. "That woman's a complete hypochondriac. She probably sneezed once and now thinks she has pneumonia or something."

Carli was quiet for a moment. "So what are you going to do?"

I shook my head, and at long last the room moved along with it. "Not tell her over the phone, that's for damn sure."

"So why not go to her mum's place and tell her there?"

"Carli, I've been drinking. They live in Margaret River, so a taxi would cost a down payment on a house and…" My voice trailed away. "Her mum thinks I'm a negative influence on Riley. We don't exactly get along. She'd slam the front door in my face before I even set foot inside."

Carli swore under her breath. "Seriously, girl, it's a miracle you've got any friends at all."

I dropped my head into my arms again. Carli was absolutely right and if it was at all possible, I now felt even worse.

****

It became a daily ritual then, that on my way home from work I'd drop past the bottle shop and buy something strong enough to knock me out until I woke up the next day. By the end of the week, Hank, the manager and my new drunken savior, would have my favorite bottle ready and waiting next to the till by the time I even walked in the front door. He never asked me the reason behind my ritualistic alcohol-induced oblivion of a nighttime. Instead, he looked at me sadly and shook his head as he swiped through my credit card.

Good man.

However, my days spent at school with Levi were emotionally exhausting to say the least. He'd tried to broach the subject of what happened between us on Tuesday morning, but I swiftly changed the conversation to effective teaching methodologies for Year Nines, and he didn't attempt to do bring it up again. To be honest, I didn't know whether to be grateful or insulted at how easily he gave up on that topic.

Anyway, the remainder of the week was spent avoiding eye contact, confined spaces, empty rooms, and any subject other than work. It sucked. And it wasn't even as though I felt the same numbness like when Dylan packed up and left. Which in comparison to this, would have been heaven on earth. Oh no, this was a gazillion times worse because I felt *everything*. I felt Levi's eyes caressing my face while I was teaching and he thought I didn't notice. I felt that powerful magnetic pull between us when we were sitting side by side and I was attempting to explain curriculum planning to him. Hell, I even felt an incomprehensible wave of despair wash over me when we parted ways in the school car park at the end of the day. So it was only at lunchtime when I hid in the freakin' staff toilets that I could finally draw breath.

Thus the alcohol.

Which was why I was seriously pissed when on Friday afternoon Martha called and requested both Levi and I attend an impromptu meeting with Serena after the final bell sounded. Dragging out my days any longer than strictly necessary was like getting a Brazilian wax just before my period was due.

Fucking painful.

Serena looked up from behind her laptop as we entered. Her measured gaze took in my murderous glare and Levi's somewhat pained expression.

"Take a seat." It wasn't a request. "I hear you've

fit in extremely well, Levi."

I raised my eyebrows in surprise. I hadn't spoken a word to anyone about his progress.

"Sophie has recommended your, shall we say, talents? Very highly."

I turned, glaring up at Levi but he ignored me.

"Have the daily debriefs with her been beneficial?"

What?

"Yeah. They've been, ah, educational."

I suddenly felt sick in the pit of my stomach. Levi had been meeting Sophie without my knowledge, every fucking day? How *dare* he? I stared down at my balled fists, imagining that in each of them was one of his testicles.

"Which is why," Serena continued, "you have now been invited to attend the National Independent Schools Education Conference. Congratulations."

"With Sophie?" The words slipped out of my mouth before I could force them back and an awkward silence permeated the office.

"Yes."

"You've got to be fucking joking."

Shit.

I really needed to get a handle on that whole head/mouth filter thing which was clearly in need of major repairs.

"Is there a problem, Grace? Your student teacher has made quite an impression on certain staff members at Geographe High School. In fact, Sophie even deems it appropriate for him to experience the largest and most comprehensive week-long networking event of the year. Surely, you're not trying to begrudge him that opportunity?" Her green cat-like eyes drilled into my own, willing me to refute with her.

103

I sat on my balled fists so I wouldn't punch her in the face. "No," I ground out.

"I thought not. Which is why," she paused, clearly enjoying pulling the strings of my fate like a fucking puppet master, "you will also be attending."

I stared at her.

"Now, I expect you to report back to me on each session you attend. I want to see detailed notes which you will then share with the staff in your department once you return. Consider it a trial run for the role of English coordinator."

Whoa.

I was pretty sure my eyes popped a good inch out of their sockets. More than anything else, I wanted to turn the English department around and make it a force to be reckoned with. Not only that, but I'd already been begging Sophie and Serena to let me attend the conference for the past three months. I mean, the best of the best were going to be there—teachers, academics and professors alike. It was an awesome opportunity but one I'd gladly forego if it meant watching Sophie get her claws into Levi.

"So, we're all going? Like, all three of us?"

A ghost of a smile reached Serena's lips. "Sadly, Sophie is currently dealing with … an illness." I snorted. That was code for a herpes outbreak if ever I heard one. Serena narrowed her eyes in warning at me. "So, unfortunately she will be missing the conference this year."

"When is it?"

Serena looked across at Levi. "Your flights are booked for Saturday morning. You arrive in the afternoon and will be staying until the following weekend."

"As in *tomorrow?*" I shrieked.

"Yes, Grace, as in tomorrow." My inability to

process this information was clearly starting to irritate her. But I didn't care. I was going to be traveling with Levi, alone, for eight days and seven thigh-clenchingly long nights.

Heaven help me.

"So, where are we off to?" Levi appeared to be handling this unexpected bombshell much better than I was. He even remembered to ask for relevant information.

"Melbourne."

"Jesus Christ." I flopped back onto the office chair with a loud groan.

****

I didn't go straight to the bottle shop that evening. Instead, I found myself once again at the beach, with shoes off and feet buried in the sand as though it were the only thing keeping me grounded. As I looked out at the azure water, my raging thoughts slowed and my shoulders, which must have been positioned up around my hairline, gradually relaxed. I breathed deeply.

Since Dad passed away, it was either in a book, a bottle or here, staring off into eternity that I found any solace whatsoever. Don't even get me started on my avoidance issues. Believe me, I was well aware. I shut my eyes and inhaled the cool, salty air. The sounds of the waves gently lapping against the shore, the gulls cawing above me and my decelerating heartbeat brought about that vague approximation of calm I was all but used to by now.

Upon opening my eyes again, I watched as the sky transformed. It changed first from yellow to orange, then to pink, red, and finally purple. At last it slipped behind the horizon, taking my emotional turmoil along with it. I didn't even attempt to organize my thoughts or create an action plan of how I was going to manage the next week. Attempting to juggle both the want and need Levi excited within me, with the abstinence that must surely follow, was going to be a headfuck of epic proportions. So I decided not to add broken promises on top of that mountain of guilt I'd already been lugging around for the past week.

Instead, I sat in the growing darkness—my feet buried, my heart full and my head strangely quiet. It wasn't until a couple strolled past, arms wrapped around each other as they murmured between themselves and then laughed openly at something one of them must have said, that I stood, brushed myself off and left.

When I rounded the corner of the internal staircase and stepped into the off-white hallway leading to my apartment, I stopped short. My newfound calm quickly dissolved as two blue eyes caused my traitorous heart to malfunction.

"What are you doing here?"

"Drink?" Levi held up a bottle of whiskey with already one-third of it gone. He must have been waiting for some time because he was spread out on the floor. One leg was straight in front of him, while the other was bent with a notebook flattened against it and he held a pen in his right hand. Levi's hair looked as though those delectable fingers of his had raked through it a few times. Whether it was out of habit or frustration, I wasn't sure.

I shrugged my shoulders and unlocked the door. We might as well get the awkward conversation over with. I mean, not talking about anything but work for the past week had been exhausting and getting it done with a bottle between us seemed as good a time as any.

Levi stood and followed me inside. For a man who'd already ingested a good portion of whiskey, he still looked as sober as a saint. He detoured straight to the lounge room, before dumping his belongings onto the coffee table and then collapsing on the couch.

When I returned from the kitchen, and even in my emotionally comatose state, my body gradually kicked back to life at the sight of him. I blamed the fact that he had changed his outfit. Levi looked sinfully sexy in dark jeans, a white t-shirt and black combat boots. The guy couldn't appear any further removed from the local surfers if he tried. I truly pitied the seams of his top though. They were clearly struggling to hold the scraps of material together over his chiseled torso and wide shoulders. Poor things. They hadn't a hope in hell.

I swallowed, then sat down next to him, busying my itching fingers by pouring very healthy shots of the amber liquid into our two short glasses.

Levi raised an eyebrow at the generous portions but said nothing. I just threw my head back and downed the whole drink in one go.

"Thirsty?"

"You've no idea."

He smiled and raised the glass to his lips, his eyes glinting at me as he took a mouthful.

I looked down and poured myself another. Once I'd downed that one too and was then onto my third, I nodded my head in the direction of his notebook. "You writing your last will and testament there, sport? Because after that shit you pulled on me with Sophie, you should be."

He smiled across at me again and casually leaned back, his arm draping along the headrests of the couch. "Kitten, after that number you pulled on Monday, you sure as hell don't get to play jealous girlfriend now."

"After being with Sophie all week, don't reckon I'd want you anyway."

He chuckled and my petulant mood lightened instantly. With him everything was so easy and yet so hard.

So hard and yet so fucking easy.

I leaned back, my head resting just below Levi's hand and took another sip. Slower this time. I even got to taste the whiskey before it hit the back of my throat.

Bliss.

We sat there, drinking and silent for a long time. It wasn't uncomfortable. In fact, even sitting at the beach earlier hadn't made me feel this centered. Which was yet another terrifying realization to add to the list that was growing infinitely larger by the day. It was strange really, how one person could have me so wired that I couldn't formulate a cohesive thought in my head, let alone verbalize it out loud. While on the other hand, that one person could also soothe me like nothing and no one else. Even whiskey didn't stand a chance against Levi.

I was well and truly fucked.

"Lyrics."

"Mmm?"

"I was writing song lyrics before you got back."

I rolled my head to the side and gazed up at Levi. His face was in profile, his eyes were closed and if it weren't for his fingers tapping out a beat on the sofa just behind my head, I could have sworn he was asleep.

"How's it going?"

He opened his eyes and languidly looked down at me. "I've got plenty of material. It's just…"

"What?" I was choosing to ignore my heart which had somersaulted at his last insinuation. Scarily enough, I also had to firmly remind myself to continue breathing as his gaze melted into mine.

He'd done it again.

I'd gone from relatively composed to panting in under five seconds.

"It just … doesn't feel right. Being here."

"With *me?*" There was no point in wishing my hysteria to have been less obvious, or for those words to have been unsaid.

"No, I didn't mean that." His eyes caressed my face and I visibly relaxed under them. "I mean being here, in Geographe Bay. It's just too ... mellow. You know?"

I nodded, completely understanding. For the past year I'd felt far too angry for this laid-back place. It was like I had been the only person who continuously felt jarred by these idealistic surroundings because they served as a reminder of how much I didn't deserve them. And how much I didn't belong. After all, how could I *not* feel contented under the blue skies, the gum trees, the tiled roofed buildings, and the lingering gaze of sun-kissed strangers? No idea. But somehow I'd managed to.

Freak that I was.

"And when you let me have it at The Hole, I knew you felt it too."

"I was a bitch, Levi. Nothing more."

"No. I mean, yeah, you were." He laughed and I smiled back at him. "But that wasn't all I saw in you. Not even close."

And I couldn't look away.

The fact that he'd immediately recognized this internal struggle I had been grappling with for what felt like an eternity, and also felt it too, suddenly made the intensifying connection between us so much more tangible. It wasn't just physical anymore. What we shared was ... *real*.

There was now a hell of a lot more to lose.

"Have you ever been to Melbourne?"

I shook my head, suddenly incredibly tired. "Have you?"

"Once, when my mum took me and Dom there to

get away from Dad for a while." He quelled my curious, though no less sleepy stare by adding, "That's a story for another time, kitten. You look beat. I should go."

"No, stay."

He smiled.

"Tell me about it. Melbourne, I mean."

So, he did. For hours his voice caressed my ears while I shut my eyes and let it wash over me. That strange, comforting feeling only he could conjure spread throughout my mildly drunken limbs. And for once, I completely relaxed. The last thing I remembered before slipping off into blissful oblivion was him gently removing the empty glass from my hands and the feel of his calloused fingers as they stroked my hair.

Heaven.

Chapter Seven

My suitcase is packed, I'm leaving.
My key to the lock is in your head,
The future's bright for all.
-MONDEZ, "Riot"

When I woke the next morning, I felt strangely rested and knew that for once it wasn't from the alcohol. I sat up and sleepily pushed the hair out of my face, catching out of the corner of my eye a folded piece of notepaper propped up against a novel on my bedside table. I didn't even attempt to figure out how Levi had managed to maneuver me from the couch to my bed. Or even into my Hitchcock t-shirt. Instead, I focused on the note he had written and scowled when it read:

You're beautiful, even when you snore. Pack a warm jacket.

What the hell did he mean by *'snore'*? I huffed. Never in my life had I *snored*. Ever. At least Dylan never mentioned it. Ignoring that embarrassing possibility, I decided to look closer at his handwriting and tried to match the man I had come to know with the dark scrawl emblazoned on the page. It was confident yet undeniably artistic script, particularly in the way he completed his 'f' and 'y' with a flourish. It was almost as though his ideas couldn't be contained within the printed blue lines of the page. God, even his scrawl was arrogant.

I smiled.

I checked the clock on my phone that was laying next to the note and almost wet myself. *Ten-thirty*. I was supposed to be leaving for the airport in under an hour and hadn't even packed yet. So I frantically fought off the covers, jumped out of bed and raced towards the bathroom, grabbing random items of clothing on the way. After quite possibly the shortest shower of all time, I threw on some ass-hugging blue jeans, ballet flats and a fitted black top. I knelt down and searched under my bed for the warm jacket I knew existed somewhere and thankfully found it next to my dusty suitcase. I dragged them both out, wiped them off and set about hurling inside whatever I could find that was both warm and clean. Once done, I quickly ducked back to the bathroom and scooped my toiletries into a small bag, before running back to my bedroom again and dropping it amongst what had already been packed.

I stopped and took a deep breath. In an attempt to slow my racing pulse, I took stock of what had been gathered and what was still needed. *Books*. I needed books. So I rummaged through the towering stacks on either side of my bed, threw half of them in my suitcase and an extra two in my handbag for good measure. I still felt off though. Surely, I'd forgotten something important. Levi had the tickets. He'd mentioned it in my semi-comatose state last night, so that couldn't be it. It suddenly dawned on me.

Riley.

She was going to be arriving home today and would have no idea where I was. Apart from the occasional text message asking after her mother, I hadn't been in contact with Riley. Though, she did say her mum was on the mend and that she was really looking forward to returning home again. Who wouldn't after spending a week with that woman? But other than that, we hadn't spoken.

Needless to say, I hadn't said a word about what happened between Levi and I in the school cafeteria. Except to mention that the gods had conspired against me and he was now my student teacher. She'd replied with so many excited emojis that I had to delete the message to stop myself from printing it off, turning those fuckers into a noose and hanging myself with it. As horrible as it was keeping this secret from my best friend, I needed to be with her in person when I told her everything. After all, it was such an asshole thing to do to someone—*hear that Dylan, you dickwad*—to hide behind a text message or phone call when delivering bad news. I owed her that much at least. Only, there had been no time. Between the act itself, Riley staying at her parents' and me heading off to Melbourne, the opportune moment had never arisen.

So, I quickly texted her about the conference and was ready to dial a cab when my ringtone started going gangbusters.

"Hey," I answered, cringing at my breathy tell-all voice.

"Hey yourself, kitten. You ready?"

I nodded. Not my most intelligent of moments.

"Well?"

"I'm nodding."

Levi chuckled and my knees almost gave way. I swear, that guy was going to be the death of those pathetic joints. "Okay then, get your ass downstairs. We're waiting."

"Who's we?"

"Me and Dom. He offered to drive. Says he can't wait to see the back of me for a while."

I smiled. "Just give me a minute, I need to lock up."

After hanging up I searched my room, ensuring that nothing had been overlooked. Once satisfied, I slung a bulging handbag over my shoulder before wheeling the suitcase through the apartment and out the front door.

It closed with a resounding thud behind me.

Levi was leaning up against a red and white 1959

Ford Thunderbird. Dad was a classic car enthusiast, he taught me well. Anything past 1983 was a wasted effort as far as he was concerned.

What, so now the guy was a male car model too? His ability to stand in the general vicinity of inanimate objects and suddenly make them look as sexy as all hell was seriously getting beyond a joke. My panties couldn't take it. Which was probably why my eyes greedily raked his body from head to toe.

Sweet God.

Black Ray Bans hid blue eyes, while a faded gray tank hung off his wide shoulders, exposing his muscular arms to mouthwatering advantage. The front of his shoulders and what I could see of his chest were completely covered in ink work. The tattoos must have coated his entire torso as well. It was official. I would gladly offer my soul on a pristine silver platter to Satan himself for just a glimpse at the rest of that body.

I gulped.

Levi's tank was carelessly tucked into the waistband of a small section of his black jeans. Jeans that hugged his narrow hips in a way I futilely wished I could myself. On his feet were the combat boots that must have walked me from the lounge room to my bed last night.

I gulped again.

Damn it, girl, you're gonna miss the flight at this rate.

I shook my head and fought the suitcase down a couple of stairs before Levi noticed my losing battle and came to the rescue. Like a knight in fucking armor. I rolled my eyes in annoyance at him and the corners of his mouth quirked up into a smile. Well, that was before he picked up my luggage and threw it over his shoulder, caveman-style. After that I just uselessly clung to the handrail for a minute because my knees had all but given up on me by this point. The way the muscles in his back and shoulders rippled with the ease of the movement as he strode back down the stairs was ridiculous.

Jerk.

When I blessedly reached the car, still upright, Levi had already deposited my suitcase in the boot. He stood waiting by the open rear door. Since his eyes were covered, I couldn't read his expression as easily as I'd like, but I noticed a dangerous smile playing about the corner of his lips.

It matched my own.

I ducked my head and scooted into the backseat, grinning up at Dom. "Nice ride."

"My pride and joy." He grinned back.

Levi lowered his sunglasses and rolled his eyes at me. He then closed my door, strolled around to the front passenger seat and comfortably seated himself before shutting the front door behind him.

I took one last glance at the apartment complex as we roared out of the car park and could have sworn I spied Mrs. Jenkinson peeking out from behind her lavender curtains. The entire block will think I've eloped with two men by sunset. But I didn't care. I had the windows down, the warm breeze teasing my unruly hair and Levi and Dom finally settled on their music choice for the journey. I leaned back. Contented. What was it about this guy that made me feel so damn … good?

One heck of a pent up sigh escaped me.

"So what's in Melbourne?"

"For fuck's sake, Dom. How many times do I have to spit it out? It's a conference for Christ's sake."

"The thing is, bro, your mouth moves and words come out, but I honestly don't give a shit."

"Then don't fucking ask."

Dom winked at me through the rearview mirror

and I smiled back. Listening to the two of them banter like fishwives was strangely comforting. And an irritated Levi was kinda hot.

I squirmed in my seat.

"How'd Riley pull up after our gig last week, Grace?"

"Pretty good, considering."

"Yeah, she doesn't seem like much of a drinker."

"Did you figure that one out before or after she passed out on you, Dom?"

He laughed. "I knew we'd be buds, Gracie."

I grimaced at the nickname and Levi snorted from the front seat. So I kicked the back of it. Hard.

"*Jesus, woman.* Watch the interior."

"Sorry," I mumbled to Dom, not in the least bit apologetic. Levi snorted again and I glared at the back of his head, willing it to explode all over the leather detailing through negative thought alone.

"So what does she do then? Riley, I mean."

Levi turned to face Dom. "What's with the sudden interest, bro?"

Dom raised both of his hands off the steering wheel in mock surrender, "Hey, no interest, man. I'm just having a chat with my good friend Gracie here, that's all." He looked at me through the rearview mirror again. "He's been whining like a bitch all week. Must be that time of the month."

Levi punched him in the arm and the entire car shuddered from the impact. "Shut the fuck up." Only, Dom didn't seem in the least bit injured. He just smirked at Levi's obvious annoyance.

I wasn't the only one who had experienced the longest week on record then.

Interesting.

"Say, Gracie?"

"Hmm?" I looked up at Dom and didn't for one second trust the glint in his eyes.

"Maybe you should get my bro here laid while you're in Melbourne. Consider it a school project or something."

I swore under my breath and narrowed my eyes at him, relishing the sound of Levi's second punch as it hit home.

My heart quickened as we pulled into the express drop-off lane at Perth Airport. All of the overthinking I'd tried desperately not to do during the last twenty or so hours rolled towards me like a seven-foot barrel wave. I tried to find my Zen through some deep breathing, mantra-style, only this time it did absolutely nothing. By the time I'd not-so-gracefully exited the car, Dom had already popped the trunk and Levi was placing our combined luggage on the footpath.

Combined luggage.

As in, we were both going away. Together. Days would be spent sitting next to each other in conference halls. Nights would be spent in adjoining rooms. And I somehow had to function rationally enough so I could report back to Serena on all the content covered over the five days. All the while trying not to kill anyone stupid enough to distract me from that colossal task. I groaned. It would take all of my energy trying to stop myself from acting on my pent-up sexual aggression alone.

Lord help me.

"Later loser." Dom snapped me out of my inner meltdown by dragging Levi into a man hug of epic proportions. I was surprised there were no bones broken or teeth shattered during the exercise.

"Later."

Dom turned and ruffled my hair, like I was a preschooler who'd finally learned not to eat from the sandpit or something. "See ya 'round, Gracie."

I smacked his hand away and he grinned.

"Feisty." He then jumped back into his Ford, revved the engine until my ears almost bled and careered out of sight.

While standing on the footpath in the residual exhaust fumes, I felt that barrel wave of nerves peak, and crash into me. Knocking me backward.

I futilely wished Dom would miraculously return so he could act as a buffer between what I wanted to do so badly that it actually became a physical hurt, and what I knew I shouldn't. But of course he didn't. So, instead I attempted to gather my disintegrating splinters of self-preservation and hid them under a shitload of Smart Mouth.

Time to bring your A-game, Grace.

Turning around, I looked at Levi who was in the process of organizing his gear. Thankfully, I stopped short. "Really?"

"What?"

"A *guitar?* You brought a fucking guitar?"

He grinned at my disbelief.

"You're planning on being the lunchtime entertainment during the next week then? Will you be taking special requests?"

"And how many books have you got in that case of yours, kitten?" He nodded in the direction of my luggage. "I've seen your bedside table. That bag's full to the brim with Conan Doyle, am I right?"

"It's none of your damn business what I pack," I retorted, clutching my handbag closer to my side in an attempt to disguise the other two.

"Exactly. Let's go." He turned on his heel, leading the way through the entrance and towards the check-in counter.

Two minutes down, another billion or so to go.

I'd totally nailed it.

I didn't nail it.

Not even close. Once the woman behind the desk managed to wipe away the drool which was simply oozing down her chin at the sight of Levi, and our luggage was safely placed onto the conveyor belt, we moved through security. Only, the closer we got to our departure gate, the quicker my resolve evaporated. Which meant that before long, I was a bundle of nerves.

I can't do this. I can't be here, with him. Honest to God, it's fucking impossible. This dawning realization irritated me like you wouldn't believe.

"What is it?"

"Huh?"

"What are you thinking? You're doing that tongue thing again."

"Nothing. I'm not thinking anything. Enough with the third degree already, fucking hell."

See?

We walked on in silence for a bit longer. I felt guilty for being as rude as all hell to Levi without good reason and the man himself remained strangely quiet. When we reached our gate, I couldn't take it anymore. I immediately turned away and stalked towards the floor to ceiling windows, trying everything I could to lose myself in the planes bowling down the tarmac and taking off into the cloudless sky above. It didn't help. But at least I had something to look at during my internal crisis.

God, I wished Dad was here. He always knew what to say when I felt like this. My mind traveled back to just over a year ago.

"Dad, do you ever get scared?"

He looked across at me, concerned. "Well, that

119

depends on what you're referring to, Monkey."

I shrugged one shoulder. "I dunno. Life, I guess."

"That's a lot to be scared of."

I stared out at the gray stormy water. Today, it perfectly matched the thick blanket of clouds hovering threateningly above. And my mood. "I just sometimes get this feeling, you know? Like, life as I know it is this temporary moment in time and at any second everything's going to change. Only, I can't do a thing to stop it."

Dad nodded his head slowly, taking in what I'd just said. "But what's to say change is bad? Maybe it's exactly what's meant to happen?"

"But I like my life the way it is now."

He chuckled deeply and pulled me in close, kissing the top of my head. "Don't be scared of change, love. Be scared of living an apathetic existence."

"Kitten?"

I blinked, staring straight ahead. My memory faded and I found myself looking at Levi's reflection in the window over my left shoulder. More than anything in the entire world, I didn't want to turn around. If he saw my eyes I wouldn't be able to hide exactly how fragmented I'd become.

All because of him.

"Hey." A featherweight touch trailed down my arm and I shivered. Once it reached my hand and entwined with my fingers, I closed my eyes, distractedly trying not to lean back into him for comfort. I then felt a tug and my eyes blinked open as Levi gently turned me around to face him.

"What's wrong?"

I averted my eyes. If he only fucking knew.

My chin lifted from the pressure of his fingers and

our eyes finally met. "Are you afraid of flying?"

"No. Not of flying."

His eyes were unbelievably tender as they took in my exposed vulnerability. He slowly nodded in understanding. "Come here." Pulling my hand, Levi led me towards a row of empty plastic seats before sitting down. He deliberately removed the handbag from my shoulder and carefully placed it on the seat next to him. I felt beyond awkward standing in front of him like this and flashes of what had happened between us in the school cafeteria flickered before my eyes, making my pulse race. He gently tugged at my hand again and drew me down onto his lap.

Cradling me like a child.

I kid you not, if it had been anyone else, I would have punched them straight in the throat. Seriously. That is, before using every last vernacular at my disposal to tell them exactly what I thought of their outrageous assumption. But because it was Levi, I cuddled in closer, my cheek flush with his chest as he wrapped his arms around me. When his chin rested on the top of my head, I felt a security that had long been absent from my life gradually descend from above and settle itself over me.

Like a second skin.

Levi's ribs expanded as he took in a deep breath and then contracted as he slowly exhaled. His heartbeat was strong and sure, it spoke directly to my own frazzled one that gradually eased its erratic tempo in response. Once calm, I leisurely trailed my fingers across his skin, tracing the outlines and patterns of the tattoos visible on his chest. It seemed the most natural thing in the world, to be curled up on Levi's lap in the departures lounge of Perth airport.

Some time later, I couldn't tell you how long exactly because it felt as though we were in a vacuum of timeless space, our flight was called. I slowly untangled myself from Levi and stood, plowing fingers through my wild hair. Levi stood next to me, then bent to retrieve my handbag before placing it on my shoulder. He smiled, winked and took my hand again, leading me to the snaking line of people who were waiting for our flight.

It wasn't at all strange that no words had been said. Truth be told, his reassuring heartbeat and steadfast embrace said all I needed to hear anyway. Now, it was just a matter of trying to figure out a way forward from here. Which was where I drew a blank. I mean, I couldn't even put a label on what we were at that moment, let alone decide where we were headed. All I knew for certain was that something between us had just shifted and I couldn't put my finger on where or how exactly, but it was as though we had realigned in a slightly different place. Somewhere deeper. Somehow connected.

I was screwed.

While filing into the aircraft, I chose once again to ignore the openly appreciative glances from the flight attendants, both male and female. If Levi was aware of the stares, he didn't show it and I allowed my heart to warm to him that little bit more. He just kept moving through the galley and holding my hand until we found our seats. In *first class*.

Whoa.

Sophie must have really wanted to pull a number on the guy. God knows if the school had organized the flights, we'd have been in the back row next to the toilets. I couldn't help an inward smile, Sophie would be so pissed knowing that I was here in her place. Served the bitch right for hijacking Levi each day right from under my nose. I shook my head. This burgeoning possessiveness was really disturbing.

"Window seat or aisle?"

"Aisle."

Levi nodded and moved past me to sit down, but not before brushing his thumb across my bottom lip and murmuring in my ear, "Stop thinking."

My knees gave a huge sigh of relief as I collapsed into the seat and composed myself long enough to stow my handbag by my feet.

We were given some refresher towels and I tried not to laugh at the disinterested face of the attendant as she ran through the safety procedures. Seriously, you'd think they'd at least *look* confident in their ability to survive a forty thousand foot drop in altitude. Apparently not. I didn't care. If I was meant to die, then so be it. At least my last moments would be with Levi and there were worst places to die than in the arms of a sexy man. So I settled back, surprisingly comfortable.

I'd never traveled much as a kid. Well, not out of Western Australia anyway. On a single salary, and even one as generous as Dad's, the cash only stretched so far. It wasn't until Dylan took me to Brisbane last summer, that I'd even been inside a plane.

I loved them.

There was something about rocketing down the runway before being simultaneously thrust back and downwards in my seat during takeoff, that I found strangely liberating. I think it was the inevitability of it all, the fact that I had to surrender all control to the pilots and trust them not to fuck up completely. It was somehow cathartic.

Ironic really.

"You're looking more like yourself, kitten."

My eyes were shut and I was enjoying the way the plane had just dipped and then rose farther up in the air. It was freakin' amazing. Levi was right, I was feeling much better. I turned to him, smiling. For once it was both wide and true. The corresponding sharp intake of his breath at my exultant expression set off a swarm of butterflies in my stomach. It felt like they were high on energy drinks.

"Fuck, Grace—"

But I didn't let him finish. This three and a half hour flight wasn't nearly long enough for everything I wanted to do to him if he completed that train of thought. When he looked at me like that, like I was a precious marvel, I felt undone. And there was no way in hell I would be able to control myself within the confines of an airplane seat if I didn't distract myself. First class or no. Besides, we'd be arrested for noise complaints as soon as we disembarked at Tullamarine anyway. Oh, and there was Riley to consider. I'd almost forgotten Riley.

True friend that I was.

"You've been to Melbourne before, haven't you?" It wasn't a question. It was a desperate plea to change the subject to less treacherous waters.

Levi sighed. "Yeah, when I was nine and Dom was seven. Dad's side of the family lives there."

"So why'd your mum need to get away from your dad?"

He turned to look out the window, clearly not comfortable with the question.

"It's just that you mentioned it last night and I … it made me wonder, I guess."

Levi's eyes met mine again but they were suddenly foreign to me. The mocking glint I'd come to know and loved to hate had disappeared completely. In its place was a cold, dead stare.

I suppressed a shiver.

"He's a fucking asshole, Grace. Unless you want to see me completely lose my shit, we need to change the subject. *Now*."

As much as I wanted to help him out, this whole

Jekyll and Hyde thing had completely thrown me. "I, ah, I mean—"

"Welcome aboard. Can I offer either of you a refreshing beverage?"

I almost launched myself at the overtly gay flight attendant in elation at his timely interruption.

"Yeah, I'll have a—" I quickly checked the time on my phone to see if it was noon yet. It had gone past twelve. I was good to go. "Whiskey neat, thanks."

"Ah, sure." He tried not to judge my obvious alcoholic dependence through a thinly veiled mask of professional politeness. "And for yourself, sir?"

"A beer. Whatever's strongest."

"Another excellent choice. I'll be right back."

As he minced his way down the aisle, I just knew we were going to be the talk of the cabin. But then I stopped myself. Let them talk, I didn't give a shit. What I did care about was the man sitting next to me. *Hear that, heart? I said it. Out loud. Now leave me the heck alone.*

"Look, Grace."

I turned to face Levi. He was rubbing long fingers across his forehead, clearly agitated at what had just passed between us. Seeing him like this was awful.

"Levi, stop." I pulled his hand away and held it in my own, reaching out with my other to brush the worry lines from his brow. "I get it, it's fine. We've all got our shitty baggage. Some of us just throw it back when we're asked about it uninvited, that's all." I smiled, caressing his cheek. "Trust me, I know. I've had plenty of practice."

He took the hand that cupped his cheek and turned it skyward, kissing my palm. His eyes peeked up from behind long lashes, totally rocking being simultaneously apologetic and sexy as hell. "What am I gonna do with you, kitten?"

I shrugged one shoulder, mesmerized by his lips as they made contact with my palm once again. I barely suppressed a shudder at the feel of them against my heated skin. "Simple," I breathed, "you're going to tell me all about it. But only when you're good and ready."

"I'm gonna do a lot more than that."

There was suddenly not nearly enough air in my lungs.

"When you're good and ready, of course."

Chapter Eight

Under the waves, I'm heading down again,
Noise in my head, I can't let go if it.
-MONDEZ, "This Life"

I was ready.

At Levi's last words my heart slowly unraveled and stealthily crept its way to the forefront of my mind, like the freakin' stalker it was. Once settled there, this dawning recognition hit me like a thunderbolt in the panties. Somewhere, between Perth and Melbourne it was settled. I wanted him to know that I was ready.

Screw everything else.

Okay, so that was a slight over-exaggeration. I did care about other things, especially Riley. After all, she was my family. So to be honest, I wasn't entirely reconciled with my decision to move forward with Levi but knew that I was going to ignore those nagging doubts. I was going to do it anyway.

Horrible person that I was.

It just truly sucked that she was going to hurt because of me and the thought weighed on my conscience like a lead balloon. She'd done so much for me. She was everything I could ever ask for in a friend, and then some.

But I was *tired*.

I'd had the hardest week of my life trying to be more deserving of her. All I got in return was outright misery and one very cranky liver. After all, when Levi first appeared it was like my world suddenly flipped on its axis. Don't get me wrong, he was seriously frustrating at times. But something in him spoke directly to a part of me that I could have sworn had shriveled up and died a long time ago. Surely, people who felt this kind of pull, both physical and emotional, grew closer because they were meant to be? They weren't all selfish pricks who were backstabbing their nearest and dearest at the first chance they got—were they?

I sighed.

Either way someone was going to suffer. And I hoped that after one year and a week, maybe that someone could be somebody other than me. I just wished it wasn't going to be Riley.

That thought left me with a seriously bitter aftertaste.

Levi sensed my growing anxiety and hastily changed the subject. He asked me to tell him all about what to expect at the conference and I was thankful for the distraction. To be honest, I was genuinely looking forward it. So I talked and talked, moving further away from the contentious decision I'd just made in my head and the guilt which came along with it. A small part of me couldn't help but notice that he held on to my hand throughout it all.

Yay heart.

Levi's eyes never left my face either and his answering grin at my growing excitement only made me lose my train of thought once or twice. When I finally ran out of steam, we had already finished our drinks long ago and the plane was descending. I now felt completely different, liberated somehow. This acknowledgment only served to quadruple my newfound energy because not only was I pumped about the conference and about what might happen between Levi and I, but I also loved plane landings too.

Levi chuckled at my embarrassingly childish behavior. I had literally just stopped bouncing up and down in my seat by this point. He slowly leaned in close and brushed his lips over mine. He was so gentle and the contact so fleeting, that I could have sworn I imagined the whole thing. It was only when he murmured in my ear afterward and a fireworks display detonated in my nether regions, that I knew it was for real. "You have no idea, do you? Of how fucking irresistible you are."

Luckily, I didn't have time to overthink what had just transpired. Or what I was going to do with the knowledge that he was clearly ready too. Though my poor knees did have to kick back into action as the plane pulled to a stop and we were free to disembark. While exiting unsteadily up the walkway to Tullamarine's arrivals terminal and still slightly dazed, Levi once again took my hand. It was a good thing really, because in my current headspace who knew where I would have ended up? No doubt in the opposite direction of where I was supposed to be.

Once we'd found the luggage carousel, grabbed our bags and Levi collected his guitar from the oversized luggage desk, we headed towards the exit. It was then that I finally snapped out of my epiphany-induced stupor.

"Jesus Christ."

Levi looked at me and then in the direction my eyes had traveled. They eventually rested on a suited chauffeur who was holding up a printed sign which read, 'DiAngelo and Mondez'.

"That woman's a fucking joke," I muttered. We walked forward and explained to the driver the slight change of plans. He just politely nodded, suggested I put on my jacket since it was cold outside and carried our belongings through the glass sliding doors. To what was arguably the longest and most obscenely luxurious black limousine *of all time*.

I swore under my breath.

The driver deposited our luggage in the trunk

while I shrugged myself into an extra layer of clothing. He was right, even in spring this place was freezing. Though most places would be when compared with Geographe Bay, I guessed. He then opened the door. As Levi and I ducked inside, seating ourselves on tan leather seats at the rear of the vehicle, I was dumbstruck. Not so much by the opulence—though given enough time I'd probably be shocked by that too—but by Sophie's sheer audacity. After all, it was a conference we were attending in two day's time, not the fucking school prom. I just couldn't believe how desperately she wanted to get into Levi's pants.

As delectable as they were.

Levi smiled at me. "You're loving this, aren't you, kitten?"

I narrowed my eyes at him, arrogant Levi was back. It was lucky really, because Smart Mouth was the only thing that was going to help me survive the torment of being this close to him. And with my clothes still on.

"I bet this was all your doing, deviously changing your last name of Thompson to Sophie's DiAngelo so I'd never suspect it was you masterminding the whole thing. A perfect ruse I might add, old Conan Doyle would be so proud."

"Yeah, because a fucking limousine is my car of choice."

Levi laughed at my scorn. "Well, I've seen how you are behind the wheel and chauffeur driven vehicles are a much safer option. For everyone. Besides," he grinned, "you'd better get used to it. Once Mondez makes it big I'm not traveling in anything less than a twelve-seater."

"You're such an arrogant prick, have I ever told you that?" I turned away from him, muttering, "God knows I've thought it often enough."

Levi laughed at the barb and I turned back to him, my eyes narrowing even further.

He was sending me out of my mind.

If only it were out of my clothes.

So I changed tack and said sweetly, "Let me guess, the twelve-seater is so all of your groupies can come too? I'm sure they'd all love to line up, one-by-one and give you a blowjob on the way to a gig. Hey, maybe Sophie could go first? I bet she's just," I leaned in closer, "*gagging* for it."

It was now Levi's turn to lean in close to me. "There will be no groupies, kitten." He stared at my mouth. "Just. You. And. Me." The way he punctuated the last four words sent a thrill down my spine and I tried not to squirm in my seat.

I couldn't shy away from his smoldering look if I tried. Maybe the cool Melbourne air had chased away the last of my inhibitions and made me crave bodily warmth—in Levi form. For once I gave my anger-fuelled desire free reign because the thought of it being just the two of us in a darkened, secluded space at long last exhilarated me beyond measure.

Maybe it was time to accept that the gravitational shift between us was a result of so much more than simple banter and chemistry. Maybe I was now far enough away from Riley to naively pretend that she wouldn't be as affected by what was going on. Or maybe, traveling to this city had simply revealed my selfish and ridiculously horny inner bitch.

Irrespective of my justifications, I refused to look away from him and swore that this time *I* would have the final word. Leaning even farther forward, my lips hovering just above his, I whispered, "Levi honey, you wouldn't be able to survive my lips on your cock."

I slowly settled back in my seat again, a smug

smile dancing across my face. Levi's eyes glazed over, his mouth dropped open and his hands gripped the legs of his jeans like they were the only thing keeping him upright. It was a pretty awesome sight seeing him so affected by my Smart Mouth. My grin grew wider.

That is, until he launched himself at me.

I squealed. Yep, apparently I was a squealer as well as a giggler. The crash of his body threw me back against the leather seat until he was virtually lying on top of me. His lips brushed against my ear as he growled out, "So you wanna play, do you, kitten?"

I squirmed beneath him and felt the growing bulge in his pants press against my hip in warning. It wasn't that I wanted to escape him per se, especially since the length of his entire form had now completely covered me. I just wanted to get some much-needed power back through the only way I knew how. So I hissed, "Bite me."

"Say please."

"Fuck off."

"So vicious." He nipped my ear lobe and I stifled a groan. "You want me, kitten. There's no point in denying it. In fact, I bet those panties of yours are absolutely soaked."

"If you keep talking, you'll never find out."

With a sharp intake of breath at my acquiescence, his lips then pressed into mine. They branded me with their scorching intensity. He grabbed both of my wrists and with one hand, threw them above my head, groaning into my open mouth as he shifted his weight to one elbow. Levi's lips unapologetically devoured mine as his free hand journeyed from my face, to my breasts and stomach before finally slipping behind to cup my ass. I couldn't get enough of it. Not of his hands, his mouth, his tongue or his body pressed against mine.

I groaned back and sunk my teeth into his lower lip with a ravenous hunger that literally took my breath away. I matched his growing need with my own by grinding my hips against his swollen erection. Not nearly satisfied, I threw my legs around him and rubbed tantalizingly until I heard a low moan escape from deep within his throat. It officially became my favorite sound in the whole damn world.

Sadly, before we could get too carried away, I felt a cool breeze brush the skin of my exposed stomach. A polite cough then followed. Panting, Levi and I tore our lips away from one another and simultaneously turned towards the source of the distraction. It was the chauffeur. He stood by the open door and was in the process of looking everywhere but at us.

Levi groaned and dropped his head into my chest, muttering, "Fucking hell." I just plastered a hand over my mouth to stop some burgeoning manic laughter.

We disentangled ourselves and quickly straightened out our clothing, Levi grimaced while readjusting his jeans and I snickered at his obvious discomfort. He ruefully smiled back at me, shaking his head. After stepping out of the limousine, Levi tipped the driver handsomely in compensation for his obvious embarrassment since the poor guy still couldn't make eye contact with either of us. Levi took my hand again and led me inside our downtown hotel.

As we walked through the grandiose lobby, I took in the rich tapestry-strewn carpets and the warm twinkling lights above. They were reflected in the many gilded mirrors placed on muted walls and the general atmosphere instantly became one of unapologetic opulence. We approached the front desk and the receptionist greedily eye-fucked Levi. It was strange really, because for once I didn't give a shit. Anyway, he let go of my hand and instead placed his own on the small of my back where it tantalizingly traveled downwards before pulling away and returning sharply with a resounding slap.

The man just spanked my ass.

Launching me forward.

Not a foot away from one *very* aroused receptionist.

I quickly recovered my equilibrium and turned to face Levi, essentially halting him in his tracks. My fiery gaze, which matched one very smarting behind, dared the man to speak. To explain himself.

He did.

Leaning down, lips in my hair, he murmured, "Those panties of yours had better still be wet, kitten. There's no running away from me this time."

I tingled from head to toe at the cheek of him saying this to me. And in the hotel lobby of all places. Hell, the girl behind the desk had virtually orgasmed through telekinesis. So I stepped even closer, deliberately trailing my fingers over his washboard abs and down over his belt buckle. I then slid them lower, resting my palm against his already hardening cock. Looking up at him, I shrugged. "Guess now you'll never know."

The way his gaze turned from playful to outright molten was one of the sexiest sights I'd ever seen. It was official, we needed to get upstairs and naked. Pronto.

After checking in, the porter led us into one of the mirrored elevators. He pushed the button for our floor and then professionally kept his eyes glued to the numerical digits as they rose with each level we passed. I decided to have some fun with Levi. He hadn't stopped staring at my reflection since the doors shut behind us and as a result my panties had long since given up on being anything other than a sodden mess. To restore some much-needed control over the whole situation, I oh-so-casually moved in front of him and brushed my ass inadvertently against his groin. Pretending there was a problem with one of my shoes, I then bent over to inspect it and brushed up against him once more. His hands immediately shot out and gripped my hips, fingers digging deep into my flesh. I smiled at both the pleasurable pain he inflicted and how easy it had been to rile him. Upon straightening up again, I flicked my black hair over my shoulder and flashed him a triumphant look. He said nothing but continued threatening me with that darkened hooded gaze.

When the elevator doors opened, I broke free of his grip. The porter must have sensed the crackling charge rebounding between Levi and I because he practically sprinted to the door of our suite. Fucking Sophie specifically asked for a *single* room.

Don't even get me started.

The guy swiped one of the key cards and opened the door with a flourish. Levi tipped him excessively to stop him from showing us the many features of the space. Not that I think he wanted to anyway. As he retreated to the elevator, I distinctly heard him mutter something about not wanting to be the housekeeper who had to change our bed sheets.

I stepped past Levi and moved into the hallway. There was an open door leading through to a floor to ceiling marbled bathroom on my right and a dark wooden built-in closet on my left. Farther along, I spied a ridiculously large bed which stood opposite another doorway leading to a separate room and lounge area. At the far end of both were extensive windows looking out onto the Melbourne skyline.

Wow. Sophie had gone all out.

Some of the hesitation I thought had been left in

the airspace over South Australia slowly resurfaced. I desperately hoped Riley would one day forgive me for my actions in the limousine, the lobby and the lift. But right now it occurred to me that there was more to be frightened of than losing the trust of my best friend.

Truth be told, I was terrified of sharing a room with Levi. I mean, clearly there was something between us. Something big. It was simmering away below the surface, ready to be found. I just didn't know if I wanted to discover what it was yet.

I sighed.

Yes, he'd proven himself to be more than just a physical crush of titanic proportions. Many times over. Surely, the way he soothed me last night and held me at the airport this morning confirmed this? But, thanks to the playful dry humping in the limousine and the blatant sass I'd exhibited in the elevator, that pulsing feeling between us had shifted once again.

I was so disorientated. We now found ourselves somewhere in the middle of it all. We were in a place that was fucking hot but also had an undercurrent of true connection as well. And it was that true connection which could be the end of me.

For real.

I turned to find Levi once again staring at me. He was leaning back against the closed door, his palms flat against the wooden paneling. His chest rose and fell at a heightened heart rate that my own immediately registered and then replicated.

"So, what's it gonna be, kitten?"

The man could read my mind, what a horrifying thought. I was about to turn my back to him and put as much space as possible between us but something in his eyes stopped me.

I moved closer.

Despite the arrogant tilt to his chin and the bravado emanating from his measured stance, there was also the hint of an exposed vulnerability hovering just behind his darkened gaze.

My heart clenched.

This must have been what he saw in me at Perth airport not four hours ago. Seeing him like this, open to the possible hurt I could inflict, tore away at the last of my defenses.

"Come here," I murmured.

He exhaled loudly. "You're gonna be the death of me, you know that?" Levi strode forward and wrapped his arms around me, burying his face in my hair.

This was where I was meant to be.

With him.

Here.

Now.

It was inevitable.

Levi nuzzled my neck, nipping and licking from the base of my throat up to my ear lobe. "Now, about those panties…"

I giggled. *Again.*

He lifted me up by the ass and I wrapped my legs around his middle, clinging to him as I'd always fantasized. Levi turned and pushed me up against the closed door. His lips descended, they were gentle yet insistent, molding themselves against mine. Once again, I found myself marveling at the sudden sense of déjà vu sparking between us. It truly felt like we were always meant to be connected in this way because we already had—a lifetime before.

I cupped my hands around his face and our kiss grew deeper, more urgent, as our tongues met and entwined. My insides lit up with a burning need for more. I nipped his lower lip, hoping he felt it too. He groaned at the contact and started grinding himself into me … just … there.

"Oh my *God.*" My vision suddenly swam as I tipped my head back.

"I'm pretty sure *He's* got nothing to do with it, kitten."

"Shut up, shut up. Just keep … fuck," I moaned.

Levi chuckled but then hissed as I drove my hands into his hair and tugged. Hard. He slammed his mouth back into mine, pinning me even closer to the door, his tongue and lips ravaging my own. My nails scratched his scalp and he growled. Before I knew it, Levi tore my jacket and long sleeved top off, discarding them without another thought on the floor by his feet. He stopped and gazed at me, his breathing labored and eyes bright.

What he saw while I was pinned against the door—no doubt crazy-eyed and beyond needy—I really couldn't say. I mean, I was only wearing a royal blue satin bra and skinny jeans for God's sake. But the blatant desire in his gaze helped me find my voice, so I ground out, "Don't you *dare* stop now."

A wolfish grin returned my carnal sentiments and he swung me away from the wall, carrying me into the bathroom. Once inside, he deposited me roughly on the dark gray vanity unit. He pulled my hair back and to the side, exposing my neck to him. His mouth began that torturous pilgrimage again, but this time he started at my sensitive ear lobe. He kissed and licked his way down to the base of my throat and across my shoulder, stopping only when he reached the silky azure ribbon of my bra. I dug my hands into his torso as he bit the material with his teeth and pulled it off my shoulder, leaving it hanging in a useless arc against my upper arm. He then did the same to the other side before reaching around and unclasping the remaining hooks. When the material fell away, exposing my small breasts, Levi's hands immediately covered them. He tweaked and teased my erect nipples with an expert touch that made me throw my head back and call his name in wild abandon.

"Kitten, that's the sexiest fucking thing I've ever heard."

His mouth replaced those amazing fingers and I shuffled forward, arching my back to give him greater access. As he licked and nipped at me, I buried my hands under his tank top, drawing it up. When he finally broke away, I ripped it off over his head. But before I could lose my mind at the most beautiful sight I'd ever witnessed, his lips were back, claiming mine with that insatiable hunger I desperately craved.

I pulled his head closer, needing his frenzied touch more than air. As his hands trailed slowly down my abdomen, I wrapped one arm around his neck while the other felt the smooth contours of his back, the muscles flexing and rolling under my fingers. If I could somehow get beneath his skin and stay there for an eternity, I swear to God I would have.

Without question.

When his hands reached my jeans, he unbuttoned the waistband and unzipped the fly. Lifting me with one arm, he then drew my pants down with the other, until they too met the same fate as my bra. Moments later, I was safely seated on the bench. Never once did he remove his lips from mine, never once did he falter in the intensity of the kiss. The guy was the most accomplished multitasker I'd ever met.

Levi's hands slowly journeyed up my calves and came to rest on my knees. I gasped sharply as he wrenched my legs open, stepping into them, before his fingers unhurriedly continued moving upwards once again. I could feel him smile against my lips as I whimpered, almost out of my goddamn mind in anticipation of what was to come.

"Please," I begged. Though for what exactly I wouldn't say. Of course I wanted his fingers on me, that was freakin' obvious by my uncontrollable writhing and moaning. But I also found myself wanting more than just fingers and tongue.

I wanted him.

All of him.

He chuckled deeply and I dug my nails into his back in warning. Teasing me while this enflamed with need was not a smart idea. As if sensing my growing angst, he finally—holy mother of God—skimmed over the front of my panties.

I pulled away from Levi's lips, shocked by the bolt of raw energy that suddenly reverberated throughout my entire body from the fleeting contact. My gaze burned into his as those deft fingers erotically moved the damp lace to one side and gently, so very gently, stroked my slick folds before sliding inside.

"Grace. *Fuck*."

I shut my eyes. As much as I craved more from him, the open adoration on his face was too much for my brittle fragments to take right now. So I threw my head back and focused only on the feel of his fingers inside me.

His thumb circled my clit while two fingers rhythmically pumped me. In no time at all my breathing became more erratic and, not wanting to fall into that black abyss alone, I once again opened my eyes. I gazed up at him in amazement. Desperately, I tore at his jeans, fumbling with the belt buckle in my haste. Sensing my growing frustration, Levi finished the job for me before stepping out of his pants and boxers.

Trailing my fingers down his stomach, they brushed against the soft hair below his navel before I wrapped them around his long, hard cock.

Fuck me.

The man was stunning.

There was no other word for it. Never in my life had I seen a more beautiful penis. God must have felt very generous the day he created Levi. I shook my head. It was like every good thing on this earth had been packaged up into a solitary appendage just for me. Levi sucked in a sharp breath as I started moving my hand forward and back. I relished the silken feel of his skin against my palm almost as much as the pleasurable sounds escaping from his mouth. Increasing the pace, I looked up into his eyes again.

Levi's face was a mixture of dazed wonder. With my free hand, I drew him down to me, kissing him with a recklessness I'd never felt before. I needed him to know, to feel, the extent he had rocked my world since first walking into it last Friday night.

Levi broke away from me and I almost wept at the hollow emptiness left behind. Thankfully, the loss of contact was simply to tear off my panties, his hands and lips returned to me straight after that. Between impassioned kisses, he brokenly murmured, "Are you on the pill? I need to feel you. I'm clean, I swear."

I nodded frantically, so close to the edge that formulating words right now was simply not an option.

He took a deep breath and then plunged inside me, groaning out loud as his cock stretched my entrance to accommodate his size. I wrapped my legs around him once more, forcing him deeper, closer. When he reached as far as he could go, Levi stopped and pressed his forehead against my own, panting. "Grace, I … *Jesus*."

Beads of sweat were pouring off us both and his

broken admonition helped me shape the words, "I'm pretty sure *He's* got nothing to do with it, honey."

Levi smiled and bit my lower lip. "Vixen. Say it again."

"What?"

"What you just called me, it's the second time you've said it."

"*Honey.*"

He groaned again before slowly starting to move. "That's the sweetest sound. Almost as sweet as you calling my name when you come."

My head tipped back and I was momentarily lost in sensation once again, but it suddenly registered what he had said. "You haven't heard me come yet."

"I will." And with that Levi's fingers clamped onto my hips and his pace increased.

Each and every one of his deep thrusts hit my sweet spot. I wrapped my arms around him and found his lips again. As the pleasure built, I moaned into his mouth, my sounds growing exponentially louder and louder. Our kisses became more frantic until … *finally*. My dark world broke into glittering pieces of light as my body convulsed. Levi thrust even quicker and a few moments later, climaxed inside me. Through my exhaustion I somehow found the strength to smile.

I had called out his name as I came.

My smile grew wider.

He had called out my name too.

Chapter Nine

You're masquerading as conscience,
It's alright, I realize.
-MONDEZ, "Lies"

"Here." Levi passed me one of the hotel robes. His lips brushed against my shoulder while calloused fingers trailed down my spine before cheekily smacking my ass.

"Hey."

He chuckled as I slipped the plush robe on. I just glared at the ground, frantically thinking up revenge tactics which somehow all involved abstinence from sex until he was a slobbering, begging mess at my feet. But I immediately gave up once I looked into those clear blue eyes, they were openly admiring my partially naked body and my mood swiftly brightened after that.

There was no doubt about it, sex with Levi had been the most mind-blowing experience of my life. The way his touch made my body come alive was freakin' scary because I'd never once responded to Dylan in that way. He'd always been robotic and distant. Hell, even chaste compared to the man who had literally bitten off part of my lingerie. He'd never made me feel frantic and desperate with need like Levi had done through touch alone, and there was no way he had ever looked at me the way Levi did.

Ever.

It had always been, I dunno, friendly yet mechanical. Like, we were merely going through the motions because that is what people did in a relationship. And that wasn't the least of it. Oh no. Dylan had had this arcane ability to always make me feel *empty*. I thought back to one of the many disappointing nights he'd stayed over at my place.

"Babe, you were unbelievable."

Dylan kissed my lips briefly and rolled off me. In the darkness I could make out the silhouette of him removing the condom and depositing it in the small wastepaper basket by the side of my bed. He lay back down, his breathing so heavy it sounded like he had just run a marathon.

I stared up at the ceiling. The breeze from my open window gently swayed the blind and I watched as slivers of light flickered across the dark wall. As usual our lovemaking had been ... brief and I was once again left feeling hollow, agitated.

Usually, I didn't say anything about Dylan's selfishness in the bedroom. I mean, he was my first boyfriend so I honestly didn't know how the whole intimacy thing was supposed to work anyway. I wasn't that much of a fool to believe what people said or did in romantic comedies was anything close to real life, but couldn't help wishing he'd make more of an effort. After all, it had been weeks since he last thought about my needs, and even longer since he'd actually done anything to satisfy them.

"Dylan?" I murmured quietly, suddenly shy at what I was about to ask.

He didn't reply.

I leaned over and switched on the bedside lamp, squinting as my eyes adjusted to the blinding light. "Dylan?" My gaze hardened as they came back into focus.

He was asleep.

I shook my head. Levi was completely different.

He'd focused on my pleasure first and seemed to genuinely revel in the way I came apart in his hands. I smiled and my body lit up at the memory.

I moved away from him, needing time to process it all and ended up wandering through the two rooms in a post-coital daze. Still restless, I moved towards the windows and found myself staring out at the Melbourne skyline. The clouds above matched the gray roads below. I liked how the greenery from the lush trees bordered the roads and contradicted sharply with the cutthroat efficiency of the vehicles traveling on them. It was a strange combination really. But somehow the juxtaposition worked and I was left feeling balanced.

Weird.

I turned away from the window as Levi flopped down onto the bed and motioned for me to join him. I hesitated, and his mocking smile teased my sudden restraint after the raging fuckfest we'd just had in the bathroom. So I lifted my chin before striding purposely towards him and then crawled up alongside, nuzzling his toweling robe-clad chest as I lay down. He wrapped a strong arm around me, letting it rest lightly on my hip and I once again felt that sense of calm slowly seep through my body.

I sighed.

We lay there in silence, enjoying the quiet and the warmth of one another. But after half an hour, I started feeling restless again. Being this close to him and not ravaging his body with my hands or mouth was proving difficult. As a distraction, I slowly trailed my fingers across the dark patterns on his chest. It suddenly dawned on me that now was the perfect opportunity to openly ogle his upper body while also admiring his tattoos. I figured it was a win-win situation, and quickly sat up.

"What—"

Straddling Levi's hips, I yanked the toweling robe open to just below his navel, revealing the artwork inscribed across the entirety of his stomach and chest.

Wow.

It was exquisite.

The sole silhouette of a barren tree trunk with gnarled branches emanating crookedly from it filled most of his torso. In the background was a looming full moon, partially obscured by storm clouds and wisps of fog. The words '*Darkness there, and nothing more*' were interwoven through the branches in calligraphy script and drew the eye up to the black raven that was in mid-flight on his neck.

I looked up at Levi.

His eyes had darkened and his fingers splayed across my hips. But I wasn't going to be waylaid by that predatory look. No matter how tempting the idea of fucking him senseless right now would be. Though in saying that, the image of me riding him until he called out my name in a blind passion once again may have briefly crossed my mind. I quickly repressed it though because I wasn't going to be distracted. Not when faced with such an arresting image and especially not when it was plastered all over his ridiculously sexy body. After all, I wanted to find out the reason behind this gothic image on what was an otherwise very upbeat guy.

Only he didn't say anything.

He just kept staring at me.

"Tell me about it," I murmured. My fingers gently traced the outline of a tree branch.

"What do you want to know?"

"Why this?" I motioned to the artwork. "Out of everything you could have had tattooed, why did you choose something inspired by *The Raven*?"

He shifted underneath me and I could feel him

hardening. I smiled mischievously before shaking my head in mock reproach. He wasn't going to get out of it that easily. So I lay on top of him, gently pressing my lips to a small section of a storm cloud, before resting my chin on his chest and looking at him expectantly.

"Tell me."

He took a deep breath and my entire body rose with the inhalation. As he breathed out through soft, full lips, I slowly lowered again.

"For years, I found myself drifting." He tucked a strand of hair behind my ear. "After I finished school I went from one job to the next, one party to the next, one girl to the next." He caressed my face. "Nothing meant much to me, you know?"

I nodded my head, relishing the feel of his hand as it brushed against my skin.

"I had my guitar and my bro but that was about it." He stopped talking and placed his hands behind his head. I missed his touch more than I was willing to admit, but his eyes now looked past me and were lost in another time. "Until one summer a couple of years ago, I met this girl."

I shifted uncomfortably, not at all liking where this was heading and internally kneed myself in the stomach for bringing it up in the first place.

Stupid curiosity.

"We weren't together long, maybe six or seven months, but ... fuck. She blew my world apart."

It was official. Watching him recount this story was like driving past a car accident, I didn't want to see the carnage but couldn't look away either.

"We started off okay. She seemed the type who was always laughing and joking. The life of the party, you know? But it was all a front." He laughed bitterly. "Man, she sure fooled me. It wasn't until after our first fight that I found out who she really was."

My lungs started burning and it was only then that I realized I had been holding my breath. Clearly, I was a glutton for punishment.

"I received a text from her telling me to leave her alone, to never contact her again, that we were through. It confused the hell out of me because I didn't think what we'd argued over was that big a deal. Anyway, I went straight over to her place to sort it out. Only, when I rocked up, I knew something was off. Her parents were out but the front door was open. So I let myself in," he closed his eyes, "and found her. She was floating face down, unconscious in the bath. If I had been a minute later she would have drowned for sure."

"Jesus, Levi."

"She recovered soon after and we told her parents that she'd slipped on the wet tiles, knocking herself out before falling into the water. They stupidly believed us. But after that she was a completely different person. It was like we were continuously playing some fucked up game of cat and mouse. I mean, we'd be okay one minute, fight the next, and then she'd push me away before trying to hurt herself. I swear, sometimes it seemed like she was looking for an argument, for an excuse to…"

My heart broke at the thought of Levi being so caught up in that clusterfuck. A manipulative and self-destructive relationship must have been hell. Didn't that girl *see* the man who stood before her? I mean, yeah he was an arrogant douche at times but he was also loyal, caring, smart, talented, fucking sexy and … I stopped myself.

You're entering turbulent waters, Grace.

"By the end of the seven months, I was over it. When we once again fought over some inconsequential bullshit I swore to her that I wouldn't go back, that I wouldn't chase her, that I was finished."

My mouth suddenly felt like the Sahara. During a heat wave. Multiplied by a billion.

"So, I ignored her text message." He swallowed with difficulty while my heart constricted. "And her parents found her body the next morning." Levi finally opened his eyes and the depth of pain within them echoed through to my soul.

"For a while, I let myself believe I was solely responsible for her death even though I knew deep down that if she truly wanted to end her life, she would have done it without my help. Anyway, it was during that time I decided nothing and no one would hurt me like that again. I went off the rails for a while, couldn't hold down a job. I partied even harder than before, slept around a bit."

"'*Darkness there, and nothing more*'," I quoted.

Levi looked at me as though surprised I was still even there. He smiled gently, removed his hands from behind his head and wrapped them around me.

Holding me close.

"Yeah, something like that."

I smiled shyly at him, suddenly nervous of what I saw lingering in his gaze.

"Anyway, it wasn't until I ended up with no job or true friends that I finally pulled my finger out and got my shit together." He laughed. What a beautiful sound. "All it took was a bit of persuading."

"How'd Dom do that?"

"He pinned me down and beat the shit out of me until I admitted I had a problem." He smiled and my insides melted.

The things those lips could do to me. I quickly shook my head. Suddenly Levi and Dom's behavior in the car made a heck of a lot more sense.

"So I cleaned up my act, enrolled at university and we got our band together. I decided that Poe was right and got this tattoo—it was pointless trying to find meaning in meaningless bullshit. That wasn't life. That wasn't why I was put on this earth." He paused for a minute, took a deep breath and stared at me intently. "But you, kitten, are the first woman I've wanted to find *real* meaning in for a fucking long time."

I squirmed. This conversation had turned seriously awkward. "Levi, I—"

"Relax, Grace." He pulled me towards him until my lips were suspended just above his.

I looked down into his eyes which were openly laughing at my spectacular freak-out.

"I'm not asking you to fucking marry me or anything."

I actually forgot to breathe. For real. Surely my lips were turning an alarming shade of blue? I mean, an oxygen mask was what was needed right now. Levi's hands gently cupping my face? Not so much.

"I just want to spend more time with you and figure out what this thing is between us. That's all." His thumb skimmed over my lower lip.

I felt light-headed and my vision began to blur. He would be caressing a corpse soon.

"Kitten, breathe."

A gust of air escaped me and my heart suddenly kicked back into action, evidently due to the verbal reminder.

Levi just smiled up at my dazed expression.

"You feel it too?"

He gently pressed his lips to mine. "Of course I feel it," he whispered, kissing me again.

With those words I let go. I completely

surrendered myself to him. As our lips brushed against each other's, so sweetly and softly that I almost cried, my hands tenderly cupped his face. Levi's tongue delved inside my mouth, stroking, massaging, instantly stirring that insatiable burning need within me. He let out a low moan as I responded and deepened our kiss, trying to get closer to that flickering emotion we both now knew was there.

And that's when I heard her.

Riley.

Okay, so not *her* exactly, but I definitely heard the personalized ringtone she'd programmed into my phone. I froze. A cold shower couldn't have done a better job at extinguishing the flame that had just begun to ignite.

Levi stared up at me, confused. "Kitten, what's wrong?"

"I ... *fucking shit.*" I jumped off him as though stung and ran for the phone. Taking a deep breath, I quickly tightened my robe and raked shaking fingers through my chaotic hair. While walking into the next room, I answered it. "Hey, Riley." Even to my own ears, my voice sounded forced.

"*Finally*, I thought you were never going to answer."

"Sorry, what's up?"

A deep sigh escaped her and I immediately felt like the most horrible woman alive.

"Riley, what is it?"

"I miss you, G. It's been a shitty week."

"I miss you too. How's your mum? She's all back to normal now, right?" How I could possibly maintain the facade of a normal conversation with my best friend after what I had just discovered in bed with Levi truly disgusted me. There was no doubt about it, I was honestly The Most Horrible Woman Alive.

151

"Yeah, she's back to normal."

I snorted. Okay, so maybe I was The Second Most Horrible Woman Alive. But it was still a crap place to be.

"I don't even know why I was there. Rest and fluids were all she needed. But you know Mum, she likes being taken care of."

"And you can never say no."

A short laugh escaped her. "God, I wish I had."

"Why not take some time out for yourself? After a week with that woman, you've more than earned it."

"I will. Brea and I are having a girls' night, that'll help cheer me up."

"Okay, but just be careful. That woman can down shots quicker than anyone I've ever met."

There was silence for a minute or two, and before my heart broke into a million pieces, I murmured, "Riley love, that's not all, is it?"

"No." She choked back a sob and my heart splintered even further. There would be nothing left of it soon. I'd simply be a hollow mass of empty blackness. To be fair, it was all I truly deserved.

There was an abrupt noise on her end of the line. "I'd better go. Brea must have arrived early. I'll give you a call later, okay?"

"Sure thing. Love you."

"Love you too."

After hanging up, I found myself perched on the edge of the couch with my head in my hands.

Hating myself.

I couldn't do this to her. The thought of losing Riley over what I had just done with Levi, regardless of the emotions we thought we felt, tore my heart to shreds. How could I have been so self-centered? How could I have behaved that way? Done that to her? At the first chance I got, I'd launched myself at the man my best friend wanted. And all the while she was stuck in the middle of freakin' nowhere, caring for a woman who closely resembled a goddamn troll. I shook my head. Dad would have been so disappointed. After all, he always thought of others before himself. My thoughts suddenly drifted back to a happier time.

"How'd you do it, Dad?"

It was a sultry day and for once he was joining me in ice cream bliss, though my question interrupted him mid-lick. "Do what, love?"

"How did you keep it all together after Mum left?" I shook my head. "I mean, if it had been me, I wouldn't have been able to get out of bed in the morning."

Dad stared down at his waffle cone, picking off small pieces and placing them in his mouth. He chewed thoughtfully. "Well, there were definitely days when I didn't want to get out of bed. I even tried it once. I pulled the blanket up over my head and refused to move until my heart stopped aching."

"What made you change your mind?"

"A little green-eyed girl."

I smiled up at him.

"She marched into my room, pulled down the blanket and demanded I go make her breakfast because she couldn't reach the cereal box in the cupboard."

"I don't remember that."

He took a big bite of ice cream, rolling it around in his mouth before swallowing. "I do. It was the day I realized more people were impacted by your mother leaving than just me. As much as I wanted to believe otherwise, I wasn't the only one whose life had changed. So, for you and your sister's sake, I had to make the right decision and get out of bed."

I nudged him with my shoulder. "You always make the right decision, Dad."

He chuckled. "Not always, but I did that day."

I rubbed my eyes with the palms of my hands, furious at myself. I was so sick of this shit. I was sick of it all in fact. *Fuckety fuck fuck fuck*. After taking a deep breath in a futile attempt to calm my burgeoning rage, I looked up. Levi was standing in the doorway, arms crossed, watching me closely. His eyes were dark and inscrutable as they took in my agitation.

"You didn't tell her, did you?"

I stared at him. And then lost it.

Completely.

Standing up, I yelled, "Tell her *what* exactly? That we fucked? That we 'felt something'?" I even used the air quotations. Not my finest moment by far. "You've got to be fucking joking, Levi."

He reared back as though struck, before turning and storming away. A moment later, I heard the bathroom door slam shut and then something smash and splinter as it made contact with the marbled tiles. It was quiet for a short while until something else careered into the same wall to meet its grizzly fate. The shower soon started after that.

I turned to look out the windows at the gray clouds above, loathing the fact that I had just achieved a personal best in hurting not one, but two of the people I most cared about. And in under ten minutes. Surely that was a record? I stood, walked to my suitcase and pulled on some clothes. After that, I grabbed my purse, phone and one of the keycards. As I yanked the hotel room door closed behind me, I wondered if there was enough alcohol in the bar downstairs to help me forget the epic fuck up I'd just created.

Highly doubtful.

****

Three hours later, I was still seated on a brown, plush leather stool in the lobby bar, aptly named Oblivion. The muted lights and tactfully positioned tea light candles placed on low wooden tables fit snugly in-between patterned couches. The entire ambiance was one of understated romance. I hated it. Well, almost as much as the soft instrumental music wafting through the ceiling speakers and the gentle murmurs from far too many middle-aged couples sitting nearby. I had the sudden urge to obliterate the place with an army tank.

Except, Patrick, the barman and I were now on a first name basis. He kept filling my glass, so I graciously curbed any violent tendencies. It was the start of a beautiful friendship. Sadly, however, Patrick was also a talker which meant that our emerging bond would never last without me having to sew his lips shut with barbed wire. Don't get me wrong, he was a nice enough guy, in a lanky, overly confident kind of way. But he talked incessantly, and about shit really I didn't care about. Though in saying that, it did mean I could zone out and get lost in my own thoughts, because provided I nodded or shook my head at the appropriate intervals, Patrick didn't seem to mind that I never spoke back. And since he was pouring me double shots, I didn't mind either.

Only, the alcohol wasn't working. I was trying so hard to drink and forget, but for some perverse reason the whiskey no longer soothed me the way it used to. Not only that, but I was struggling to swallow each sip too, it slowly burned while sliding down my throat.

The world was clearly against me.

So I just glared down at the ocher liquid, with Levi's last broken stare and Riley's choked sob circling around and around in my head. If only I could think of a way where we could all get out of this clusterfuck unscathed. Then, not only could we all have our happily ever after, but I could also get out of this torturous bar before dousing it in turpentine and setting it alight. I shook my head. Thankfully, it was while Patrick was recounting a sob story about … *fuck, who the hell cared?* Wanting everyone to end up living happily ever after was a naïve hope in a wishful dream. This was reality. Where people screwed one another over more often than they bathed or breathed. In other words, a heck of a lot. And for some reason, I seemed to wound more people than most.

"Grace, you gonna get that?"

I looked up at Patrick, confused. He stared pointedly at me and then at my phone which was in the process of dancing its way across the bar towards him. I must have switched it to vibrate sometime after my third/sixth whiskey. After all, I really didn't want to be reminded of what I was doing the last time I heard Riley's ringtone and she did say she was going to call back. I downed the rest of my drink before picking it up. "Hey."

"Hey, G." The sounds of heavy thumping music and loud chatter interspersed with expletives and laughter emanated through the receiver. They almost drowned Riley's voice out completely.

"Having a good night at The Hole?"

She giggled, and knowing Riley as I did, I'd say she was on to her fourth drink. "I'm having an amazing night."

"Glad to hear it. Is everything okay now? You sound heaps better than the last time we spoke."

"Everything's great. It was just a miscommunication, G. You see, we had a bit of a chat and…" she stage-whispered into the phone, I had to hold it away from my ear to save my bleeding eardrums, "I think he likes me." She giggled again.

I swallowed, begging my whiskey not to make a fool out of me by crafting a stellar repeat performance. So Levi had phoned Riley. Man, when a girl did him wrong he really didn't hang around to sort shit out. "That's great, I'm so happy for you."

"Yeah, you sound it. G, what's wrong? How come now you're the one who's about to burst into tears?"

I slowly shook my head before realizing that she couldn't see me. Right, words. They would be helpful. So I mumbled, "I'm okay."

"No you're not. Where's Levi? Is he with you?"

"Um he's ... I haven't seen him for a while."

"Have you guys had a fight or something?"

"You mean he didn't tell you?"

"Tell me when? I haven't spoken to him since he was at our apartment last Saturday."

I rubbed my forehead, beyond confused. "But you just told me you spoke with him and now everything's sorted out between you two."

"I what?" She paused for a minute. "*Oh my God.* You thought I was interested in Levi, didn't you?" She laughed and I had to grip onto the bar to stop myself from hurling the phone at the most expensive bottle of liquor I could find. There were plenty sitting on the shelf facing opposite me, so I had heaps of options.

"G, I don't like Levi. Well, not like *that* anyway."

"You what?"

"God no. He's too ... Anyway, he's not the one for me."

"But you were all over him at The Hole last Friday."

"Girl, I hugged him hello."

"And last Saturday you were making doe eyes at him while almost force feeding him a damn smoothie."

"You were going to make him coffee. I didn't want the man to die from dehydration."

"But what about the text you sent me? You know, the one with all the excited emojis after I told you he was my student teacher."

"That's because I was excited. *For you.*"

"Me?"

"Of course. As soon as I met him I knew you guys would be perfect for one another. Why did you think I invited you to their gig?"

"Riley, I ... I've got to go."

There was a deep murmur on her end of the line, followed by what I could have sworn was a drunken, sloppy kiss. I heard Riley giggle before murmuring to me, "Sure, G. I'd better go too."

"*Wait*. Who are you with?"

But the line was already dead.

I carefully put the phone back down on the bar and stared at it for a good ten minutes. Riley wasn't interested in Levi. I had misconstrued the whole thing.

Mother fucker.

So that meant every time I pushed Levi away, stopped him mid-thought or ran away from him, had all been for nothing. Which therefore meant that every growing feeling, fantasy and emotion I had experienced but continuously told myself was wrong, wasn't.

Christ Almighty.

And now I had no fucking idea what to do. I mean, I had just seriously wounded the guy after he was brave enough to open up to me about his past. Not only that, but I had also thrown back in his face the fact that he wanted to explore what was between us.

Us.

Was it even possible? Would he ever want to look me in the face again, let alone be willing to figure out what the heck was going on? If by some miracle he could, would I even be able to do the same thing? Was there any way my broken fragments could be pieced back together with the help of this mocking, arrogant, beautifully kindhearted man?

"Grace, are you okay? You don't look so hot."

I glanced up at Patrick but it was Levi's face who stared back at me. "I've got to go." I paid him way more than necessary before standing, spinning on my heel and bolting out the bar.

Chapter Ten

It's never easy, this weight pulling on my heart today,
Just stop these feelings,
Let me go, crying as I drift away.
-MONDEZ, "Escape"

I'd like to say that when I walked through our hotel room door and stepped over the threshold of the lounge room, Levi and I immediately gazed meaningfully into each other's eyes. I'd then like to say that I perfectly communicated the depth of my regret through look alone and we both ran into each other's open arms before having crazy make-up sex on the couch, the bed, and then up against the window. Though, not necessarily in that order. But I'd be lying. After all, this was reality and shit like that simply didn't happen in this fucked up world.

So instead, I left the frantic eagerness I felt in the bar at the front door. It seemed as though the closer I got to facing up to the aftermath of my cruel Smart Mouth, the more tongue-tied and terrified I became. I didn't want to lose the mocking eyes and sardonic grin Levi seemed to reserve just for me. I didn't want to lose the intensity in his gaze when he stared at me as though I was something remarkable. I didn't want to lose the comfortable companionship we had developed over the past two days, or the way he could calm me like no one before ever had. I didn't want to lose … him.

Needless to say, rather than stride purposefully into the room and earnestly lay all of my tattered cards on the table, I quietly let myself in and crept across the soft carpet. When I reached the open doorway of the lounge room, I peeked my head around the corner and saw him.

Levi was seated on the beige couch, head down, acoustic guitar perched on his lap, strumming a bittersweet melody. He would stop at short intervals, his forehead creased in deep concentration before taking the pen out of his mouth. He would then make changes in the notebook placed on the coffee table in front of him. It was truly the most delectable sight I had ever seen. Directly in front of me was an intelligent, creative and undeniably sexy man all rolled into one.

My panties wept.

No, that was the understatement of the century. They howled, screamed and then hurled obscenely inventive abuse at me. Blessedly, Levi was so wrapped up in his music that he didn't even notice. Or, if he did, he chose not to acknowledge my presence. I wasn't sure which was worse. Either way, I suddenly felt like an intruder who, if recognized, wasn't welcome anyway. So, I took one last look at the man who not hours before had given me the most intense orgasm of my life before courageously baring me part of his soul, and turned away. I dragged my miserable ass to the shower. *Maybe I could wash away my sins?* It was worth a shot.

There were shards of broken glass still scattered throughout the small room. I was surprised Levi had managed to get himself both in and out, completely unscathed. It was lucky the squat glasses left for rinsing after brushing one's teeth were not in my daily hygiene repertoire, because I didn't want to have to explain to the housekeepers why we suddenly needed more of them. They would probably want to hurl a few glasses at the wall after I told them what I had done as well. Besides, to this very day I simply cupped my hands under the faucet to gather the water needed for rinsing. I loved brazenly slurping out of them once full. And to be frank, I honestly didn't give a shit if it was offensive to whoever shared the bathroom with me or not. It got the job done. End of story.

I had a quick shower and afterward rummaged through my suitcase for my Hitchcock t-shirt. It wasn't overly clean but reminded me of home and of a time before I orchestrated this mother of all fuckups. Grabbing the first novel I could find, *Wuthering Heights*—how freakin' apt—I crawled into bed, switched on the lamp and started to read.

Only I couldn't. Normally, I could easily lose myself in Heathcliff and Catherine's anger-fuelled love affair as easily as slipping on a glove. Okay, so living in a balmy climate meant I didn't exactly ever really *need* to wear gloves, but you get my meaning. Anyway, reading was impossible. With each strum of Levi's guitar, the chords slowly and painfully pierced my guilt with their heartbroken tenor. The sounds were so melancholy that I found myself staring blankly at what appeared to be a jumbled mess of words on a page. Even worse, was the fact that this jumbled mess then gradually became more and more blurred with each passing minute. Levi humming a sorrowful harmony on top of the forlorn chords was what finally tipped me over the edge and I could no longer fight the tears that fell. They trickled freely down my cheeks.

I had hurt Levi. His music was telling me so. This knowledge wounded me like nothing I had ever before experienced. I hated that I caused him pain, and the worst part was I honestly didn't know if he would ever forgive me. Even if he did, I didn't know if I could ever begin to deserve it. Maybe after a million apologies, interspersed with groveling absolutions of what a horrible person I was, he might forgive me out of sheer frustration. It was a vaguely mollifying thought.

I dumped the unread book on the nightstand,

switched off the lamp and wiped my damp face with the back of my hand. Man, I hadn't cried in over a year, this was intense. How was it that after only one week I could feel this way? How had this man unknowingly burrowed so far under my skin that hurting him in such a short timeframe felt like an unbelievably deep wound? I rolled my eyes in the semi-darkness. Who was I kidding? I knew Levi would make me feel more than I ever had from the first moment he opened his damn mouth. A week seemed like eternity in comparison.

After settling down under the blankets, I curled onto my side, begging the whiskey to do the job it was supposed to and help me escape this hell. It didn't. For what felt like hours, I tossed and turned, saturating my pillow with angry droplets of self-loathing. It was only when the last bars of the guitar finally faded away, the lounge room light was switched off and the mattress bowed under the weight of Levi's body climbing in next to me, that I could finally stifle my sobs.

He lay on his back and as my eyes adjusted to the darkness, I could make out the shape of his profile. The man was so distant yet closer than I knew I deserved. Despite this, I selfishly stretched out to him and trailed featherlight fingers down his arm, committing to memory every dip and rise of his taut muscles. It was only when I eventually reached his open hand that I faltered briefly. I took a deep breath and then entwined my fingers with his, holding firmly. Levi didn't pull away but he didn't respond to my touch either. Mildly hopeful, I then raised our joined hands to my lips and gently kissed his knuckles. I hoped that through this contact, though brief and not nearly sufficient, he could feel some of my regret. Levi's breath caught and I could sense an uneasy stillness on his side of the bed. So, not wanting to push my luck, I moved his hand back to where it was.

But I wouldn't let go.

There was no way in hell I was letting go of him tonight.

"What are you doing here?"

My sister looked down at her black high heels, she must have come straight from work. "Can I come in?"

"No. You can't."

She looked up at me and sighed. Pain etched her features. "Look, Monkey—"

"It's Grace. My name's Grace."

She took in a sharp breath, her eyes widening momentarily. Exhaling slowly through red lips, she murmured, "I've come to apologize."

"And that's going to make everything all right, is it?" I yelled.

"Grace, please—"

"After everything you did, you think a fucking apology is going to make it all better? What kind of deluded fool do you take me for? You took everything from me. Everything.*"*

"I'm so sorry." She reached out a placating hand, but I took a determined step back. "I didn't mean for it all to happen like that. Truly, I didn't."

Tears clouded my eyes. "I trusted you."

"I know, and I'll never forgive myself for what I did."

I stared at her for a moment. "Well, I guess that makes two of us then." Turning my back to her, I slammed the front door in her face.

In the half-light of morning, I shook off the remnants of that painful dream. I hadn't dreamed about my sister in months and blamed yesterday's emotional turmoil for dredging those buried memories back up.

Needing comfort, I stretched out my hand for Levi. At some point in the night I must have let go of him and my brain suddenly registered the loss of contact through the painful simulation of a vice grip on my contemptible heart.

Only he wasn't there.

My fingers fumbled over cool, crinkled linen, which simply goaded me with the lingering musky scent of his body.

I quickly sat up and scanned the room. There was no playful note left behind, no text message, nothing. No, he had simply awoken and bailed, leaving me feeling worryingly bereft. At least his guitar and duffel bag were still propped up against the wall. He'd have to return for them at some point, right? Whether it was to collect them before leaving for the airport or not, I really didn't want to contemplate.

****

That Sunday stretched into one of the longest of my life. Somehow it felt even more drawn out than the culmination of the previous week. I mean, at least then I knew what his feelings for me were, even though he kept them carefully restrained. But as I stared out the window at the ominous storm clouds hovering above, I suddenly questioned everything.

Not wanting to leave the room in case he came back and gave me the opportunity to grovel at his feet, I stumbled out of bed and took an unbelievably long shower. The glass had been cleared up, so thankfully the whole experience wasn't as torturous as last time. When I finished he hadn't returned, so I turned on the TV. After an hour of randomly flicking from one infuriating channel to the next, he still hadn't come back so I switched it off and threw the remote across the room. After that, I tried reading but it was as useless at distracting my attention as it had been the night before. Which meant that after another hour, that too was hurled across the room. I managed to pass a solid half an hour by looking through the conference program on my phone, but then decided to stop kidding myself. I really just wanted to have my mobile on my lap in case Levi called.

He didn't.

When I eventually found myself with my forehead pressed against the glass, counting windows of the building opposite, I finally gave up and wandered downstairs.

It was late afternoon by the time Patrick, the barman, was mid-way through a one-man play on his greatest sporting achievements. Apparently, the guy was a heck of a lot more accomplished than I'd ever given him credit for. Or ever would.

Anyway, I was halfway through my second drink when I came to the conclusion that I simply couldn't take Levi's silence any longer. Acting on impulse, I grabbed my phone off the bar and texted him.

Me: **Come back.**

A minute later, I then added,

Me: **Please.**

I waited a good twenty minutes, or at least until the closing scene of Patrick's monologue and the remainder of my whiskey had been drained, before giving up. He wasn't going to reply. It was time to face facts. I'd fucked up.

Big time.

After smiling weakly to Patrick, I then drifted back up to the room again. Miraculously, the alcohol actually did what it was supposed to this time and after collapsing on the meticulously remade bed, I grabbed Levi's pillow, inhaled the remaining scent of him like some mad woman and fell into a fitful sleep.

I awoke some time later to the sensation of calloused fingers caressing my face. Surely I was still dreaming? I didn't want to open my eyes and realize that this was all some kind of cruel joke my deceptive head was playing on me, so I kept them tightly shut. Only, the fingers kept stroking me and as my sleep-induced fog slowly lifted, so too did my dejected mood.

I smiled.

"You can really snore."

I frowned.

"You do. I could hear you as soon as I got out the elevator."

At that my eyes popped open and I hastily sat up before hurling myself at Levi. The sudden movement took him by surprise and he was knocked backward onto the bed. Straddling him, I leaned in until our noses were almost touching, my narrow eyes menacing. "I. Don't. Snore."

That mocking smile of his was back and I felt an incredible lightness, like the weight of the world had finally been lifted from my shoulders. My heart progressively kicked back to life after a few false starts, and began merrily fluttering away like the fickle organ it was.

Levi rolled his eyes up at me. "Sure, kitten, whatever you say."

I froze. "Say it again."

"What?"

"What you just called me. Say it again."

"*Kitten.*"

My lips slammed into his, no doubt burning him with a ferocity that quite frankly, terrified me. The desperate need I felt for this man was beyond comprehension, beyond description, yet undeniably all-consuming. He wrapped his arms around me, squeezing me tighter, pulling me closer, and I willingly lost myself in the feel of his body pressed against mine. His hands grabbed my ass, my back, my shoulders, my neck, molding them with impatient imprints while my fingers delved into his hair, tangling themselves amongst the soft strands. As I firmly tugged, he groaned into my open mouth and as he gripped my flesh, I moaned into his. Our lips raged a bitter war invading, conquering, occupying what each felt they were rightly owed. And when our tongues met, they at long last acknowledged what had been left unsaid the night before.

Anger.

Forgive me.

Hurt.

Forgive me.

Don't fucking do it again.

Please. *Forgive me.*

By the time our raging battle eventually waned and a truce had been declared, our lips were swollen and bruised.

I rested my forehead against Levi's, panting. "I'm so sorry."

"I know."

"I spoke to Riley. I got it all wrong."

"I know."

"I'm such a fucking idiot."

"I know."

I punched his arm and he chuckled. What an incredible sound.

****

"Tell me something about yourself that I don't already know."

We were sitting on the couch later that night and I was licking the last cheesy remains of nacho goodness off my fingers. We'd ordered room service the minute Levi found out that I hadn't eaten all day. I tried explaining to him that whiskey could essentially be counted as a food group on account of the malt, but he wouldn't listen. And thank God for that because those nachos were without a doubt the best I'd ever had. However, it then led me to ponder further. Granted, not the best idea after drinking on an empty stomach, especially when I found myself wondering if it was possible to marry a culinary dish. Probably not. Though I did watch a documentary once about people marrying inanimate objects, like the Eiffel Tower, statues, cranes and shit, but quickly dismissed that notion. After all, unless it was a fridge full of nacho ingredients, the point was moot.

"*Grace.*" I felt a tug on my hair.

"Huh?"

"Tell me something that I don't already know about you."

I'd just fantasized about marrying some Mexican food? *Hell no.* So I dragged my errant thoughts back to the much more delectable present. My back was resting against Levi's chest and he was twirling a strand of my hair around his finger.

"What do you wanna know?"

"I don't know, something no one else does."

"Um, my star sign is Scorpio?"

"You're gonna have to do better than that."

"But you already know about my dad and hardly anyone knows that stuff."

"Then tell me something else."

I thought for a moment and paused, suddenly shy. After taking a deep breath, I mumbled, "I hate getting wet."

"*What?*" Levi sat up straight, pushing me off him before turning me around to face his incredulous eyes. "What do you mean, you hate getting wet?"

"Just to clarify, we're talking about water here not … anything else."

He smirked.

I looked down. "And it's not that I don't like getting *wet* exactly…" I sighed. God this was embarrassing. After taking another deep breath and looking up at him again, I continued, "Say you're swimming at the beach, right?"

He nodded.

"And you've just stepped out of the water, dripping wet."

He nodded again.

"What do you do?"

"Ah—"

"You towel yourself dry of course. Only it's freakin' impossible to actually *get* dry, isn't it? I mean, your skin is still damp, your hair is still wet and the breeze always picks up by this time so it feels like the temperature suddenly drops to below freezing." I shuddered. "And then you try and pull on some dry clothes to get warm again but they get all caught up on the residual skin moisture and … and…" I glared at him. "The whole thing is fucking horrible, okay? That's why I don't like getting wet."

Levi looked at me for a full ten seconds before throwing back his head and laughing. And laughing. And laughing.

Asshole.

I crossed my arms in front of my chest. "Fuck you."

But this just made him laugh even more. "Kitten," he choked out between chortles, "that's the funniest damn thing I've ever heard."

My glare turned dangerous but he ignored me.

"So do you ever swim at the beach?"

"No."

"The pool?"

"No."

"What about taking a shower?"

"I fucking shower, Levi."

"Okay, okay." He wiped tears from his eyes while I imagined numerous revenge filled scenarios which all somehow involved his agonizing death and guacamole. After finally noticing my less than impressed facial expression, he leaned forward and softly pressed his lips to mine. Heaven.

"The name Kitten fits you even better now," he murmured. The man was forgiven.

The corners of my mouth lifted as I gently pushed him back. "Your turn. Tell me something no one else knows."

"I'm an Aquarius."

I rolled my eyes.

"Okay." He stared at me, took a deep breath and then slowly exhaled. "I hate birds."

I blinked.

"They freak me out."

I blinked again.

"*They're the rats of the sky.* You just never know where they're gonna fly or land next. Their heads turn on weird angles and the way those beady little eyes *stare* at you," he shuddered, "it's like they're plotting your death in the most painful way possible. And don't forget that those sons of bitches have fangs attached to their goddamn feet. Those things could fucking rip you to pieces given half the chance."

I didn't say anything. Not a single word.

"What?"

"Um, honey?" I tried to bite back the incredulous laughter but failed miserably and fell into a fit of hysterics. The irony behind his hatred for the winged creatures and one being plastered all over the side of his freakin' neck completely made me lose my shit. After several minutes, I finally calmed down, even though my sides were aching and I was wholly out of breath. The man was a walking contradiction. For some reason this knowledge made me unbelievably happy.

Levi still looked slightly affronted at my amusement, so I tenderly caressed his face and after a moment he succumbed to my touch by leaning into my hand. His eyes softened as they melted into mine. But I totally ruined the moment.

Like always.

"Where'd you go today?"

He removed my hand and placed it on his lap, clasping it between his fingers. He was silent for a minute or two while I mentally stomped on my own left foot with an imaginary killer heel on my right. Just as I was about to retract my question, he looked down and murmured, "To visit my aunt. She lives just out of the city."

"Oh." Stop talking, Grace. Shift the conversation to another topic, any other topic. Tomato salsa. Mention your new-found appreciation for tomato salsa. "It must have been good to see her again."

Damn it.

He stared up at me. "Yeah, it was. Valerie's always been like a mum to Dom and I."

"Hang on, what about your own mum?" *For God's sake, woman. Okay, corn chips. Talk about corn chips.*

Levi looked down again.

"Levi, I—"

"She died a few years back."

Whoa. My other hand instinctively moved to rest

on top of Levi's and I squeezed gently. "I'm so sorry."

He half-heartedly shrugged one shoulder and continued looking down at our hands, saying nothing.

"Were you close?" *Seriously, Grace. Shut up.*

He paused before replying, "Yes and no. I mean, she was Mum so of course I loved her, but... Anyway, she deserved a better life than the one she had."

"Because of your dad?" *Shut up. Shut up.*

He looked up at me and there it was again, the sudden coldness that warned me to stop this line of invasive questioning. "Yes."

It seemed as though my defective verbal filter finally recognized the extraordinary foot in mouth situation I once again found myself in. "It's okay, you don't have to talk about him if you don't want to. When you're good and ready, remember?"

He nodded. "When I'm good and ready."

I honestly didn't know what to say to bring him back from whatever dark thoughts circled around in his head after that. So we were both quiet for several minutes. But I then decided to voice what I had really wanted to say for the past couple of hours. "I'm glad you came back."

The coldness in his eyes gradually thawed and once that quirky half grin appeared in the corner of his mouth, he began to look like my Levi again.

My Levi.

Jesus Christ.

But for once I ignored my head. I chose not to overthink this ticking time bomb which my subconscious not-so-subtly dropped into my headspace. When Levi replied soon after with, "Me too," I also refused to overthink the fact that my heart had now decided to beat at triple the normal rate for the sheer fun of trying to kill me.

So instead I simply said, "Come to bed with me."

A slow, panty-dissolving smile spread across his face as I stood and held out my hand to him. He grasped it in his own and rose also, towering above me. Bending down, he encircled me in his arms, kissing me slow and deep. He then gently stepped me backward into the next room, never once breaking contact with my lips. It was only when I felt the mattress pressing against the backs of my knees that I murmured huskily, "I meant to sleep. We've got a big day tomorrow."

He gave a low chuckle. "Sure you did, kitten."

Chapter Eleven

You wait patiently but it's too late,
By the time she arrives she's gone again.
-MONDEZ, "Timeless"

I lost myself in the luxuriating feel of Levi's lips, tongue and hands for exactly eight seconds. To give him credit, that's all it took to transport me from being a remotely sane individual to someone who was about to self-implode. I internally slapped myself across the face and then broke away from the kiss. However, a part of me, the aroused bit, knew that I'd regret this decision later.

"Kitten, what is it?"

We were both breathing heavily and Levi's pupils had dilated to the point where they took up the entirety of his sapphire blue eyes. I took a deep breath, unlocked my hands from behind his neck and rested my forehead against his chest. My palms grabbed the material of his black t-shirt, scrunching it between my fists. After taking three more deep, steadying breaths, I finally found the strength I needed to talk without my rampant hormones doing the exact opposite of what I intended to say. Once satisfied that my itching fingers wouldn't betray me, I relaxed my hands, smoothed out the fabric and looked up at him.

"More than anything in the world I'd like us to fuck right now," I began. His eyes glazed over and I quickly tried to channel my thoughts into some vague semblance of rational order so as not to reenact those very words. "But I meant what I said. I think we should just sleep tonight."

Levi tucked a stray strand of hair behind my ear,

deep in thought. After a minute or two, he murmured, "And why is that, Grace?"

I stared at his chest, trying desperately to ignore the tingling sensation of his fingers against my scalp and my embarrassingly weakened self-command because of them. Not wanting to meet his gaze, I shut my eyes and mumbled, "I don't want to hurt you again."

As Levi tipped my chin up, I flicked my eyes open. Our gazes locked and for once he was deadly serious. "I don't want you to either."

"But if we have sex right now, I will. I know it."

He tilted his head to the side, questioning.

"Look." But his proximity was too close and I couldn't think straight when he was touching me. So I broke away from his embrace, moving over to the window. For a good five minutes, I stared out at the black Melbourne sky. The bright twinkling lights of the city buildings which fringed the comet-like streaks of cars whizzing past below, spoke of a speed and a fervor that matched my head and heart space perfectly.

I wanted to explain this right. I wanted him to understand that what I was feeling was akin to Juliet for her Romeo. It was now all too sudden, too significant, too tangible for my poor heart to take all at once. Throwing our physical connection on top of the emotional turmoil I was currently trying to deal with gave me the ominous feeling that our budding relationship was likely to end just as badly. Not that we were going to die tragic mistimed deaths or anything, just that we were likely to drive one another to crazed stupidity if we didn't tread more carefully. And the thought of hurting him pained me.

A lot.

Turning around, I immediately registered the fact that Levi was seated on the bed. His legs were straight out in front of him and crossed at the ankles.

I gulped.

His head rested against the padded headboard and his curious gaze was trained on me.

I gulped again.

Why is he doing this? Why is he suddenly modeling the latest linen and bedding exclusive to boutique hotels? Now was definitely not the time to look that damn sexy.

I tore my gaze away again and spoke to the much less stimulating cobalt sky. "I think we need to … breathe for a bit, you know?" I glanced back at him over my shoulder. His expression was fathomless so I continued. "I don't mean that we should stop or ignore what's obviously between us, but I think it would be a good idea to just sit with these feelings for a while. Process them, that's all."

"You want us to slow down?"

I turned to face him squarely. "Honey," I stopped and tried again, "*Levi*, it's only been nine days. But with all the shit that has happened it feels like…" Waving my arms about me in a vague gesture did nothing to explain the enormity of what I was referring to.

"It feels like forever."

I dropped my arms back to my sides. "Exactly."

He nodded. "Okay, if that's what you want, we can take it slow."

My body sagged with relief as I moved back to the bed, crawling up next to him. "Thank you," I murmured, before tenderly kissing him and settling my body down next to his, unbelievably exhausted.

"You're killing me, you know that?"

I chuckled softly, wrapping my arms around him, cuddling in closer. "Right back at you."

****

The next morning dawned bright and clear. As my eyes adjusted to the sunlight streaming in through the open curtains, I looked down and took stock of my current situation. It was pretty awesome. Levi was sprawled across me, one of his legs entangled between my own and his arm laying warm and possessive just below my breasts. I glanced across at his head resting against my shoulder, his features had softened through sleep, making him appear younger, while dark, thick lashes contrasted with the lighter skin of his cheeks. Seriously, this was the best wake-up call I'd ever had. I slowly reached for my phone on the bedside table, not wanting to disturb the sleeping Adonis next to me, and checked the time. "*Holy fuck.*"

I tore off Levi's arm and kicked away his legs, scrambling out from underneath the covers and almost falling face first onto the plush carpet in my haste. There was a gravelly chuckle behind me and it took all of my newfound resolve not to turn around and hurl myself at the man. Whether it was to devour or thwack him, I wasn't yet decided, but either way I'd make him pay. No wait, we're taking it slow. Definitely thwack him. Sadly, before I could begin my violent onslaught I was reminded of how little time I actually had to get the job done properly. So, in the interest of punctuality, I compromised and threw a cushion at his head instead.

Once showered and dressed, I was rummaging around in my suitcase, searching for my wayward notebook and pen when Levi emerged from the bathroom.

And Oh. My. God.

The man looked like a wet dream. Truly. His gray suit pants hugged his hips in a way that made me immediately recite ten Hail Marys. The silver belt buckle winked teasingly at me as it caught the light. His crisp white shirt had faint blue checks which oh so conveniently matched the color of his fuck-me eyes. It was open at the collar and his sleeves were rolled midway up his forearms, exposing just enough skin to cause a riot in my downstairs department. Consequently, my female parts decided to protest against the decision made last night and to be fair, they voiced a damn convincing argument.

I quickly shut my gaping jaw with a snap and muttered, "You look ... nice."

Levi purposefully strode towards me. Gone was the polite, understanding guy from last night and in his place was a predatory, dangerous man.

Sweet Lord.

The spicy scent of his cologne intoxicated me with each step. I swear, he was going to be the catalyst of an outright sexual frenzy if I didn't escape from him soon. I didn't even realize I was backing away until my head bumped into a wall behind me, hitting it with a soft thud.

I held my breath as Levi planted his powerful hands on either side of my flushed face. Leaning in close, he skimmed his nose against my jawline and trailed it down my neck, before growling, "You don't look so bad yourself, kitten."

I bit my cheek to stifle a moan.

"And since we're taking it slow," he murmured, "I won't spin you around to face the wall. I won't slowly lift the hem of that cock tease of a pencil skirt you're almost wearing. I won't even raise it up over that sexy ass before fucking you from behind." He licked and nipped my partially exposed collarbone.

I gasped.

"Even though your eyes are begging me to."

"Bastard," I breathed.

"Because I won't or because you want me to?" Levi's lips blessedly stopped their sensual assault but his blazing eyes stared down at me, heated and challenging.

I glared at him. Smart Mouth was definitely needed. "No, because your self-indulgence is making us late." With that I ducked underneath his arm and quickly grabbed what I wanted before striding—as confidently as my trembling legs would allow—out the hotel room door.

After we walked into the packed foyer of the Melbourne Convention Center, I stopped. Hundreds of people from all over the country were there, animatedly discussing cutting edge teaching methodologies and the latest research in adolescent cognitive development. It was freakin' awesome. I looked up at Levi who stood next to me, ignored the wicked glint that lurked behind his eyes and said, "Don't forget that we're representing Geographe High here. Now, normally I don't give a shit about what other people think, but as soon as we put on our name badges it's important to remember that we're no longer Grace and Levi. You're a student teacher and I'm your mentor. Got it?"

"Fuck you're hot when you do that."

"Do what?"

"Get all authoritative and shit. It makes me hard just looking at you."

"*Levi.*" I disentangled our fingers. It hadn't taken him long to catch me up in the hotel corridor and had been holding my hand ever since. Not that I minded the contact. Well, until now. "Behave."

"Yes, Ms. Thompson."

I stepped closer. "You're walking a fine line, Mr. Mondez."

He grinned. "I'm looking forward to seeing what you'll do when I cross it."

I let out a combination of an exasperated and

sexually frustrated sigh, spun on my heel and stormed off towards the signing-in table. A deep chuckle trailed after me the whole way.

"Grace? *Hey, Grace.*"

I turned at the sound of a familiar low timber. "Aemon?"

The man behind me smiled widely before pulling me into a bear hug. "It's so good to see you again." He pulled back, still grasping my shoulders while appreciatively eyeing me up and down.

I could have sworn I heard a low growl to my right.

"You look sensational."

Yep, definitely a growl.

I smiled self-consciously. For as long as I'd known him, Aemon had never shied away from the fact that he wanted me. Even when I was dating Dylan and he was sleeping with yet another random girl on university campus, he'd always told me I deserved better. Apparently, he was just the guy to show me the many benefits of a committed relationship. Kind of ironic really, since Aemon never stuck around long enough to remember anything except the cup size of the women he slept with. I'd always just laughed it off, because even though he was a total player, I'd never seen him as anything more than a friend. Well, this was all back when I was nice enough to actually *have* friends.

I took a step back. "Uh, thanks. It's good to see you too. So, where are you teaching now?"

"At St. Joseph's, here in Melbourne. Moved over straight after graduation." He pushed away the lock of sandy blond hair that was forever falling in his eyes. It drove the girls wild. Most girls. He trained his hazel eyes on me. "What about you?"

"I'm at Geographe High, back home."

Aemon nodded but then immediately sobered. "Look, I'm really sorry to hear about your dad." He took one of my hands and held it. "I've been meaning to call you, but between moving states and starting this new job…" He gave my fingers a squeeze. "If there's anything I can do, just say the word, okay?" His face lit up. "I know, how about I take you out for dinner sometime this week? We can talk, drink," he smiled, "reminisce."

"That won't be necessary."

I shut my eyes and prayed to the gods of justifiable eye-gauging that we would all make it out of this conversation alive. Retracting my hand, I smiled apologetically. "Aemon, this is my student teacher, Levi Mondez."

"Student teacher?" I could tell he was desperately trying not to look too incredulous at the sight of Mount Testosterone. But he failed. Completely.

Levi took a step closer to Aemon, his body partially shielding me while narrowing blue eyes at him.

I knew what he was doing. The jerk was stamping his authority like I was some freakin' prize to be fought over. So I maneuvered myself in between them both to glare up at him. Only, he was far too busy eyeballing my old friend to notice the silent warning.

"Levi, this is Aemon," I said through clenched teeth. "We went to university together."

"I'll bet."

I watched both men sizing each other up. The differences were incomparable. Levi was tall to Aemon's short, strong to his lean, simmering to his serene. If we were anywhere else, I would have found their pissing contest hilarious. Only we weren't, so it was annoying.

I yanked on Levi's shirtsleeve. "Come on, we'd better go find our seats." He refused to be deterred and I ended up having to pull him away by the arm. "I said, let's go." Levi gave Aemon one last passing scowl and I rolled my eyes.

"See you around, Aemon."

"You can count on it, Grace."

Strangely, once we moved into the conference hall and sat down, Levi didn't mention Aemon. I was expecting him to interrogate me about what type of friendship we'd shared or in the very least, comment on the preppy good looks of the damn guy. But he remained silent. Even worse, was that for the remainder of the day, Levi acted like a true professional. I couldn't help but wonder why he wasn't specializing in drama instead of English and for some reason this complete change in personality pissed me off like you wouldn't believe.

I mean, to start with he appeared enthralled throughout the entirety of the first keynote speaker who was a professor in child psychology. Needless to say, by morning refreshments I was mildly irritated. But then Levi sat at a professional distance during the middle session which was led by the principal of a rural area school. He even nodded in agreement at many of the ideas raised. So by lunch, I was annoyed. However, when the guy actually had the audacity to take notes during the final address of the afternoon, run by the inventor of a new online educational portal, I was *fuming*.

Fuming at what exactly, I couldn't say. The fact that I hadn't seen Aemon again so couldn't rub his attraction for me in Levi's ridiculously handsome face? The fact that he had actually done as I'd asked and acted sensibly? Or the fact that I desperately wished he'd ignored my demands and felt me up in the back row? Regardless of all three possibilities, by the end of the day I was so outraged that I stormed out of the conference hall. I strode far quicker than I ever thought imaginable.

Hell, even an Olympic power-walker would have been proud of my efforts. I just had to get back to the hotel before tearing a hole in the next person who dared to speak to me.

One look at my livid expression was all it took for Patrick to pour me enough whiskey to drown a bearded sailor. I snatched the glass off the bar and swallowed its entire contents in one mouthful.

"Tough day?"

"Gimme another."

He raised an eyebrow at my abruptness but did as I asked, turning and grabbing the bottle of my favorite numbing potion off the shelf behind him. While refilling my second glass, Levi stepped into the bar looking like the Grim Reaper of panties everywhere. He sidled up next to me and purred, "So, do you come here often?"

I rolled my eyes, though was somewhat placated by the warmth of the alcohol as it spread throughout my tense body. "Cut the crap, Levi."

He nodded to a curious Patrick. "I'll have a glass of the same, thanks."

The barman glanced between the two of us, looking as though all the mysteries of the universe had finally revealed themselves.

Levi cleared his throat. "I couldn't help but notice a certain," he paused, tracing a finger through the condensation left on the bar from my glass, "*negativity* radiating out of you today." He dropped his voice as he leaned into my ear, murmuring, "What's up with that?"

I stared at my drink, trying to formulate the words needed to explain my anger-fueled confusion without sounding like a walking hypocrite. It was useless. To pretend my behavior at the conference meant anything other than wanting to go back on my decision from not even fifteen hours ago, would insult the intelligence of both Levi and myself.

Time to face the music, Grace.

So, after taking a deep breath I looked up at him again. "You did what I asked."

A brief smile of understanding crossed his lips before disappearing again. "Yes, I did what you asked."

"It sucked."

"Big time."

"Kiss me."

"Hell yes."

And for the next little while we were lost to the other. As Levi's lips moved against mine, the anger receded. As his tongue worked my own, it dissipated further. And as he pulled me closer against him, arching my back while he deepened our kiss to celestial proportions, it disappeared completely. I was left feeling renewed, revived but as freakin' horny as the devil himself.

This time Levi was the first to pull away. "Kitten, if we don't stop now, I'm going to fuck you where you stand," he growled.

"Do it."

But he shook his head, his eyes laughing at my brazen disregard for Melbourne's public indecency laws. "At least let me buy you dinner first."

A five minute taxi ride later, on account of the blisters generated by my Olympic power walk qualifying time, we were strolling through the Queen Victoria Markets. With Levi's hand in mine, he weaved me in and out of post-work shoppers, tourists and university students all purchasing incredibly fresh ingredients from the myriad of food stalls available. The noise was extreme, ricocheting off the tin walls and wrought iron roof, seeming to grow in intensity the farther we ventured inside. I loved it. I loved the chaos, the color, the flurry of activity, the exotic smells, everything.

Levi gazed down at my enthralled face and smiled. "I knew you'd get it." He then led me through to the other side of the market and as we stepped back outside I could immediately smell the fumes from the cars racing past. A ripple of nostalgia for the endless sandy beaches and clear blue skies back home washed over me but I shook it off quickly, determined not to pine for anything when Levi was nearby. As we headed south, we passed an insanely long line leading to a fancy Indian restaurant before entering Italia Bar, next door to it.

The place wasn't large, maybe about the same size as the joint living and sleeping quarters of our hotel room. I had to step around the gigantic rectangular pillar situated smack bang in the center. It was covered with newspaper articles haphazardly stuck all over it, showcasing the bar's many gastronomic achievements. There were a few mismatched tables and plastic chairs to my left, with a glass display cabinet and a bar with stools either side of it positioned on the right. Up above the display cabinet was an enormous chalk menu board suspended from the exposed metal ceiling, advertising an array of mouthwatering Italian dishes. My stomach immediately registered that it hadn't consumed anything in a heck of a long time. A millennium in fact, if my saliva glands were anything to go by.

We took a seat on the bar stools since all of the tables were taken and Levi turned to me, excited. "Are you ready to be blown away by the best meatball roll this country has to offer?"

"Um, yeah?"

"Sweet." And with that, he hopped off the chair to go order at the register. I shook my head in amusement, how a grown man of his height and stature could pull off being boyishly cute as well as absurdly handsome was quite simply beyond me. But Levi somehow managed it. Effortlessly.

Once returned and seated as comfortably as an impossibly tall man could on a bar stool, he then said, "It's a great place, am I right?" I nodded, indulging his cocky enthusiasm. "Our Auntie Val would bring us here whenever we visited. Apart from being allowed to play with her insane collection of musical instruments, this place was definitely the highlight of the trip."

I stockpiled that tidbit of information away for another time and instead asked, "So, it's been around for a while then?"

"Yeah, I think it's run by the third or fourth generation of the same family. Cool, huh?"

"Impressive."

Our conversation waned then and I didn't really know what to say after that. To be honest, it was mainly because I wanted to explain my self-diagnosis of bipolar. On the walk through the markets I'd been trying to think of different ways to broach the subject and explain why I kept acting like a glutton in a patisserie shop who would intermittently declare themselves on a sugar-free diet. Only, I somehow didn't think the simile would explain it coherently enough. So the words wouldn't come.

A thumb brushed my bottom lip making me start and my eyes instinctively flew to Levi's. "Tell me what you're thinking."

My mouth popped open and then closed. I even verbalized a guttural sound at one point. But other than that, it just wasn't going to happen. No words on the subject, smart or otherwise, were making themselves heard tonight. So I ended up shrugging my shoulders and hoping that by some miracle he could read the depth of my intended meaning behind that gesture alone.

"Okay, how about I start then?"

I nodded, slightly perturbed not only by my lack of articulation but also by the sudden gravity expressed in Levi's features.

"I'll be honest, kitten. I'm finding it pretty hard to keep up with you at the moment." I bit my lip and even though his eyes dropped to the movement, he continued, "One minute you're hot for me, the next you want to slow down." He spun my stool around to face him squarely and rested his palms on my sheer stocking-clad knees.

I bit my lip again. Harder. I wouldn't even need a meal at this rate.

"I just want to know what's going on in that crazy little head of yours."

"You'd have me committed if you did." *Thank Christ, words.*

"Try me."

I looked down, tracing my fingers over the width and breadth of his hands. God they were huge. Strong. Warm. *If I shift my body this way slightly they'll be so close to my ... Grace, focus.* I shook my head. "I don't really know what I want. No wait, that's not true. Hang on, let me start again." I shut my eyes, thinking hard while desperately trying to ignore the touch of his hands traveling up my thighs. "I know that I want *you*." I peeked at him again, glancing up from beneath my lashes.

"Glad to hear it."

I smiled. "And I know that I want to be *with* you. But," he stared at me intently, "trust is a big issue for me."

"You don't trust me?"

"I do, I think. But that's not what I mean. You see, it's *me* who I don't trust."

He raised an eyebrow, clearly perplexed and I didn't blame him. I might as well have been speaking in

Haiku. "I'm explaining this in the shittiest way possible." I took a deep breath. "It's like my head is telling me not to trust my heart, you know? Like, what I'm feeling right now is too good to be true, will never last and I'll once again end up comatose on the couch surrounded by a sea of fucking tissues and empty whiskey bottles." I lowered my voice. "I was in a fucked up place after Dylan left and I don't want to go back there again."

"So, how are we going to do this if you don't trust what you're feeling?"

"That's the thing, Levi, I don't freakin' know. One minute, I'm telling myself to ignore my head and follow my heart, while the next minute my heart freaks out and it's back to listening to my goddamn head again."

"What does your gut tell you?"

"That I'm flippin' *hungry*." I paused. "Commit me, please? Or at least get me some decent drugs so I won't have to live with this fucked up dichotomy of shit that circles my brain non-stop."

Levi smiled sweetly. "No drugs, no asylum, just this." He leaned forward, tenderly kissing me. Far too quickly, he pulled back and I could smell the whiskey on his breath as he murmured, "Trust in this, Grace."

I pulled his mouth back to mine. To the feel of his lips, to the emotion barely contained within them, and the faith that they openly sought. Was it possible? Could I expose myself to potential hurt once again? Was being with Levi worth the risk?

Yes.

Fuck yes.

It was on the tip of my tongue to say it. Hell, after that heart-melting kiss I was ready to yell and scream the word before orchestrating a musical number and sashaying my newfound certainty around Italia Bar. I'd even use the other patrons as backup dancers. And the manager. But I was ruefully interrupted by the arrival of our meal.

"*Christ Almighty*," I exclaimed, staring down at the meatball roll that was bigger than my shoulder blade.

"It's a good thing we're sharing."

I nodded, mesmerized by the triple bypass on a plate in front of me. Levi cut it in half, picked up his portion and bit into it with a gusto that was quite simply awe-inspiring. I mean, the guy didn't spill a drop. I followed suit and God in heaven, it was sinfully divine. "This is the best thing I've ever tasted."

Levi winked at me. "Give it time, kitten. I can think of something else you might like more."

I blanched and almost asphyxiated myself on a chunk of meatball before quickly swallowing. "You're very sure of yourself, Mondez," I stated flatly.

Levi's smile just grew wider and my panties almost shimmied themselves down my legs all of their own accord. Jerk. However, before I could suggest a creative place to shove that sexual insinuation, his phone rang. Levi looked down at it puzzled, then recognition cleared his features and he answered it. "*Hey, Katrina*." Holding up his index finger and gesturing that he'd be one minute, Levi then stood and moved outside the restaurant. I just shrugged one shoulder in nonchalance. Who was I to give a shit if he answered his phone or not?

Four mouthfuls of carb-laden bliss later, he returned, practically bursting with pent up elation. It was kind of adorable.

"Good news?"

"*Abso-fucking-lutely*. Katrina's band, Adrift, is playing this Thursday night and she's put my name on the door."

"Great."

"With a plus one if you're interested?"

I grinned. "Sure, sounds fun."

"They're pretty heavy, but I think you'll like it. Reckon you're a dark horse when it comes to music."

"Piss off."

He smiled wide. "Anyways, you'll get to meet Katrina after the show. She's an awesome girl."

I nodded, not trusting my head/mouth filter because as much as I wanted to blame the amount of food I'd just ingested on that sudden stomach twinge, I'd be lying. For some reason, the sheer mention of this girl's name sent warning signals shooting throughout my brain. It also caused my insides to tighten unnaturally. Was it possible to hate someone I'd never even met?

The answer didn't bode well for Thursday night.

However, I managed to shove the last morsel of culinary genius into my mouth to avoid any possible verbalization of what I'd just realized. Once we'd both finished our meals, Levi took my hand again and led me outside. "C'mon, let's head back to the hotel. I wanna get you naked before your head takes over again."

All thoughts of Katrina flew out of my mind. Instead, I was immediately flooded with images of Levi in various stages of undress while he contorted my body and ravaged me senseless. "And who ever said that romance was dead?"

"Kitten, you'd fucking hate romance. You'd turn and run at the first sight of it."

I nodded. The man had a point.

Chapter Twelve

It's raising us, bending and molding us,
It's raising us, it's reverberating.
-MONDEZ, "Reverberate"

It had been a hectic day. The café was incredibly busy from the mass influx of tourists all on summer holidays. My entire shift had been a whirlwind of taking orders, delivering food, cleaning tables, restocking condiments and trying not to let the seemingly endless chaos be the cause of my emotional ruin. So I was glad to finally step onto the beach, sink my feet in the sand and sit down next to Dad.

I began tracing nondescript outlines and patterns with one finger as my mind ticked over an unusual conundrum.

I had been asked out on a date.

For the first time in my life, a guy had shown an interest in me. An attractive one too, in that healthy guy-next-door kind of way. It sucked he complained about his meal though. Total bullshit by the way, I'd even read the food order out to him before taking it to the kitchen. Anyway, now I didn't know what to do about the phone number he'd slipped me with the tip.

I stopped and gazed out at the water, it was calm now that the breeze had died off. The glassy ripples turned a dusky purple, mirroring the color above as the sun dipped low. I tried to locate the exact point on the horizon where the sea met the sky but couldn't find it, so instead shut my eyes, inhaling deeply. A minute later, I slowly exhaled. I breathed out all the pent-up stress from the past five hours, all the uncertainty over the napkin burning a hole in my pocket, everything. When I opened my eyes again and watched the sun as it set, I felt renewed.

I looked across at Dad and couldn't help but smile. He must have had a lot on his mind too. The hole he'd dug was twice its normal size and almost three times as deep. I could tell he was finished because the customary stick was nowhere to be seen and he was staring at the waves as they rolled into the shore. Dad sensed my gaze and turned to look at me. He grinned.

I loved these moments. They were the times I felt pure, unadulterated joy. So I came to a realization. I wasn't going to overthink this. I was going to take my time and breathe. Life would somehow figure itself out and I would end up where I was meant to be.

Eventually.

"Do you want another?"

"Yeah, thanks." I was relaxing on the couch in our hotel room and had been reminiscing about a time when I'd felt equally as contented. My head was leaning against the cushion, my eyes were closed and my feet, still encased in nude leather pumps, were blessedly resting on the coffee table. I'd have to wear flats tomorrow. Turned out there was a reason why high heels weren't a part of our national race walking team's uniform.

Who would've thought?

Contrary to what Levi had threatened as we left the restaurant, he didn't tear my clothes off as soon as we stepped into our suite. I was slightly peeved at first, frustration didn't sit well with me at the best of times, but after a couple of drinks and Levi's hand languidly tracing abstract nothings on the material of my pencil skirt, I relaxed considerably. He always did that. Calmed me with his touch and through his presence, calmed me until

I could sit with the quiet, envelop myself in its stillness and not feel the need to scream at it anymore.

Levi soundlessly rose from the couch and even though my eyes remained closed, I could feel him gone. My left side felt cooler as the warmth which emanated from his body and seeped into mine just seconds before, slowly dissipated.

So now I can't even sit by myself on a fucking sofa?

Christ.

This growing dependence on the guy was seriously disturbing. After taking a deep breath, I made a vow to think nothing but amatory thoughts. For tonight at least. Tomorrow however? I shook my head. Who freakin' knew.

"Here you go."

My eyes opened and Levi stood before me—a sexy culmination of all my teenage rock band fantasies mushed together. His arm was outstretched and a whiskey dangled tantalizingly in front of my face. Christmas had come early this year. My eyes dropped to the drink—and New Year's too if the amount of alcohol in that glass was anything to go by.

"Thanks." I slowly took a sip and teasingly licked the corner of my mouth afterward. Refusing to break contact with his lustful gaze, I murmured, "Mmm, delicious."

Levi's eyes darkened. He slowly placed his own glass on the coffee table before leaning down and gently nipping my bottom lip. "Tease," he growled.

I chuckled softly but then almost whimpered out loud when he stood and moved away. *Now who's the damn tease?* Rummaging around in his duffel bag, he pulled out an iPod and then moved into the bedroom, connecting it with the dock on his side table. A few seconds later, soft piano chords wafted through to the lounge. It wasn't exactly what I was expecting, but seemed pleasant enough.

I raised an eyebrow at Levi as he sat next to me, resting his right arm behind my head on the back of the couch. "Give it a minute," he said.

A short while later, I smiled. Deep, dirty guitar riffs layered the original gentle melody of the piano, like a grizzly bear balancing on top of a water sprite. The contrast of both those guttural and sweet sounds somehow seamlessly complemented the other and the intensity slowly swelled as the tempo increased. It then plateaued for a minute or two, only to take me by surprise as a tight drumbeat, accompanied by some smooth rolling bass lines suddenly kicked in.

Whoa.

The entire combination was heavy yet soft, profound yet playful and undeniably ingenious throughout. I kept waiting for the vocalist to make themselves heard over this cacophony of interlinked yet markedly dissimilar musical sounds, only they never appeared. Smiling, I realized that this band was in no way lacking without one.

"This genre is what us musicians like to call stoner rock. Intense, huh?"

I turned to face Levi. He was looking at me while slowly moving his head back and forth in time with the heavy beat.

"Stoner rock?" I smiled wider. "The name fits."

Levi lifted the arm that rested behind my head and gently skimmed the backs of his fingers down the side of my face. "You're so beautiful, Grace," he murmured, before tucking some hair behind my ear.

For some reason I felt the need to hold my breath. No idea why.

"I never thought I'd feel this way about anyone, but…" He shook his head slightly. "How is it that you mean so damn much to me?" His eyes searched my face and I could feel that instinctive pull between us strengthen. "You feel it too, I can tell."

I nodded slowly but then looked down, suddenly awkward. Surely, a man couldn't look at a woman like that after only ten days. I mean, he'd already moved past my prickly shell, sidestepped my Smart Mouth and snuck under my feeble deflections. And here he stood at the base of my last defense—a raised, weathered, drawbridge. It pathetically attempted to protect one very fragile core. Only, Levi was slowly pulling the rotting wood apart with his bare hands, inspecting the brittle pieces and telling me that they were irrelevant in the first place.

He was asking me to let him in.

How did he make it look so easy? What he said he meant, what he felt he showed.

I didn't even know where to start.

"Look at me."

My gaze slowly traveled back to his again.

"I'm falling for you, kitten."

The final bars of the first song slowly faded and we were left cocooned in what felt like a cozy bubble of tenderness. Only I burst it spectacularly by mumbling, "Um, thanks?"

Levi stared at me as the opening chords of the second song began. He blinked once, twice and then his face broke into a lopsided grin that wreaked havoc on my female parts. Unlike my head, they were all up for this type of conversation.

"Thanks?" he repeated.

I squirmed in my seat as a mixture of some powerful emotion I refused to put my finger on, desperate need, and sheer embarrassment washed over me. "Well, what am I supposed to say? You know I'm not good at this shit."

He chuckled, low and deep. "You don't have to say anything."

I looked at him for a long minute then, searching his face and trying to determine exactly how I was going communicate the true extent of what I was feeling. Once decided, I carefully placed my glass on the low table and standing up, turned to face him.

When I deliberately stepped in between his legs, Levi looked up at me, openly curious. But he remained silent and I was grateful. It was a nice change not having to contend with my foot-in-mouth or his mocking quips, and ironically, this lack of conversation gave me more confidence to say exactly what I wanted without convoluted words getting in the way. So, when I reached around to the back of my skirt and slowly lowered the zip, Levi's eyes darkened.

He knew exactly what I meant.

Smart man.

As I let the skirt skim over my hips and flutter to the floor at my feet, he sharply inhaled. After I intentionally stepped out of the pooled material and kicked it away, his expression changed to something different entirely.

I smiled coyly at the hunger burning in his eyes, and then unhurriedly unbuttoned my pale shirt, taking my sweet time with each and every fastening. Upon completion, I pulled the material wide and let it leisurely drop from my shoulders. I watched, empowered, as Levi momentarily shut his eyes, breathing raggedly. He was clearly attempting to deal with an internal struggle of paramount proportions and it emboldened me beyond measure.

He opened them again and an acutely ravenous gaze deliberately raked my body. It traveled from my high heels to the lace band of my thigh high stockings before coming to rest on the delicate confection of scarlet material that tied at my hips with satin ribbon. Levi's eyes questioningly flicked to mine and I smiled wickedly, nodding slightly while twisting my waist and visually confirming that yes, it was a g-string. He let out a deep breath and slumped back onto the sofa, rubbing strained fingers across his eyes.

I giggled.

After a minute, Levi appeared to gather more strength. He dropped his hand as blazing eyes once again continued journeying upwards. They took in my navel, followed the sweeping line of my waist, preyed on the matching crimson bra, and finally settled on my face.

It was only when his eyes locked onto mine, stunned, yet enamored, that he breathed quietly, "Grace, just look at you." He shook his head but then stopped abruptly, narrowing his eyes. "Have you been wearing this," he gestured to my present state of near undress, "under that sexy librarian outfit *all fucking day?*"

I shrugged my shoulders, feigning indifference but secretly loving his incredulity. "Sure, why not?" Okay, so maybe my subconscious secretly wanted this very moment to happen as I was selecting lingerie this morning. I mean, I sure as hell would never have chosen these scraps of material posing as sexy underwear otherwise. And okay, it probably also contributed to my raging quest for Olympic glory after the conference too. But I was choosing to graciously ignore both possibilities. I mean, at the time my head had decided to take it slow, remember?

Levi's eyes turned predatory then. He leaned forward, quickly picked me up by the waist as though I weighed no less than his acoustic guitar, swung me around and unceremoniously deposited me on the couch with a resounding thump.

I swore.

Fluently.

Even though I'd landed safely, the sudden movement took me by one heck of a surprise. Thankfully, my mother and I were no longer on speaking terms because if she had seen me, she would have been mortified. My head rested on the cushioned armrest, hair in flagrant disarray. My back was on the couch itself, arms gripping Levi's biceps and head still reeling from how fucking amazing those muscles felt as they contracted with the movement of hurling me onto the sofa. One of my feet was in contact with the floor while the other had disappeared somewhere behind Levi's hip. Along with any remaining decorum.

Altogether a very interesting position.

Levi grasped my right ankle and lifted it up. After closely inspecting my leather pump, he murmured seductively, "I think we'll leave these on."

I squirmed on the cushion, aroused by the dangerous glint in his eyes and his slow, deliberate movements.

Levi rested my ankle on top of his shoulder and I inhaled sharply as he began kissing his way up my leg. *Holy fuck.* Even through the nylon, his lips were absolute magic. Once he reached the lace band of my stocking, he stopped, smiling devilishly. "I think we'll leave these on too."

I bit my lip, stifling a groan at the prospect of what he was going to do to me and how much I was going to explode if he didn't get started on it soon. But determined to see me self-combust, Levi continued his tortuously measured journey towards the apex of my thighs. His lips were now touching ridiculously sensitive skin on the inside of my legs, sending shockwaves directly to the most intimate part of me and I moaned. Loudly.

Levi chuckled.

Bastard.

When he reached the soaked material of what used to be my g-string, he broke away and smiled up at me. I glared down at him, annoyed that he had stopped and that I was quite literally panting.

"But these will need to come off," he murmured.

"Do it already."

He snickered again. "Patience, kitten. It'll be worth it, I promise."

I threw my head back on the cushion with a huff, like a petulant toddler having a temper tantrum. *Stupid patience. It's completely overrated.*

Ignoring my physical outburst and even worse, finding it funny, Levi grinned before licking and nipping his way across my hip.

I moaned again. Honestly, I couldn't help it. The man had the most amazing lips and tongue I'd ever experienced. So those, combined with the sensation of his slight growth as it scratched my heated skin, almost made me lose my freakin' mind.

When he eventually reached the bow, he took the ribbon between his teeth and pulled. *Seriously, what is it with this guy and eating my underwear? Fuck, who cares, it's hot.* He then traveled to my other side and untied the second piece of satin just as sensually.

My lingerie fell away and Levi stared up at me exultant, looking like all of his underwear-eating fantasies had suddenly come to life. But rather than begin his carnal onslaught on my female parts, he instead moved back, gently placed my right foot on the floor and switched his undivided attention to my left.

"*Please*," I begged, writhing and squirming and almost on fucking fire as he began yet another tortuous ascent.

"Kitten, I've been wanting to do this to you for a *very* long time." At last he reached my inner thigh. "I'm not gonna rush it."

"Honey, we've only known each other for *ten fucking days*." I panted, as he moved ever so closer. God, even in this arousal-induced fervor I was still attempting to delude myself.

Levi nipped my flesh and I unashamedly moaned. "Don't give me that shit, you know we're more than that." His lips continued higher, he was almost there. "As far as I'm concerned," he breathed, "we've known each other for an eternity."

I groaned. "An eternity is how fucking long it's taking to get your mouth on me."

He snickered and nipped me again, though harder this time. I'd have a mark tomorrow. The thought made me smile.

I was swiftly dragged back to the present when his tongue finally found me. "*Fucking hell*," I cried to the ceiling above.

Levi snickered from between my legs and I reached down, tugging his hair in warning. But my grasp immediately loosened because his tongue ... sweet God. His tongue worked me slowly, rhythmically and ever so purposefully. It was as though he already knew my every contour and response elicited through mouth alone. This beautifully talented man crafted quite simply, the most insanely awesome sensation I'd ever felt. Letting go of Levi's hair, I threw my arms above my head, gripping the arm rest behind me as my body bucked and bowed in reaction to each of his masterful strokes. One of Levi's hands then trailed down my thighs, leaving tingling waves in its wake, before two fingers slipped inside me, rhythmically pumping while stars formed before my eyes.

I moaned as a coil of raw energy formed inside of me. *Good God, this looming orgasm is actually going to kill me.*

"That's right, kitten," Levi hummed, "I wanna hear you call my name."

I moaned louder. The combination of his fingers, tongue and words forced the sensation to build incrementally stronger. My world became dark as I concentrated solely on that one ball of bright, glowing energy.

"I wanna hear you call it so loudly, the floor above us knows who I am."

I moaned. Really fucking loud. I was so close. I was petering on the edge of a black precipice and ready to free fall into that pool of sparkling light glittering just below.

"Come for me, Grace."

I fell.

The sphere of raw energy detonated and reflective light blinded me as my body came alive, screaming, convulsing and shuddering from that long-awaited-for, hallowed release.

Levi's tongue kept working me throughout it all—through the buildup, the fall, and the aftermath. Even as I lay there minutes later, trembling, breathless and slowly trying to gather together everything he had catastrophically blown apart, he gently lapped me. When I stilled he at last stopped, before reverently kissing me once again and then looking up at what had to be my ridiculously dazed expression. A self-indulgent grin stretched across his face.

"I'm pretty sure the whole fucking building

knows my name now."

I turned my head away, exhausted, as he laughed quietly.

Levi sat up, removed his shirt and slowly crawled towards me. He kissed, sucked and murmured how fucking sensational I tasted the whole way. I was still reeling from that orgasm and did little except watch his worshipful progression up my body as though from a distance. Once he reached my face, he looked down at me, his clear eyes taking in my genuine bafflement as I stared up at him.

How does he do it? How does he make me feel so full? So complete. So … I couldn't even bring myself to think the word.

"Grace—"

But I still wasn't ready, so I pulled him towards me and demanded his lips instead. That bombshell had to wait for another day. For a time when I could let the emotion sink in and openly claim my heart without fear pushing it away or my sense of unworthiness annihilating it totally. I could taste my own saltiness in his mouth and my tongue dove inside as eager hands seized his face, dragging him closer still.

Levi responded with unleashed fervor, pushing me deeper into the cushions of the couch while his tongue commandeered my own. He groaned as I trailed my fingers down his chest and over his stomach, before slipping around to splay across his back, nails digging into his flesh.

"I need to be inside you," he ground out against my bruised lips.

A brilliant idea.

My fingers immediately found his belt. I unbuckled it and did away with the top button and zip of his pants with a ruthlessness which surprised me.

Thankfully, I gentled before reaching inside to take hold of him.

"*Fuck*," he hissed into my mouth, as I released his erection from his boxers and slowly started working the silken shaft.

Unfortunately, I didn't have long to enjoy the feel of him hardening even further under my exploratory touch because I suddenly found myself flipped over onto my front. "*What the fuck?*" I grasped the armrest for support, head still spinning, as Levi propped me up on my knees.

While I tried to process what the heck was going on, Levi's hands leisurely trailed up from my heels. They deliberately moved across my calves, thighs, over my ass, back and shoulders. He then gathered together the loose hair that had fallen about my face into a vice-like grip and pulled down firmly. My head shot up and I gasped out loud, immediately soaked and wanting.

"You ready for me, Grace?"

I warbled out some strangled acquiescence and rubbed my behind against him in case he didn't speak crazy.

Gradually he entered me, filling and stretching my insides to accommodate his size. He groaned, "Oh my God, this feels…" But he didn't finish and I moaned in agreement at what was left unsaid. He paused for a minute, letting me acclimate to the feel of him, before grounding out, "Hold on, love, this is gonna get wild."

I didn't even have time to react to the endearment. Let's be honest, it was probably for the best anyway, because he eased out almost the whole way before taking a deep breath and slamming back into me.

"*Levi*," I cried out, momentarily blinded by the exquisite ache that suddenly sprung from deep within and reverberated throughout my body.

He immediately stilled. "You okay?"

"Don't fucking *stop*."

He didn't.

With each thrust, the world as I once knew it concaved around me. When his grip on my hip tightened, my head swam. At each of his adoring exclamations, my breathing hitched. As the front of his thighs unremittingly slapped the back of mine, I lost all sense of reason. How this man could turn an otherwise rational individual into a bundle of electrified, floating fragments, I had no idea. But he did.

That gradual ache once again built inside of me. "Jesus," I whimpered, seriously not liking my chances of surviving a second orgasm.

Levi groaned my name as I tightened around him. The knowledge that he was as completely undone by me as I was of him, gave me the strength not to splinter and crumble. Somewhere buried amongst the tottering mountains of arousal-induced sensation was my logical thought still ticking away, so I made a decision. I was going to embrace each and every fiber of fervent sensation as though it were the last time I would ever feel it.

I pushed back.

"Grace."

My world grew darker, I pushed back again.

"Grace," Levi hissed.

And again, flecks of light appeared.

"*Fuck*."

With his broken admonition, I came wildly. It was earth-shattering, life-changing and every other clichéd reference to dramatic transformation I could think of but not vocalize in my disjointed state of mind. As he came too, Levi somehow managed to hurl apart my very being, expose its broken remnants and gaze in wonder at the dazzling light caught in their reflections.

When the last of our joined cries finally eased he bent forward, wrapping one arm around me, gasping for breath. He held me close, effectively stopping me from collapsing since my limbs refused to function and keep me upright.

"Reckon the whole building knows my name too," I mumbled into the cushion.

Levi shook his head against my back, too shattered to speak.

Chapter Thirteen

I'm stuck in yesterday's memories.
You, you can't remember at all,
Tell me there's a tomorrow,
Today's driving me fucking crazy.
-MONDEZ, "Entries and Exits"

I honestly tried to concentrate during the second day of the conference. I even had my notebook out, with pen poised over the paper in anticipation of the torrent of words which were going to fly out of my mind and onto the blank page.

Only it was useless.

Levi sat next to me, dressed in dark gray suit pants and a light blue tieless shirt, sleeves once again rolled up over his forearms. His upper thigh was pressed against my own, for God's sake. I mean, how was I ever going to think straight when he was actually touching me?

I couldn't tell you about a single topic from the seminar that morning. Not one. Hell, I wouldn't have been able to spell my own freakin' name had someone asked me. In other words, I was a sodden mess of want and need wrapped tightly in my favorite green and black structured work dress. And ballet flats. God knows there was no way I would have been able to sit still in *those* nude pumps. I wouldn't have been able to leave the hotel room for the rest of the week if I dared put them on again. Sadly, I had to report back to Serena on all things educational and prove I was just the woman for the English coordinator role. So, living out my every sexual fantasy with the man seated next to me was going to have to wait for a couple more hours at least.

I sighed.

This was shit.

As we filed out of the conference hall and into the foyer for lunch, with Levi's hand resting possessively on my lower back, I decided that I had to say something. So I led him to a corner, turned around and stated flatly, "This isn't working."

"*What*?"

"This." I gestured to the both of us standing far too close for a mentor and her student teacher. "It's not working, Levi. I'm supposed to be taking notes on each of the sessions, only with you right next to me all I can think about is—" I stopped and my face flushed. Most likely bright red.

Levi smirked.

"I'm serious. I need to have something to show bitch-face Serena when I get back and so far all I've got is this." I shoved my blank page accusingly up at him.

"Don't worry about it, kitten. I've got plenty of notes you can use."

I rubbed frustrated fingers across my forehead. "That's not the point."

"You wanna slow down again, is that it?" He looked hurt, I could almost see the indignation building and then rolling towards me in a monstrous tidal wave. "Are we seriously going back there again? Because after last night, I thought you were over hiding behind that bullshit."

I stepped closer. I no longer cared about any onlookers, they could all go fuck themselves. "Honey, no. *No,*" I reached out, resting my hand on his chest. "I don't want us to slow down and I don't for one second regret anything that happened last night. It was," I stared directly into his eyes, wanting him to know that I spoke the absolute truth, "the most unbelievable night of my life."

Levi placed his hand over mine, moving it slightly until it rested over the steady beat of his heart. "Mine too."

I shut my eyes and breathed deeply, drawing up the courage to look at him during this crucial moment. So I slowly opened them again and we stood there, gazing unflinchingly at the other for what could have been seconds, minutes, hell—even days. *Whoa*. I could tangibly see the emotion in Levi's clear blue eyes. It was no longer hidden behind his mocking stare, this depth of feeling was blatantly sitting at the forefront, just waiting for me to accept it.

I tore my gaze away, immediately terrified by what I had seen and even more so by what I felt. I shook my head.

"Look." But I then had to stop and try again because my voice turned husky. "*Look*, the session after lunch is broken into smaller workshops." I stared at my hand wrapped in his, not wanting him to let go of it. Ever. "Maybe we should both go to separate ones and meet up at the end of the day?"

Two fingers gently lifted my chin and our eyes locked. "Is that what you want?"

"No," I whispered, "but yes."

Levi slowly nodded and gently brushed the backs of his fingers down my face. He'd done it again. Through a look and with a touch he calmed my burgeoning storm, soothed my frantic emotion and eased my total confusion. He made everything right again.

"Okay, then. Have it your way."

"Doesn't she always?"

Levi and I turned.

Aemon stood close by, his fitted white shirt and navy pants emphasizing a lean build and tan skin. That mop of blond hair fell into hazel eyes, eyes that were intentionally looking between Levi and I. *Crap*. I took a quick step back but Levi gripped my hand tighter, refusing to let it go.

"Looks like you're both ... getting along well."

Levi's stare turned cold. "What of it?"

Aemon ignored the question and turned to me. "I missed not seeing you again yesterday, Grace. I'd like us to spend some more time together while you're here."

I could hear Levi grinding his teeth.

"So ... I thought I'd come over to see what session you'd signed up for after lunch."

I checked my program. "Um, I was thinking of going to *The Modern Classroom*."

He grinned mischievously. "What a coincidence, me too. In that case, I'll save you a seat." Aemon winked. "See you after lunch." With that, he turned and strolled away. I was surprised he wasn't whistling a jaunty tune, he looked that damn pleased with himself.

"Asshole."

"He's harmless, Levi. Forget about him."

Levi turned and cupped my face between his strong hands. "He wants what's mine."

I narrowed my eyes. "Possessive much?"

"You're mine, Grace. I've never wanted anyone so fucking bad in my entire life, and if that dickhead thinks he can just—" He took a steadying breath. "If he so much as touches you, I'm gonna kill him."

Despite the macho bullshit, I kinda loved hearing him say that. So, I stood up on my tiptoes and softly kissed his lips. "Come on," I murmured, "let's go somewhere else for lunch. If I have to choke down another stale ham and cheese roll, *I'm* gonna kill someone."

We decided on a hipster café not far from where

the conference was held. The place came complete with wooden crates for seats and glass jars with paper straws to drink out of. It was hilarious. Levi and I spent the hour talking about pretty much everything other than the deep and meaningful conversation we kind of had in the foyer. And Aemon. What game was he playing at anyway? Surely, he knew I wasn't going to be another sexual conquest. I mean, we'd known each other for years and I'd never even touched the guy. Well, except when he hugged me, put his arm around me at any chance he got, and tried to kiss me that one time… Probably best not to dwell on the past.

Anyway, Levi and I spoke about his music and my work. At other times, we just as easily lapsed into companionable silence. It was during these periods that I finally accepted how much I truly cared about him. Turned out, it was a heck of a lot. I mean, what I felt for Levi after only eleven days was incomparable to what I ever felt for Dylan. And we had been together for a year. But I still couldn't shake the sense of foreboding which shadowed my every move and elbowed me in the ribs every time I smiled, laughed or dared to feel happy. I tried to ignore it, really I did.

But it was relentless.

"We need to head back."

I nodded, seriously hating my earlier decision even though I knew it was the only way I could actually get some work done. Once again, Levi took my hand and we walked towards the convention center, markedly slower than the speed in which we had left it. Just as we were about to enter the packed foyer, he pulled me aside. Levi gazed at me, tenderly trailed the backs of his fingers down the side of my face before leaning forward and murmuring in my ear, "Keep your phone on you."

I looked up at him, confused, but he simply

brushed his lips against mine and walked away. In no time at all he was absorbed into the throng of people moving towards the smaller rooms just off the main entrance.

After shaking that conundrum off, I located my next session. There was still some time before it began so I was surprised to see Aemon already there. He smiled at me as I sat down next to him.

"Good lunch?"

"Yeah, much better than the shit they give us here." I took my phone out, switched it to silent and then placed it in my lap.

Aemon threw his head back and laughed. It was a nice sound. "I'd forgotten how honest you were, Grace."

I looked down. "More like socially inappropriate."

"Hey." My gaze went to his and he was staring at me intently. Too intently. I shifted in my seat; the atmosphere had suddenly changed and I felt beyond uncomfortable.

"Don't look at me like that."

"Like what?"

I narrowed my eyes at him. "Don't play innocent with me. You forget that I know you, Aemon Thomas Barker. I've seen that look before, many times over in fact, and it always leads to trouble."

"Don't you mean it always leads to a woman riding my cock?"

"Well, there's a mental picture I'd pay to have removed," I muttered.

He grinned. "I've really missed you, Grace. Seeing you again reminds me of all the fun times we used to have. We were always so good together."

"We were never together, Aemon."

"No." His eyes saddened. He paused, and when

he next spoke his voice was low. "But I wished we were."

I looked down at my phone. Nothing. *Shit*. I sighed, turning back to him. "Aemon, we've been through this, I'm not the girl for you. A lot has changed since I last saw you and the person you're reminiscing about is not the woman I am today. Trust me, she's long gone. Now, can we please change the subject already?"

"Why? Because you're fucking your student teacher?"

I stood and glared at him. "Screw you."

Aemon put out a hand to stop me from storming off, he had a strong grip. "Grace, I'm sorry. I had no right to say that, I just…" He sighed, loosening his hold on my arm slightly. "I just didn't realize how much I missed you until I saw you with that guy yesterday, that's all. Please stay. If you do, I promise to keep all jerk-like tendencies to a minimum."

I stared at him for a moment. His hazel eyes were contrite and the rest of him seemed genuinely apologetic too, so I warily sat again. Somehow, the conversation had gone from playful banter to me wanting to castrate him in under thirty seconds. It didn't bode well for the remainder of the afternoon.

Aemon turned and gave me his most winning smile, no doubt it was the one that detonated panties everywhere. "Let's start over."

Grudgingly, I nodded.

"Good lunch?"

I smiled.

The workshop itself was awesome and I was grateful for the distraction from the awkward conversation Aemon and I just had. A young teacher from a private school in Darwin was taking our group through a heap of interactive online programs designed for greater student engagement. Since Geographe High had a laptop program in place, the ideas she discussed were easy to implement in my classes. Well, the ones that didn't have Mark in them, of course. Because I just knew he'd find a way to mess the whole thing up. Dickwad.

So, it wasn't until my phone vibrated in my lap, immediately giving me vivid flashbacks of last night, that I realized an hour had already passed. I checked the text message.

Levi: **Bored. Can't concentrate without u**

Aemon gave me a questioning look but I shook my head. Tilting the screen away from him, I surreptitiously replied.

Me: **Try harder.**

Levi: **Nope, not working. Still want u ... wet**

I gasped, and then tried to disguise my not-so-subtle exclamation with a cough. It clearly didn't fool Aemon because he quizzically looked at me again, but I refused to meet his eyes.

Me: *Levi.*

Levi: **Fucking amazing when u called *that* out last night ;)**

I put the phone down, shut my eyes and took a deep breath. Was the man trying to kill me? Now my mind kept replaying our scorching nocturnal activities in high definition and with surround sound. I thought back to the feel of his lips against my silken folds, the way he teased me with his tongue and gripped my hips as I—

Aemon touched my hand and I almost jumped out of my skin. "You okay?" He mouthed.

"Fine," I whispered.

In all seriousness, I really wasn't.

Me: **Concentrate, Levi. Are you taking notes?**

Levi: **Sure am. Detailed too. About how great ur pussy tasted, how sweet it felt being inside u. Even**

wrote about the look on ur face just before u came.

Levi: **Twice**

I squirmed in my seat. Aemon glanced at me again, his eyes registering my heated cheeks, shallow breaths and, I looked down. *Fuck.* Erect nipples. I turned away.

Me: **I don't have a 'look'.**

Levi: **Yeah u do. See?**

A minute later, Levi sent me a photo. It contained the comprehensive dot points he'd taken of our mind-blowing sex from last night. I had to give him credit, the man was thorough. There was even a—I gasped.

Me: **Is that a freakin' DIAGRAM?**

Levi: ☺

"Grace, what's going on? You're acting … weird."

My eyes shot up to Aemon's worried face. I must have looked completely unhinged because he actually shifted back in his seat. I tried to ease his concern by whispering, "Quit fussing. I'm fine, really."

"Want me to get you some water or something? You're looking a bit flustered."

"Thanks, but I'm okay."

He nodded once and then turned his attention back to the guest speaker, so I took a calming breath before once again glancing down at my phone.

Lord, give me strength.

Sure enough, there it was. A stick figure sketch of me being fucked from behind by the stick figure representation of Levi. He'd even given me a speech bubble where I was quoted as saying, 'Oh Levi, you sex god'.

Me: **Okay, this is complete bullshit for three reasons: 1. I never said those words, 2. Honey, you're big but you're not *that* big, and 3. You wouldn't even** know what my expression looked like because *I was facing the other way.*

Levi: **It's my artistic impression**

Me: **Your artistic impression is shit. You look like you've got a python growing out of your dick and I look like a wombat having a seizure.**

Levi: **Fine, when we have sex tonight I'll make sure we're facing each other. That way tomorrow's diagram will be more accurate, ok?**

My eyes glazed over.

Aemon leaned in close and murmured in my ear, "It's a good idea to have a personalized blog for each class, don't you think?"

I internally slapped myself across the face. "Um, yeah."

Me: **What makes you think I'm going to let you fuck me tonight?**

"Not too sure about writing a post after every lesson though, seems like a lot of extra work to me."

"Mmm hmm."

Levi: **Want me to fuck you this afternoon, then?**

"Hey, maybe we could collaborate and set up a trial blog together? You know, cross-school curriculum or something?"

Levi: **In half an hour?**

"What do you think, Grace?"

Levi: *Fifteen minutes?*

"*Grace?*"

I looked up at Aemon but all I saw was the exit behind him. "I'm really sorry, but I've gotta go."

Me: **Meet you out front in five.**

Levi and I practically sprinted the whole way back, hand in hand, to the hotel. By the time we reached the elevators, I was red-faced and gasping. Of course,

Levi had barely raised a sweat and I blamed the fact that his legs were almost three times the size of mine, which meant that I had to work three times as hard to keep up. But I did. With thoughts of what we were about to do dancing before my very eyes, I could have run another five blocks. At least.

Levi looked down at me as he pressed the button and his eyes instantly turned dangerous. "Fuck, I love seeing you like this."

"Like what?"

"All hot and breathless," he smiled sensually, "it reminds me of last night." Stepping closer, he murmured, "Want me to lick your pussy again?"

"What, *now*?" I gaped back at him, out of breath for another reason entirely. I swear, my panties almost self-combusted on the spot.

"Elevators have a stop button, kitten. Come here."

He didn't have to ask twice. Hell, after he murmured 'come', I practically launched myself at the guy. Drawing his face towards me with desperate, frantic fingers, our hungry mouths met and I was instantly on fire. *How does he do it? How does he enflame me with this need that is never sated unless his lips are on mine?* I simply couldn't get enough of him. He consumed me.

The elevator doors slid open and a flustered someone rushed past. But we didn't move inside. Instead, Levi pushed me up against a gilded mirror on the wall, his hands in my hair, his tongue working mine and his hips—

"Fuck me," I exclaimed softly into his mouth.

"I intend to."

"Levi, is that *you*?"

Levi tore his lips from mine and turned at the sound. I was left leaning heavily against the cold glass, feverish and disorientated, wondering who on earth could have distracted him so completely from our frenzied kiss.

And there she stood.

"*Katrina*?"

The girl at least had the decency to appear uncomfortable at what she'd just interrupted, and her alabaster cheeks flushed a subtle shade of pink. Bitch. Whenever I blushed it looked like I had third-degree burns. She stood there awkwardly. A tall, slender brunette, with the darkest brown eyes I'd ever seen. She was in her early twenties and the poor woman clearly wasn't expecting to see Levi passionately devouring anyone in the hotel lobby if the surprise on her flawless face was anything to go by.

"Shit, I'm so sorry. When you said you were in town I thought it was for your band, not…" She looked at me. I was partially hidden behind Levi and clearly uneasy. "Well, this is embarrassing."

We were all silent for a minute and I suddenly wished I was anywhere else. Stranded in the Andes maybe? At the bottom of a canyon? Fuck, even being torn alive by a tank full of flesh-eating piranhas would have been more enjoyable.

"I should go." She hastily turned to leave.

"Katrina, wait. Stay. It's fine, isn't it, Grace?"

I stared up at Levi. Was he out of his freakin' mind?

But he missed my incredulity because he had already turned back to her. "At least have a drink with us since you've come all this way."

I kept staring at him, silent, before looking away.

Katrina glanced between Levi's earnest face and my hopefully blank one. "Um, I'm not sure that's a good idea."

"Please."

I felt sick.

"Okay, but just one. It looked like you guys were in the middle of," she paused and blushed again, "something."

I stared at the floor. Bring on the piranhas.

We all moved into Oblivion. I trailed behind the other two, desperately trying to figure out what the heck was going on. What was Katrina doing here? It sounded like she'd traveled a long way, so why was she so hell-bent on seeing Levi after phoning him just last night? *Is she interested in him?* Fuck. That must be it.

Surely, it would account for her arriving unannounced and looking so damn gorgeous in a freakishly natural way. I mean, she wore denim skinny jeans with Converse high top sneakers and an oversized red and black checkered shirt. It was open at the neck, unintentionally revealing some very healthy cleavage yet she somehow looked like a model straight out of a street fashion magazine. The girl had obviously never been near concealer in her life. Okay, so maybe I'd never used it either but that was because I refused to put shit on my face, not because I didn't actually *need* to. A completely different reason, I might add.

Christ. Levi and I were supposed to be naked and raw in the elevator right now. We were supposed to be calling out each other's names as though our lives depended on it, not having a damn drink with an absurdly beautiful third wheel. She seemed nice too, which just made the whole fucking thing even worse.

Kill me now.

Levi bought a round of drinks and wandered back to where Katrina and I were mutely seated. I refused to open my mouth unless alcohol was being poured into it, while Katrina looked as equally in need of inebriation herself. It seemed saying anything that wouldn't exacerbate the awkwardness any further was quite simply beyond her. If I didn't resent her presence so much, I'd almost feel sorry for the girl.

"One mid-strength beer for you." Levi placed the frosted glass bottle in front of Katrina, who smiled warmly up at him in surprise.

"You remembered."

"Of course, I remembered."

I looked away, nauseous.

"And a whiskey neat for you." He smiled down at me and his eyes crinkled in the corners. *How have I never noticed that before?*

"Thanks," I murmured.

Levi took the seat next to me on the low couch, one of his hands rested on my exposed knee, while the other held his beer. There was an equally low table in front of us, complete with stupid tea light candles. Two upholstered armchairs with what looked like fern fronds regurgitated on them were facing us opposite. Katrina was perched self-consciously on one of them, looking like she wanted to be somewhere else.

If only.

We were all quiet, sipping our drinks and staring in different directions. Personally, I was eying the door. To be honest, I didn't know what to say and was determined to speak as little as possible so my head/mouth filter wouldn't betray my current feelings of frustration and foreboding.

After quite possibly the most awkward lapse in conversation *of all time*, Katrina put down her beer and cleared her throat. "Um, Levi?"

He looked up at her.

"You haven't introduced me to…" Her chocolate brown eyes looked pointedly in my direction and I instinctively threw my head back, taking another mouthful of what I now wished was arsenic.

"Shit, you're right. Sorry." He chuckled before looking at me. "Grace, this is Katrina." He looked back at her, smiling. "We practically grew up together. And Katrina..." He gazed down at me once again. "This is Grace, my..." He paused, his eyes softening before stating simply, "Grace."

I melted.

I'd never even thought to categorize Levi and I. I mean before now we had always been *us*. It was a deceptively simple word. However, together or apart we were anything but. I mean, to call me his girlfriend didn't cover the width or breadth of what we shared, and yet to say we were lovers implied that our connection was purely sexual. Clearly, the sex was freakin' hot but there was also a heck of a lot more substance behind us than that. Partners? Too domestic. Sweethearts? Hell no. So, Levi calling me *his Grace* felt strangely ... *perfect*.

I smiled up at him, entwining my fingers with his and wishing beyond hope that this was going to be the fastest drink in the history of the universe.

"So, how long have you both known each other?"

Levi kept gazing at me and a small smile tugged at the corner of his lips. "Eleven days."

I grinned wider.

"Wow. Not long then."

I stared across at Katrina, daring her to continue.

"Oh, I didn't mean—it's just that you guys seem so," she paused, "*wow*." Katrina picked up her beer again before looking away and taking another drink. It was markedly longer this time.

There was another long silence, before Levi asked, "So, how's Adrift going?"

She relaxed then. It was like the question had been the code breaker that unlocked her self-assurance, because she put the beer back on the table, leaned forward and began talking animatedly. Sadly, Katrina was also highly intelligent *and* motivated. She spoke of the music her band was producing and the opportunities they were creating for themselves. Apparently, they had just been signed to a Melbourne-based record label and were in the process of organizing an east-coast tour over summer before heading to Europe after that. If it was at all possible, she was even more stunning now. Her eyes were bright, her smile wide, and yep, there it was—a fucking dimple materialized on her left cheek.

Jesus Christ.

The more she spoke, the looser Levi's grip on my hand became and before long he let go of it completely. Mimicking Katrina's body language, he also leaned forward, elbows resting on his upper thighs as he asked interspersed questions. The two continued like that until I drained the last of my drink and stared at the bottom of the empty glass for what seriously felt like hours. I discretely checked the time on my phone. Fuck, it literally *had* been hours. The fact that they were talking about music terminology I didn't understand, people I didn't know and places I'd never been, only exacerbated my disconnection. It also highlighted how much I didn't know Levi.

What a sobering thought.

So, I gave it another twenty minutes. But when they finally stopped talking about music and instead started rehashing childhood stories, I was officially over it. Standing up, I mumbled something about getting another drink and slowly headed towards the bar. Not that either of them even noticed. They were too busy laughing about Dom getting his arm stuck in a swimming pool filter when he was a kid, so I could have cartwheeled my way towards Patrick and they wouldn't have batted an eyelid.

I felt a conflicting sense of sheer annoyance and heavy sadness as I rested my palms flat on the bar. It reminded me of when I was little girl...

I had been playing with my stuffed toy dog in the lounge room. We weren't allowed any pets, so I was pretending to teach it how to sit and roll over. Mum sauntered into the room, bright pink acrylic nails clicking against the crystal wine glass in hand. She flopped dramatically onto the couch, spilling some of her drink on the black leather. I turned away. I hated it when she was in one of her moods.

Earlier, I had heard Mum and Daddy arguing. They were yelling more and more at each other these days. I would go hide in my bedroom and look at the brightly colored pictures in my storybooks, imagining that I was one of the characters being cuddled by a forever smiling Mummy and Daddy.

Mum didn't say anything for a while. Instead, she took deep mouthfuls of her drink and stared dejectedly at the framed wedding photograph hanging on the wall. I tried to ignore her and play with my dog, but her loud sighs kept reminding me she was there.

"Never trust in happiness, Grace," she slurred.

I looked up at her but didn't say anything. I just wanted her to leave.

"It never comes to any good." Mum raised her glass to the photograph and drunkenly toasted, "To marriage." She tipped her head back and drained the rest of her wine before passing out unconscious in front of me.

I shook my head and glanced up at Patrick. For once, he didn't say a word as he poured me another whiskey. I half smiled, half grimaced my thanks in return.

However, it was the sympathetic look in his eyes as I downed it in one mouthful that really pierced a hole in my heart. I carefully placed the glass back onto the bar, tipped him generously and turned to leave. As I walked out of Oblivion, I took one last glance at Levi and Katrina, she was sitting in the spot on the sofa I had vacated and the two of them were smiling into each other's eyes. It took all of my willpower not to collapse in a heap on the lobby floor as I headed in the direction of the elevators.

Alone.

Chapter Fourteen

Tear off that blindfold,
Open your eyes.
-MONDEZ, "Echo"

I was standing, facing the window, having long given up on reading any of the novels I brought with me. What a waste of time. So far, none of them did what they were supposed to, none of them had distracted me long enough to feel anything other than a torrent of tempestuous emotions. I sighed, pressing my forehead and hands against the glass, relishing the sharp snap of cold as it fizzled against my fevered skin.

I sensed rather than heard Levi walk into the room. The base of my neck prickled and a faint ache in the bottom of my stomach slowly uncurled. I'd have a freakin' ulcer by the time this week was through. But I refused to turn around. Hell, I wasn't even going to separate my eyebrows or fingers from the damn window. To be fair, leaving them glued to the icy surface was a far better option than backhanding him across the face, which was what I really wanted to do. So, as far as I was concerned, he could just deal with the back of my head and consider himself lucky.

"You left." The man was gifted in the art of stating the freakin' obvious.

"You noticed that, huh?"

"Why'd you leave?"

Is he fucking serious? I spun around to face him. "For the same reason you chose to stay."

He looked confused. "I thought we were all having a good time."

"No, you and Katrina were having a good time. In fact, you were both having such an amazingly good time

225

that neither of you realized you had an audience—*me*. And I got to watch the whole Katrina and Levi Are Having a Fucking Good Time Show for over two goddamn hours."

"What's this really about, Grace?"

His sudden change of tack pulled me up short and I stopped. But I was angry. Oh boy, was I still angry. If I thought about it long enough, I'd come to realize that I was more pissed at myself than anyone else. I mean, I had just wasted yet another day of the conference mooning over his sexy ass. Once again, I'd allowed my insatiable female parts to distract me from doing what I needed to win my dream job. Not only that, but I'd also allowed myself to develop feelings for the damn guy. Fucking strong ones.

I swore under my breath.

"Katrina and I are just friends, there's nothing between us anymore. What we had finished a long time ago."

"Anymore? *Anymore?* Jesus Christ, Levi, you might want to run this newsflash past Katrina because I'm pretty sure she didn't get the memo."

He stepped closer, his arms outstretched as though trying to placate a wild animal. "Grace, calm down."

I shot him a withering look, breathing raggedly.

"Katrina and I grew up on the same street, okay? We played together as kids, and yeah, when we were old enough, we fooled around a bit. But it was never anything serious."

"Try telling her that," I spat, though somewhat mollified by what he'd said.

"Kitten, there's nothing to tell." He paused. "What's with you weirding out on me all of a sudden?"

Turning around, I gazed out the window, only it was now dark so all I could see was my own reflection.

The girl staring back at me appeared lost. She looked like she was wading through a post-apocalyptic wasteland and couldn't find anything remotely familiar. The bewildered expression on her face quickly dissolved any lingering fight I had left in me. My forehead hit the glass with a soft thud. "I can't compete with Katrina."

"What?" Levi moved closer until he was standing directly behind me. I could feel his breath move the wisps of hair which had escaped from this morning's attempt at a sophisticated updo. Though after the day I'd had, my hairstyle now looked like a rodent had crawled onto the top of my head, unwillingly entangling itself in my chaotic strands and subsequently died a slow, agonizing death.

I turned around to face him, my eyes searching his. "I can't compete with her, Levi," I repeated softly. "She's a better fit for you than I am. Seeing you both together just proved it."

He raked frustrated fingers through his hair before moving away, pacing back and forth in front of me. "So we're back to playing these character roles, are we?" He stopped. "Hang on a second, what was my line again?" Levi stepped in close, his eyes piercing. "That's right, now I remember: *I'm not interested in her.*"

The man's sarcasm was seriously irritating.

I pushed him away. "Just shut up and listen will you?" Taking a deep breath, I ticked off each reason on one of my fingers. "Katrina's beautiful, she's talented, she understands your music in a way I never will, she wants the same things you do, *and* she wants to get into your pants. She's the whole fucking package, damn it. But me?" I spread my arms wide. "This is it, Levi. This is all I am." I let them fall dejectedly back to my sides again and looked down at my feet. "I can't compete with her. I can't compete with someone who's so freakin' perfect for you." Looking up at him again, I added, "I mean, you guys have a history for God's sake, a *long* one."

He got angry then. If it wasn't directed at me I would have found it unbelievably sexy. Who am I kidding? The man was eye candy regardless of who he was yelling at. "You're talking shit, you know that?"

That got my attention. Even more so than the way his broad chest heaved with each breath. I glared at him. "Excuse me?"

Levi leaned in close, his nose almost touching mine as he murmured, "You heard me. You're. Talking. Shit."

I glowered, wishing him a pile of dismembered body parts at my feet.

"Don't give me some sob story about how 'This is all of you' and 'This is all you've got'." He even used the air quotation marks. I was officially ready to kill him. "They're fucking excuses, bullshit lies and you know it."

I raised an eyebrow in warning.

"Ever since we first met—"

"*Eleven days ago*," I yelled.

"*Yes, eleven days ago. Deal with it already.*" He took a calming breath. "Ever since we first met, you've always held back. You've never shown me who you really are." His eyes blazed accusingly as he planted his hands on the window either side of my face. "Not once. And all because you don't trust me enough to open up. So don't give me this crap about how you've martyred yourself and still come up lacking, or that you don't know me better than anyone else. Because what you're telling yourself is fucking bullshit."

A red mist descended. "You're such a *hypocrite*."

He stepped back, incredulous. "Me?"

"Yes, *you*." I mimicked the incredulity in his voice. "How dare you stand there and accuse me of holding back, what about you, huh?" I stepped forward, poking him in the chest. "What have you refused to share with me?" It was a low blow. I knew it the moment it came out of my mouth, but I was so beyond angry, I truly didn't care.

He stilled, his voice deadly quiet. "I'll tell you when I'm good and ready."

"And I'm telling you," I spat, poking him in the chest again, "you're a fucking hypocrite." I spun away from him, slamming my hands against the window, rattling the glass in its frame. "Just go fuck your lap dog downstairs," I threw over my shoulder. "I bet she's still waiting for you."

"*Watch your goddamn mouth when you talk about Cat.*"

I froze. Not because he'd yelled at me, that I could handle. I froze because of the possessiveness he'd just shown. I froze because of the nickname he'd given Katrina. And I froze because it was a nickname uncannily similar to the one he'd given *me*.

Ouch.

After all, if he cared about her the same way I thought he cared about me, and if what they shared was anything similar to what I thought we did, then Levi had been in love. So the guy could say whatever the fuck he wanted, but categorizing their past relationship under the pathetic guise of *just fooling around*, was a complete and utter fallacy.

I purposefully turned around. "What did you just call her?"

He faltered slightly, immediately registering his blunder.

"*What did you call her, Levi?*"

"Cat. I called her ... Cat."

Nodding slowly, I murmured, "Thought so." I

pushed past him. "You're a fucking asshole." And I ran into the bathroom, slamming the door behind me.

Once inside, I braced myself against the basin. It was the only thing keeping me from crumpling to the floor and never getting back up again.

We were finished.

What Levi and I had fleetingly experienced, that sense of us being pieces of the same jigsaw puzzle, was now obliterated. Even if by some miracle we managed to once again fit into the places prescribed, surely the gaps between us would only serve to define how utterly cracked we were. I mean, the fissures would be too obvious, too difficult, too impossible to ignore. I shook my head. I guess we'd both kept secrets. Neither of us completely trusted the other, and as much as we wanted to delude ourselves, a relationship couldn't be built on half-truths.

I couldn't even look in the mirror. My wretched heart was too bruised and sore. Stupidly, I'd wanted to give it to Levi, but he'd already given his to Katrina— *Cat*—years ago. How could I ever trust in what he'd told me? How could I ever believe in what he'd made me feel?

The pain was unbearable. I couldn't stand feeling that naked anguish for another second, so I picked up the first object I could find and hurled it at the wall. Glass shattered everywhere, rebounding off the marbled surfaces, spraying the room with glinting daggers.

"Fuck." I looked down at a sizable shard that had somehow become lodged in my upper arm. Blood slowly seeped through the material of my sleeve. It began gravitating its way downwards, eventually trickling over my exposed skin and then dripping onto the tiles, creating a small pool at my feet. I stared at it, mesmerized. Strangely, when compared to the agony I was

experiencing on the inside, the searing pain that I should have felt merely resonated as a low hum.

"Grace?" I could hear Levi calling me. His voice sounded so far away. "Grace, are you all right?"

I didn't say anything. I was too fascinated by the trail of blood oozing steadily out of the wound and soaking the fabric of my entire sleeve.

Levi threw himself at the door and broke through, frantically searching the small space until his eyes found me. They instinctively dropped down to my arm and the mess I was making on the floor. "Grace?"

I looked up at him, dazed, though the room swam dangerously with the movement and I could suddenly hear the faint roar of the ocean in my ears.

"*Shit*." Levi quickly grabbed a washcloth and the dustbin from below the vanity unit. He brushed the scattered pieces of glass off the counter, before putting the cloth inside the dustbin and dropping it back onto the floor with a crash. He strode towards me, hastily picking me up by the waist and then gently sitting me on top of the vanity unit. Grabbing my bleeding arm, he raised it above my head.

I grimaced at the sharp pain that shot through my body. My head spun violently and I swayed, but kept silent.

Levi looked down at me. "Don't move. Stay right where you are, got it?"

I blinked, not trusting my ability to follow his instructions if I nodded again.

Then he was gone. And I don't mean he moved out into the bedroom, I mean he was *really* fucking gone. Levi left the hotel room entirely. So I remained partially collapsed, slumped against the chilled bathroom tiles and looking like a drunk student asking to be excused from class so I could go throw up in the toilets.

And still the blood flowed.

Though at least it was now heading in the opposite direction, neatly balancing the crimson carnage it wrought on my favorite work dress. To be honest, I didn't want to look at it. So I stared straight ahead, purposefully keeping my mind as blank as the marble in front of me. I refused to remember the last time I was sitting in this spot. I wasn't going to dwell on the savage argument we'd had leading up to this moment either. And I definitely wasn't going to ponder the bitter repercussions yet to come. I would fall apart at the seams if I did. Instead, I just sat there and concentrated on my breathing.

In and out. In and out. In...

Levi finally returned, carrying what looked like an industrial-sized first aid kit in one hand and a soft drink can in the other. I could only assume he grabbed them both from downstairs, probably from the receptionist who eye-fucked him at the front desk. By the size of the kit, it looked like she'd been overly helpful. Christ. Judging by the dimensions of the box, he could have treated a whole squadron of soldiers, not one hotheaded glass thrower with a shitty right aim.

He dumped the first aid kit on the ground and handed me the open can of Coke. "Drink." The man was going to make an awesome teacher one day.

I shut my eyes and took a deep mouthful, spluttering as I swallowed and bubbles fizzed the back of my nose. The sugar helped. I was already feeling a little less dazed and more ... broken. Maybe I should throw the can at the mirror too? With any luck it would ricochet back off it and strike me dead.

"My dad wasn't around much when I was a little kid." Levi spoke softly and I looked across at him, surprised. He was bending over the open plastic box, pulling out scissors, tweezers, antiseptic cream, gauze and a bandage, refusing to meet my enquiring gaze. "So it was always Mum, Dom and I at home."

He stood and moved towards me, placing all the items on the counter. I tried to read his face, to figure out why he was telling me this, but he still didn't look at me. "Dad was detective inspector of the WAPD. He was based in Perth, so he would drive off at the start of every week and sometimes return home on weekends. Mum loved what he did, she would worship the fucking ground he walked on when he was back and never stopped talking about how important his work was when he was away. Man, she'd go on for hours about how his dedication to the police department meant people all over the country were that much safer in their beds at night. She loved his paycheck too, a *comfortable life* was what she called it. I guess that's because we always got everything we wanted since money was never an issue."

Levi used the scissors to carefully cut open the sleeve of my dress. I didn't care it was my favorite, I just wanted him to keep talking. He placed the scissors back on the counter and picked up the tweezers. "And she was right in a way. We did have everything we wanted. A big house, heaps of expensive stuff, a swimming pool, even a tennis court, not that anyone used it. The whole lot. But it wasn't until I turned nine that I found out where all the money came from." I heard the chink of glass as it dropped into the dustbin and was amazed that I hadn't even felt Levi take it out. I was too engrossed in his story.

"I woke to the sound of Mum and Dad arguing one night. It wasn't unusual, they fought all the time when he was home. Dad would get so sick of her following him around the house like a," he paused before continuing quietly, "like a lap dog."

I grimaced, hating myself.

"She'd try to preempt all his needs like a fucking servant. But there was something about that fight which sounded different. It scared the shit out of me when I heard something hit the wall pretty hard. I mean, Dad had never been violent towards *her*. So I ran to their bedroom and threw open the door. I didn't really know what I was gonna do if Mum had been hurt, I was pretty small for my age back then. It didn't matter anyway because it was Dad's briefcase that made the noise, the one he took with him whenever he went away. He was so protective of it. If Dom or I went anywhere near the thing, he'd fucking lose his mind and beat the shit out of us. I learned that lesson the hard way."

Levi unzipped the back of my dress. There was nothing sensual about it, yet the closeness of him sent shivers through me. He carefully peeled it off my blood-soaked skin and let it drop down to my hips. Next, he found another clean washcloth, wet it and began meticulously cleaning my skin. Never once did he look me in the eyes.

"Anyway, Mum was holding a heap of photos and documents in her hand, screaming and waving them at Dad. But he ignored her. He just kept picking them up off the floor. I think Mum must have sensed me in the doorway then, because she turned to find me staring at them, confused. She raced forward, gathered me up and ran to grab Dom out of his bed too. We were on the next flight to Melbourne and stayed with our Auntie Val, Dad's sister, for a while. Mum didn't have any family of her own, you see, and Auntie Val more than made up for it. Her and Dad were never close. They hated each other, though I'm not really sure why. Anyway, she was an obvious choice when Mum had to get away from him because Tyler and Finn were there to keep us boys entertained."

The other band members were his cousins. Interesting.

Levi put the blood-soaked washcloth into the basin, collected the antiseptic cream and opened it. "So, one night I came downstairs to get a glass of water. As usual I couldn't sleep and when I walked past Auntie Val's bedroom, I overheard her and Mum talking. Well, Mum was howling really, so it was pretty easy to figure out what she was saying. Apparently Dad wasn't the hero she once thought. He'd been accepting bribes for years in return for turning a blind eye to some of Western Australia's most notorious criminal networks." Levi gently rubbed the cream into my cut, which didn't look at all life threatening since the blood had been cleaned up. Not that I gave a shit. I was too busy reeling from Levi's words to give a damn.

"The photos Mum found were of pedophiles and kids from a child sex ring that Dad was supposed to have infiltrated and then busted. Only he didn't. He just accepted a wad of cash in return for his silence and pretended the investigation had turned cold. He fucking ignored the whole thing."

I gasped, too shocked to do anything else.

Levi placed some gauze on my arm and then started wrapping a bandage around it. "And after a month Mum went back to him." He laughed bitterly, clearly disgusted. "She always went back to him. He would promise her that he'd change and she'd believe him every fucking time. She never ratted the son of a bitch out either. Not once. I think that hurt the most, when the two people you thought most trustworthy turn out to be most criminal."

Levi finished bandaging my arm and slowly started packing the items away. "I didn't say anything about it to anyone either, and I've never forgiven myself.

At the time, I thought no one would take me seriously because I was so young. But now I just think of all of the damage done to those innocent kids the whole time I stayed silent." Self-loathing was etched all over his face. "As soon as I was old enough, I got a job and talked Dom into moving out with me. I didn't want any part in what Dad did. I didn't want his money or anything that it bought."

He closed the first aid kit, snapping it shut with a click. "The whole cover-up was exposed a couple of months after Dom and I found a new place. It was all over the news and Dad's been serving time ever since." Levi straightened then, gripping the handle of the box so tightly the whites of his knuckles showed. He stared at the blood-soaked floor. "I hope he rots in there. It's the least that motherfucking bastard deserves."

I watched spellbound as Levi walked out the bathroom. Just before he opened the hotel room door, he called over his shoulder, "And the thing between Katrina and I? It really *is* over, Grace." He left without a backward glance and the door shut softly behind him.

By the time Levi returned, I had cleaned up the mess in the bathroom, changed into yoga pants and a tank top, and was sitting cross-legged in the center of the bed. My hands covered my face and I clamped my eyes shut as tightly as they would go. But I could still see them. The images of children having their innocence torn away, Levi included, continuously circled my brain. The story he had told was heartbreaking, there was no other word to describe it. And the fact that I had accused him of holding it back, as though it were a test of his depth of feeling, made me feel sick. I truly regretted how I'd acted. I felt so ashamed.

So I decided to repay him for his honesty. It was important he knew how much I valued the trust he'd given me. What happened between us after that? I wouldn't even contemplate. Couldn't. But I was going to try to show him that I could be a better person if he would just give me the chance to prove it. I owed him that much at least.

My head shot up from the unexpected dip in the mattress as Levi climbed onto the bed. I hadn't heard him return, so quickly brushed my tears away, suddenly embarrassed. He sat facing me, in torn jeans and a dark t-shirt, his expression searching. But I looked down and started picking at the threads of the coverlet, too frightened that his eyes would turn cold because of my actions from earlier.

"Dad and I were always close," I began.

Levi said nothing. He didn't ask me to leave the room in disgust either, so that was a good sign.

I continued, "Three times a week, after he finished work and my shift at the café ended, we'd have what he used to call 'Daddy and Daughter Time'." I snorted. "It was a shit name, he was so unoriginal when it came to stuff like that. But I looked forward to spending time with him more than anything else in my entire week. Even more so than Dylan, which should have sounded an alarm bell right from the start."

I traced the patterned outlines on the fabric with my index finger. "Anyway, Dad and I would meet down at our favorite beach. He'd always buy me a caramel ice cream first, like I was five or something, and I'd let him. For some reason it always tasted sweeter when he did. We'd just sit in the sand and talk literature or he'd tell me about his day and I'd talk about whatever crap happened in mine. Sometimes we wouldn't even say anything, we'd just stare at the water and the sun as it set in front of us. Reckon those were the times I loved best."

I swallowed. "I was living with my sister then.

Her and Dad weren't as close, not that they argued or anything because they didn't. They just didn't seem to connect in the same way Dad and I did. Anyway, my sis and I moved into the apartment together when I was eighteen and we always got along really well. Though she's older than me by seven years. At the time, she was math coordinator at a school nearby and encouraged me to study education when I finished my senior year. I guess she knew I loved learning and thought I'd be good at teaching kids how to enjoy it too."

I paused for a minute, collecting my thoughts before continuing. "I'd met Dylan the year before, when I served him at the café and he complained about his food order. He was always a dick like that. I'd never had anyone show an interest in me before that and apparently being a jerkoff was his way of saying he liked me, so…" I sighed. "Our relationship was okay, I guess. It wasn't exactly fireworks and fucking rainbows or anything but we traveled along all right. I thought I was in love and he told me he loved me all the time, if not in person then by voicemail or text. Weird really, because he said all that stuff but when we were together it was," I shrugged one shoulder, "I dunno, boring I guess. He never looked at me like I was anything special. I mean, it wasn't as though he'd ever pinned me against a wall and talked dirty to me, or got so caught up in the moment that he wanted to fuck me where we stood. Not like—" I stopped, flushing.

Shaking my head, I continued, "That summer Dad died of a heart attack." I rubbed tense fingers across my eyes, wanting to keep my shit together despite the painful memory. "I was a mess. Dylan would come over and try to comfort me," I shook my head again, "but shoving a reheated frozen dinner in my face and calling me ungrateful for not eating it didn't exactly help. If I hadn't been so wrapped up in my own bubble of despair, I would have seen the signs. Hell, I might have even done something about it, who knows? They were so freakin' obvious. At first, my sister and Dylan both decided that giving me *space* was the best thing, so they'd head out whenever he dropped by. Then there were the covert glances when we were all pretending to watch a movie. I even overheard a whispered conversation in the hallway one time. They must have thought I was fucking deaf or something. And then the text messages started. If one of them was out while the other was with me, they were forever on their phone. They'd both wear the same secret smile that if I'd been in a better frame of mind I would have picked up on straight away. But I didn't. I didn't care about anything other than the agony I felt in losing Dad."

I stopped tracing patterns and instead went back to playing with the fabric of the coverlet. "So, when I woke up one morning and read a text from Dylan that said we were finished, I wasn't exactly devastated. To tell you the truth I didn't scream, didn't cry, didn't feel any worse off than I did the night before. I just got out of bed and walked to my sister's room to tell her. Only she wasn't there. And none of her stuff was there either. I checked the rest of the apartment. All of her belongings, clothes, toiletries, plates, cutlery, fucking *everything* was gone." I laughed bitterly. "Man, they must have moved at the speed of light to get all her shit out of there in under eight hours."

Taking a deep, steadying breath, I continued, "Riley found me that afternoon. I was sitting in the spot where the couch used to be, staring at the wall where the TV once belonged, completely lost in a bottle of whiskey. That girl was fucking amazing. She moved in straight away, never once asked what happened and when I was," I glanced up at him, "good and ready," I looked back down at my restless fingers, "I told her that my sister and I'd had a fight, Dylan and I were through, and I was still distraught over Dad's death."

I scrunched the fabric between my fingers, creasing it. "I refused all contact with both of them after that. They could die in the flaming pits of hell for all I cared. Though six months later there was a wedding invite in the mail. Fuckers. I burnt it." I shook my head. "I never told Riley the whole truth; I don't really know why. But she stayed and I'm thankful for it every day of my life. Which is why she's more family to me than my own sister and more of a friend than I've ever deserved."

We were silent for a while. I kind of wished telling Levi about my darkest betrayal would help me feel somewhat liberated. But I didn't. I didn't feel anything other than total exposure and absolute vulnerability. Hell, I would have felt more comfortable had I been sitting there naked. And the worst part was that I didn't know what else I could say. I genuinely had no idea how to communicate what he meant to me, how much I truly wished he cared for me too. It sucked. With each breath we took it felt as though the space between us was getting heavier, denser, harder to navigate.

I looked up at him and my breath caught. Levi was staring at me intently, his head to one side. I couldn't look away. So I came to a decision, my eyes were going to speak for me. Even if he didn't want to hear a single word more, they weren't going to stop until he knew the truth.

All of it.

I took a deep breath. *Tread carefully*, my eyes said. *Be gentle and kind because I'm fragile. And even though you sit at some distance from me, you now hold my heart cradled in your palm. You can break it*, they said. *I have given you that power. Please, don't break it.*

Don't break me.

Levi's eyes turned liquid. "I love you, Grace."

I took a deep breath, savoring his words. "I love you too, Levi."

Turned out, falling in love was as simple and as complex as that.

Chapter Fifteen

Unfortunately time will never slow down the ticking clock,
It's not as if you care at all or that you even give a fuck.
-MONDEZ, "Chaos"

Levi reached for me and I moved to sit astride him. His hands cupped my face and I sighed as feather-light lips chased my eyelids, cheeks and jawline. I wrapped my arms around his neck, losing my fingers in his tousled hair. Finally, I gave into the compulsive need to touch him, to feel him, to reassure myself that this was real. I thought I'd lost him. And that emptiness at the base of my stomach felt exactly the same as when Dad passed away. It suddenly became clear. Levi was my world.

My everything.

He pulled back slightly and gazed at me, his eyes the brightest blue yet. "It's true. I love you."

"Never stop."

"Not a chance."

"Even if I fuck it up? Because I'm going to, sooner or later."

"Grace, I'll never stop loving you. No matter what happens, my heart has your name on it."

I leaned forward, grazing my lips over his. "That's kind of gross. But I'll never stop loving you either."

Levi groaned and deepened the kiss, his tongue delving inside. I responded fervently, pressing closer and pulling his head by the hair. But he was still too far away, so I ran my fingers down his chest and grabbed the hem of his t-shirt, pulling it up and over his head. It was discarded over my shoulder without a moment's thought. My hands roamed his tattooed skin, engraving each rise and dip of his torso with my heated touch as his muscles tightened and rolled beneath them.

I had to get closer. "Lie down," I murmured.

Levi slowly lowered himself back onto the bed, his eyes never leaving mine. He looked so fucking mouthwatering, I couldn't look away. I crawled on top of him and briefly touched his lips, before slowly kissing my way down his chest. He cursed when my tongue licked his sensitive spots and sucked in sharp breaths when I gently nipped his flesh.

It was awesome.

I unbuttoned Levi's jeans and unzipped the fly, peeking up at him from beneath my lashes.

"What'll it be, kitten?"

"I'm going to put my mouth on your cock. And I'm not going to stop until you beg me to."

He swore. Loudly.

Chuckling, I gently traced the outline of Levi's hard length through his boxers. "Or, we could just skip to the begging part." I grinned.

"You wouldn't be that cruel."

"Wouldn't I?" I gripped him firmly, teasing him through the material and smiling wickedly when he threw his head back, groaning.

But then I took pity on him. After pulling down his jeans and boxer shorts in one go, I threw them in the general vicinity of his t-shirt. Sitting back, I gave myself a full minute to take him in. His gorgeously open face looked at me with hungry adoration, and those black tattoos boldly recounted an even darker tale. I gazed at Levi's strong arms, they held me close when I needed it, and closer still when I thought I didn't. I admired his long fingers, they healed me when I hurt and ignited me when

I ached.

Christ.

"How did I ever come to deserve you?" I whispered.

Levi sat up. He took my face in his hands and kissed me passionately. His lips drank from mine until I saw the stars, could taste the moon and felt the beginnings of eternity stretching before us. When we finally drew breath, he murmured, "Holy fuck, *that* was intense."

I nodded in agreement. We were definitely going to need an eternity together, a lifetime wasn't long enough. As always, I was impatient to get started so I gently pushed him and he flopped back down onto the bed with a crooked grin. I moved between his legs and bent forward, coyly looking at him while grasping his erection in one hand. Slowly and deliberately, I licked the beads of moisture gathered at the tip, "Mmm."

Levi inhaled sharply and reached down, running a calloused finger over my wet lips. I opened my mouth and sucked on it.

"I've been dreaming of this ever since you bit my finger in your classroom. Do you remember?"

I smiled wide. *How could I forget?*

After releasing Levi's finger, I turned my attention back to his hard erection. As his pupils dilated, I smiled. I relished the deep sounds he made at the back of his throat as I ran my tongue languidly up the shaft. When I reached the head, slowly taking him in my mouth and drawing him even farther inside, he swore. "Fuck, Grace."

Suddenly, his pleasure became mine. I increased the pace, working him ravenously with my mouth. I wanted to own his every breath, his every sound, his every exclamation. I wanted to greedily wrap them all up and store them safely inside me.

It wasn't until Levi gently pulled me away, growling, "Kitten, stop. I'll come if you don't," that I realized how long I'd been relentlessly devouring the man. My lips were swollen and my jaw ached slightly, but I didn't care. I had lost myself in the moment and loved every second of it.

Sitting up again, I wiped the corners of my mouth with my fingers.

Levi's eyes turned molten. "Come here."

I went willingly. He grabbed my arms, rolled me onto my back and covered me with his body. He kissed me with a force that awoke a passion so strong I truly feared we'd explode if I reciprocated it fully.

I broke away, panting. "Please."

"What do you need, kitten? Tell me and I'll give it to you."

"*You*. I need … Please."

Levi's weight shifted to his elbows as he gazed down at me. "You need me, huh?"

"Yes," I breathed, "and you fucking know it."

"You're right, I do. I just love hearing you say the words."

"Bastard."

He chuckled but soon sobered as his eyes turned predatory. He ruthlessly tore off my clothes until at last, I was naked beneath him.

I arched my hips and angled myself in line with him, imploring him to enter.

He did.

"*Levi.*"

He smoothed the hair away from my face and looked down at my stunned expression. I was attempting to process the incredible sense of completeness that washed over me when we joined. A mixture of emotions flickered across his face. "Mine," he murmured.

I wrapped my arms around his neck and my legs around his hips, drawing him deeper. "Mine."

Levi groaned, bent down and kissed me, his chest flush with my own. The contact sent a shiver through me and I held tight. I could even feel the pounding of his heart, we were that close. Never before had I been this intimate with anyone. I'd always shied away from it, screamed and yelled at it. But with Levi, being connected in this way felt right. It felt ... *perfect*.

He began to move.

I framed his face with my hands and stared up at him, awestruck. He gazed back down at me and we met each other, thrust for thrust. Our bodies came alive then. We fed off the heat created, the pleasure given, the sounds echoed. Beads of sweat appeared, they trickled down our fevered skin but still we looked on, eyes wide and worshipful.

I could feel that energy begin to smolder inside me as my entire body transformed into a blazing mass of careening electric currents. Levi sensed how close I was and increased the rhythm, deepening his movements. "Come for me, Grace."

My eyes never left his face as I lit up around him. I came for Levi, for the love he showed, the trust he'd given, the bravery he inspired. I came for the betrayals we shared, the family we lost, and the life we found.

Once my tremors subsided, Levi let go and came too. His eyes grew wide and he called out my name as though in fervent prayer. I drew him down to my lips, kissing him with abandon as his body convulsed, trembled and then grew still.

"Holy fuck*,* " I murmured against his mouth. "Now *that* was intense."

He smiled.

****

I was in a much better state of mind on day three of the conference. I hadn't yet seen Aemon, which was a relief. After all, I wasn't looking forward to explaining my hasty exit yesterday, and for some reason, being around him made me even more honest than usual.

My arm throbbed slightly but it was nothing I couldn't handle, and my white shirt all but covered any evidence of my hot temper anyway. In fact, during the morning session, I completely forgot about it. Instead, I slipped in and out of blissful daydreams.

After we made love the night before, Levi and I once again ordered room service. We devoured it, and then each other. Several times over. As I shifted in my seat, balancing a notebook on my knee while trying to remain focused, my lower body ached in the most delicious ways possible.

Levi's phone buzzed in his pocket. Thankfully, the overzealous speaker from New South Wales drowned out the vibration. I glanced across at him. He stared down at the caller ID, frowned and then canceled the call. After meeting my eyes, Levi winked, and my insatiable female parts were suddenly ready for another round of insanely hot action.

Sweet God, the things he could do to me.

Levi's eyes hungrily lingered on my lips, but before I could embarrass myself and moan out loud, his phone buzzed again. He considered it for a moment, clearly uncertain.

"Just answer it already," I hissed.

He showed me the name on the screen and my stomach instantly dropped. "I'll just see what she wants and be right back, okay?"

I stared down at my pen, it was in the process of being snapped in two.

247

"Stop it. You're overthinking things, kitten." He quickly skimmed his thumb across my bottom lip and then left to take the call.

Fucking Katrina.

I swear, that woman had a damn radar that sent out warning signals whenever Levi and I were in a good place. Her ability to miraculously appear on cue was uncanny. I shook my head. Negative thoughts were only going to lead me to a bottle of whiskey and it wasn't yet noon. I took a deep breath.

Chill the fuck out, Grace.

After all, Levi and I were in love. We openly shared our deepest secrets last night and then solidified our strengthened connection through insanely passionate sex. Lots of it. So Katrina could call Levi. Hell, she could talk to him until her phone ran out of battery, for all I cared. But if she ever laid a finger on him, I would have it removed and shoved into her ear hole. She would walk around all day unknowingly flipping people the bird. With that comforting thought, I reverted back to Mr. Overenthusiastic and continued taking notes with my slightly warped pen.

When we broke for morning refreshments, Levi was nowhere to be seen. I was totally okay with it. Really. And as fate would have it, I bumped into Aemon.

Oomph.

Literally.

"You okay, Grace?"

I rubbed my sore arm and tried to disguise the dull, pounding pain. "Yeah, I'm all right. You?"

He laughed. "Of course. I'm stronger than I look, you know."

"Sure you are."

He laughed again.

Uh-oh, here it comes.

Aemon's eyes turned serious. "Where'd you get to yesterday? When a woman leaves me like that, it's usually because she's doing the walk of shame."

I averted my eyes. "I ah, just had something I needed to do."

"I see."

My eyes flew back to his. He did see. *Shit.*

"So where's your student teacher?"

"He has a name, Aemon. I introduced you, remember? It's Levi."

"Okay then, where's Levi?"

"Ah, I'm not exactly sure. He took a call during the last session and didn't … um, come back."

"And you're okay with that?"

"It's a free country. I can't exactly get pissed because he answered his damn phone, can I?"

"That's not what I meant. I was referring to if you were okay with him not coming back."

I put my hands on my hips and glared at him. "If you've got something to say to me, then just say it. Quit with the bullshit already."

Aemon's eyes narrowed and he took a step closer. "All right then, I will. I don't think he's the guy for you, Grace. There, I've said it."

I rolled my eyes. "And let me guess, you are?"

But Aemon ignored me. "He's not gonna stick around. I've seen his type before, they say all the right things and make you feel like a million bucks, but when another opportunity comes up, they move on to it the first chance they get."

He must have noticed my dangerous expression because his tone then softened considerably. "Look, we've known each other a long time. I just don't want to see you get hurt, that's all."

I counted to ten in my head. And then to twenty.

"Grace, say something."

Thirty. I held up my finger, telling him to wait. Forty. Once I reached fifty, I spoke. "Aemon." My voice was measured. "I get that this is your perverse way of looking out for me. Believe me, I do. But I'm not going to justify my relationship with Levi to you. Now, if you want to keep your balls, I suggest we change the subject. Quickly."

He sighed. "Don't say I didn't warn you." I moved threateningly towards him. "*Okay, okay*. Let's just go back inside, the next session is about to start."

"Good idea," I muttered.

Aemon and I made our way back into the conference hall and sat down. I actually did really well during the next two hours. I mean, I didn't even let the empty seat on my right serve as a distraction. After all, there was no way I was going to let Aemon's words torment me.

Much.

Okay, that was a complete lie. They continuously churned over in my subconscious and then randomly popped up in the forefront of my mind when I least expected it, paralyzing me with fear. Clearly, my brain was a sadist. *Is there any truth in what Aemon's prophesizing? Will Levi ultimately leave me? Is this phone call the catalyst of a catastrophic downward spiral? Can my internal monologue possibly get* any *more dramatic?*

I shook my head. I had to trust in what we shared. Surely our relationship was strong enough to survive a freakin' phone call. After all, what else could I do? Pray?

I snorted.

By the time we broke for lunch, I was mentally drained. It felt as though I had been dragged through the most exhausting obstacle course ever created. However, despite my internal battle between merciless negativity and determined positivity, I somehow managed to take notes. Lots of them. In fact, many pages had been filled with my dogged efforts. Katrina's name only appeared five times. And there were only two references to Levi dumping my ass. I scribbled them all out until the words were smeared patches of blue ink on white paper.

I guessed that Levi was at the café we went to yesterday. After mumbling something comparable to a farewell to Aemon, I negotiated my way past countless people standing in between me and the main glass doors of the convention center.

He was out front, pacing up and down the footpath on his phone, face creased in concentration. "What about Finn's symbols? His high hats?" Levi paused, listening to the person on the other end. "Right. And how many sticks does he have left?" He paused again. "Well, tell him to get up and go get some. *Now*." Levi spotted me standing a couple of feet away and his eyes instinctively softened. "Have you sorted out the special delivery?" He nodded. "Okay, text me when you hear back. Later, fucktard."

My eyebrows rose in surprise. He wasn't still speaking to Katrina then. "Everything all right?"

He nodded, eyes bright. "C'mon, let's go eat. I'm starving." Levi grabbed my hand and we walked to the café, he bounced excitedly on the balls of his feet the whole way.

Twenty minutes later, we were part way through our lunch and I was internally laughing at myself. I was officially eating off a wooden chopping board and admiring a table number stamped on a ten-inch vinyl record. Hipsters were awesome. I wasn't going to ask about what was up with Levi. Clearly something big was unfolding, but if he didn't want to tell me, then I wasn't going to force the issue. I was growing as a person. Who would've thought?

"Katrina called earlier."

I swallowed with effort. "I know, I was there."

"She told me that Tsunami pulled out."

"Who the fuck's Tsunami? And what did they pull out of?"

Levi shook his head in amusement. "I love that mouth of yours, kitten. It's so sweet." I narrowed my eyes at him and he laughed. "They're the second band in tomorrow night's lineup." He noticed my blank expression and sighed. "You know, the gig Adrift is headlining? The one we've both got tickets to go see?"

"Oh, right."

"Well, turns out Tsunami can't play. Their lead singer has tonsillitis and his voice is fucked. Which means…"

I put down my organic, fair trade, free range and God-only-knows-what-else slider. "*Yes*?" I drew out the word until it had at least seven syllables, forcing Levi to finish his damn sentence.

"Katrina wants Mondez to play."

"What?"

"After you went up to the room last night, I showed her our latest EP recording."

I looked at him, confused.

"It's saved on my phone. Anyway, she loved it. So when Austen from Tsunami canceled on her, she phoned, asking us to play instead."

Sitting back on my wooden crate, I stared at him, bewildered.

"I've been calling the boys all morning trying to get shit sorted. We need to organize our instruments, hardware, plane tickets, *everything*. It's fucking hectic."

"Plane tickets? When do they get here?"

"In four and a half hours. We're gonna check out the venue later on tonight. After we've seen what it's like, we can figure out what we need to borrow from the guys in Adrift tomorrow. We've never played anywhere except The Hole, so it's gonna be unreal performing in front of a large audience. Katrina says The Ruby Room holds up to two hundred people and I've heard that Adrift pull a decent sized crowd."

I shook my head, stunned.

"Crazy, huh?"

"Crazy," I agreed, trying to take it all in.

****

The afternoon session was weird, to say the very least. Aemon sat on my left and Levi on my right. They'd both been polite enough when we first sat down, but I could feel an undercurrent of seething hatred festering between the two of them. Which meant that whenever I glanced at Levi and he was on his phone, I only had to look at Aemon to see him frowning at me. That knowing look on his face was freakin' annoying.

I sighed, forcing myself to focus on the guest speaker. Only it was beyond impossible. The child psychologist from Adelaide was, without a doubt, the most boring presenter I'd ever had the misfortune to sit through. If anything, I was glad for the constant vibrations coming from Levi's direction, at least they jolted me awake at periodic intervals. The combination of a late night, an exhaustive internal battle and this guy's droning monotonous voice was a recipe for a well-earned sleep.

At last we filed out the main doors. The cool Melbourne breeze slapped me awake and I instantly felt more refreshed. I turned to face Aemon. "Guess, I'll see you tomorrow then."

"Look, if you feel like going out for a drink or

anything tonight, you know, to catch up on old times…"

"She doesn't."

I glared at Levi, who in turn, was glaring at Aemon.

"How about you let Grace talk for herself?"

Levi moved until he was standing within spitting distance of Aemon, hands clenched in tight fists. "How about I beat the shit out of you for making a move on my woman? Show some respect, you conniving dick."

Whoa. Levi's temper is so goddamn sexy. I mean, focus, Grace.

"For fuck's sake, both of you calm down." I pushed Levi to the side and looked at Aemon. "Thanks for the offer, but I'm not really in the mood for a trip down memory lane tonight. I just want to head back to the hotel." Softening my rejection, I then added, "But I'd really like us to hang out before I head back home."

Levi growled, it resonated directly with my enraptured female parts.

Aemon smiled at me. "It's a date."

I gritted my teeth. "No, it's not. Man, if I give an inch you take the whole damn mile, don't you?"

He grinned wider.

"You won't be smiling when I'm through with you, asshole," Levi threatened quietly.

Aemon's grin faltered briefly when he met an unblinking steel blue glare. He'd clearly just failed some testosterone-fuelled test because Levi nodded. "Just as I thought." Levi turned his back to him and faced me instead. Stepping in close, he threaded his fingers through my hair, leaned down and kissed me.

Deeply.

Minutes later, he pulled back, nipped my bottom lip and murmured, "Ready?"

I melted. Sighed. And quite possibly swooned. To

be honest, I couldn't even comprehend his simple question. I just wanted him to touch me again. We'd gone almost twelve hours without this type of heated contact and it almost killed me.

"Let's go."

Aemon was nowhere to be seen, so Levi and I strode back to the hotel, hand in hand. As we walked through the foyer, he asked, "Drink?"

"God, yes."

When we stepped into Oblivion, I instinctively noticed that the bar felt different. There seemed to be more people, even though the place was in no way full. In fact, on closer inspection I could only see two new additions to the usual corporate and elderly types. But something in their youthful vibrancy made the place feel less suffocating than usual.

Levi let go of my hand and stared straight ahead. I gazed up at him, perplexed.

"Prepare yourself, kitten."

"Huh?"

"*Gracie, Dickwad.*"

I turned my head in the direction of the sound, just in time to be twirled around in the air like I was starring in a freakin' ballroom dancing contest. "Fucking hell, Dom, put me down."

He laughed, before plonking me back on my feet and ruffling my hair like I was three.

I punched him in the stomach and my arm screamed bloody murder. *"Goddamn it."*

"You all right?"

I grimaced up at Levi's concerned face but nodded, rubbing my hand over the smarting pain.

"You throw punches like a girl." Dom chuckled, completely oblivious.

Narrowing my eyes at him, I threatened, "Want

me to try again?"

"How about I take a look at that arm for you?"

My face lit up. "*Riley*." She'd been standing behind that annoying mountain of muscle and jest. I shoved Dom aside and threw my arms around her, immediately ignoring the thumping ache. "It's so good to see you." Pulling back, I stared at her. "Hang on, what are you even doing here?"

She smiled broadly down at me, looking as faultlessly gorgeous as always. "Levi thought you might like some company at the gig tomorrow night." She shrugged one shoulder. "You know I never pass up a chance to watch the boys play, so I swapped my shift with Mae, booked a room here and *ta-da*." She opened her arms wide.

I smiled at Levi, mouthing a heartfelt, *"Thank you."*

He grinned and winked at me, while I quickly gripped the back of a nearby chair. *Useless knees*.

Dom stepped closer to Levi, inspecting him up and down. A teasing smile played about the corners of his mouth. "If I didn't know any better, I'd say Gracie here got an A plus on that school project I gave her."

"What school project?"

"Ignore him, Riley. He's talking out his ass," I muttered.

"So who was it, bro?" Dom persisted, "Don't tell me it was that woman who kept shoving her tits in your face? You know, the one from school you told me about? She was supposed to be here too, right?"

I glared at Levi, who glowered at Dom.

"I mean, correct me if I'm wrong but I always took you for an ass man myself."

"Shut the fuck up."

Dom stared hard at Levi, then looked at me, and

back to Levi again. His roguish eyes widened when recognition finally dawned. "You sly dog." He punched Levi in the arm.

"Leave it, Dom," Levi growled out.

"It was Gracie here the whole time, wasn't it?"

Levi swore under his breath while Dom bent over double, slapping his thighs and hooting with laughter.

Putting fisted hands on my hips, I directed my glare at Dom. "What's so funny? You got a problem with me or something?" I couldn't help but notice Riley smiling gleefully in my peripheral vision.

He raised his hands in mock surrender. "Not the fists, anything but the fists. I'm still hurting from your last hit, Gracie."

"Jerk," I muttered.

Dom wrapped Levi in a one-armed man hug and congratulated him on finally getting laid. It looked like he was presenting him with a fucking award or something.

"You're going to tell me every last detail," Riley whispered in my ear as we watched the two men. I smiled, nodding.

The boys finally broke apart. "Ready to go?"

"Now?" Levi looked confused. "But where's Finn and Tyler?"

"They're still dropping our gear off at Auntie Val's. Katrina's going to drive them in. Finn couldn't get on the plane fast enough when he heard we were coming here, you'd think he'd be over her by now." Levi shook his head sadly. "Anyway, we're meeting them at The Ruby Room in half an hour."

Levi looked at me, his eyes downcast. "Mind if we rain check that drink?"

Dom rolled his eyes and made obscene whipping gestures in the background.

Ignoring him, I pulled Levi closer by the belt

hooks and reached up behind his neck. *Pain? What pain?* I drew his face to mine. "It won't taste as good without you."

He kissed me, his hands resting lightly on my hips. "I love you," he murmured, quietly enough so the others wouldn't hear.

"I love you too."

"Wait up for me?"

I nodded. "Now go. The sooner you leave, the sooner you return."

With a final wink and mischievous smack on my ass, Levi turned away. He smiled goodbye to Riley but then caught Dom making melodramatic doe eyes behind his back, so punched him in the ribs. Surely he'd broken at least four? Apparently not. Dom just laughed it off, yanked Levi into a headlock and manhandled him out of the bar.

"You had to sit next to *that* the whole flight over?"

Riley sighed. "Yeah."

"Girl, you deserve a drink. Come on, let me introduce you to Patrick. He'll pour you something strong enough so you can forget all about him."

"I highly doubt it."

We spent most of the evening in Oblivion, drinking, eating, and catching up on two weeks' worth of news. Patrick was completely enamored with Riley. He reenacted all of his most heroic stories for her. I'd already heard most of them and watched in fascination as she politely nodded and smiled for a heck of a lot longer than I ever could. That was the thing about Riley, she always made you feel like the most interesting person alive. Even when you weren't. She had the patience of a saint.

We eventually got away from Patrick, though not before he slipped Riley his number, and headed up to her room. It was on the very top floor of course, and her corner suite had the most breathtaking city views.

I whistled. "Not bad."

She rolled her eyes at me, moved into the next room and settled herself down on the seven-seater sofa, tucking slender legs beneath her. Riley stared at me as I sat beside her. "Okay, spill."

"Spill what?"

"Don't play coy with me, Grace Anne Thompson." I grimaced at the permanent reminder of Mum's first name. "I've been waiting days for an update on you and Levi. Did it ever cross your mind to call me back? Or text? I mean, I wanted to give you space and all but, *God*."

I looked down, guilty. Between the whole fight, sex, fight, injury, and falling in love thing, I'd completely forgotten to call her.

"*Days*, Grace," she repeated.

"All right, all right." I glanced at her. "What do you want to know?"

"Everything."

Now it was my turn to roll my eyes.

"Let me refresh your memory then, the last time we spoke you had this ridiculous notion in your head that I liked Levi—"

"Hey, that reminds me, who—"

But she held up her hand, halting me. "And you guys just had an argument. Now, judging by the way you were locked at the lips earlier, I'm guessing it's all been dealt with. But I still want to hear the whole story." She sat back, arms crossed and expectant. "Spill."

"I've missed you."

Riley's eyes softened. "Me too. Now talk."

I did. I told her as much as I could, from how Levi and I first connected at the gig twelve days ago, right through to when we kissed in Oblivion earlier. She listened to every word, enraptured. The only parts I glossed over were about Levi's dad, my arm, and the truth behind Dylan leaving me for my sister. I mean, the former wasn't my story to tell, there was no need for her to worry about a superficial cut, and if I was truly honest, I really liked the idea of Levi knowing me better than anyone else. It meant that what we shared was somehow more … special.

By the end of it, she looked completely stunned. "So you're telling me that after twelve days, you guys knew you were in love?"

I nodded, raising one shoulder. "We knew after eleven actually."

Her face lit up like it was New Year's Eve. She squealed and pulled me into a tight hug which left me gasping for breath. "*I knew it.* I knew you'd be perfect for one another." She paused, holding me at arm's length. "And the sex?"

"There are no words."

Riley squealed again, clapping her hands and bouncing up and down on the couch. However, she quickly quieted down after looking at her watch. "It's getting late. I need an early night if I'm going to hit the gym tomorrow morning."

I rolled my eyes again.

"And I don't want to keep you from your next orgasm."

With that delicious possibility, I checked the time on my phone, it was past ten. Levi would start to wonder where I was if I didn't get back soon. After all, he'd asked me to wait up for him, so it would be a bitch move if the guy arrived back and I wasn't even there. I leaned forward, gave Riley a final hug and then left.

As I exited the elevator and strolled down the

corridor to our hotel room, a secret smile crept across my face. I couldn't wait to see Levi, to hear all about his evening and tell him about mine. I couldn't wait to lose myself in his arms and show him just how much he meant to me. I shook my head wryly. Man, I'd be singing fucking love songs soon enough. My smile grew wide as I stepped through the doorway and called his name. Though it immediately wavered when my own voice echoed back.

The room was empty.

I couldn't help it, my mind instinctively flashed back to when I was five.

I was searching for my doll. It had been a birthday present from Grandma before she fell sick and I loved to cuddle it. There was something about inhaling the scent of lavender from the hand-sewn fabric that always reminded me of her. I hadn't seen the doll all morning, but knew Daddy would be able to find it. After all, he found my skipping rope and that had been hiding behind the washing machine since before Christmas.

When I moved closer to the lounge room, I heard raised voices. Well, Daddy's mostly, which was strange because he never yelled. "Don't give me that story, Anne," he shouted, "I know for a fact you weren't with Dianna this afternoon."

"Are you calling me a liar, Peter? Is that what you're saying? That you don't trust me anymore?"

"What I'm saying is that you weren't with Dianna. Just after he hit a hole in one, Barry mentioned that she was taking Michael to the doctor at two o'clock."

Mum spun around to face the window. She flicked long brown hair over her shoulder and planted hands on her hips, agitatedly tapping one foot.

"Who were you with?"
There was silence.
"Who were you with, Anne?"
"I told you, Dianna."

Okay. So that memory didn't help. Like, at all. I quickly changed into my Hitchcock t-shirt and climbed into bed. But as much as I wanted to refrain from jumping to stupid conclusions, my mind was all over the place. Time and time again, my head sprouted out the most unhelpful question in the history of the universe.
Where the fuck was Levi?

Chapter Sixteen

Driving in a getaway car, imitating victory,
Breathe fresh air, you're unaware, fading into
memory,
    Memory.
    -MONDEZ, "Chaos"

I had a horrible sleep. I kept twisting and turning, entangling myself in the bed sheets. Levi didn't come back. Even by four in the morning, as I was scrolling through our previous text messages like they somehow held the key to his whereabouts, he still hadn't returned. At first I didn't call him. I tried to play it cool. I mean, it was no big deal. I was *so* the bigger person for not letting his absence affect me.

A fucking lie.

Half an hour later, terrifying images of Levi crumpled in a backstreet alley, covered in his own blood and gasping his last breath, appeared before my sleep-deprived eyes. I couldn't dial his number fast enough after that. Only his phone didn't respond. There wasn't even a dial tone. My cruel brain then filtered through even more images of Levi—now he'd been mugged before being left for dead in said back alley. So I slammed my phone back onto the side table, cursed out loud when my arm started hurting and angrily swapped pillows. His lingering scent calmed me instantly and I berated myself for not thinking of this idea earlier. At long last I fell into a troubled sleep.

By morning refreshments Levi still hadn't shown. Tension marred my every thought and movement which meant that even though my arm felt heaps better, once again I retained next to no information. It pissed me off. I was sick and tired of my continual inattention. I mean, how was I ever going to land the English coordinator role if I had nothing to show Serena? I gritted my teeth.

Aemon stupidly tried to ask me about Levi during the break but my death stare was enough to stop that line of questioning dead in its tracks. As much as I enjoyed seeing him again, his persistence in trying to win me over was unbelievably annoying. He even tried pressing his leg against mine during the next session. Thankfully, it was only a Q&A, so taking notes wasn't a requirement. Instead, trying not to stab him with my pen became the priority.

I purposely sat adjacent to the aisle in the second to last row when I at last felt Levi sit behind me. The skin on the back of my neck suddenly tingled so I knew it was him. But if I needed further proof, the collective sharp intake of breath from the women next to him was a freakin' strong indicator of his arrival. Aemon must have realized it too because he shifted even closer, if it was at all possible. I didn't move away.

As my body registered Levi's spicy cologne, I couldn't help but breathe it in. The fragrance immediately reminded me of what it was like to have my legs draped around him as he groaned into my open mouth. I internally kicked myself in the shins, reminding my quivering female parts that I was angry at the guy and not in any way, shape, or form, aroused. After all, Levi stood me up. All fucking night. And without a single word for God's sake. As the anger slowly descended, like an old friend returning home from a long vacation, I started to feel more like my old self again.

The phone in my lap suddenly vibrated.

Levi: **Tell that asshole to get the hell away from you or I'm gonna deck him. Oh & i'm sorry** ☹

I made no move to do what he'd asked.

Levi: **He's actually gonna die. Look, it all**

ended up taking heaps longer than we thought & then my phone ran out of battery

Still nothing.

Levi: **I'll make it up to you, i promise. Just as soon as i've disposed of the body**

I sighed.

Me: **Where were you?**

Levi: **The Ruby Room & then Katrina's**

Breathe, Grace. Just breathe.

Me: **You slept at Katrina's place?**

Levi: **Grace, it's not what you think**

I turned my phone off and then whispered something inane to Aemon. It wasn't funny but he laughed anyway and I was glad. A twisted part of me just wanted to hurt Levi in the same way he'd hurt me. I could have sworn I heard his muttered oath from behind.

When we broke for lunch, I told Aemon I needed some air and stormed out the conference room. Part way down the crowded hallway Levi grabbed my arm, stopping me. Turning around and ignoring the curious stares from the people pushing past, I glared up at him. "Let go of me."

"Not until we talk."

"There's nothing to say. You asked me to wait up for you and instead spent the whole fucking night with Katrina." I was panting with rage.

He stared down at me, his face impassive. "Are we going to talk about this somewhere private or do I have to pick you up and carry you there myself?"

I stepped closer. "You wouldn't dare."

"Try me."

There was a steely determination in his eyes I didn't trust, though my girly bits practically begged me to take him up on his threat. So I growled, nodded curtly and then stomped into an empty room off the main corridor.

Levi shut the door behind him and turned to face me. I stalked over to a disused table and plonked myself on its edge, arms crossed in front of my chest. As much as I wanted to remain furious at him, the fact that we were both now alone and he was so temptingly close seriously messed with my ability to stand without support.

Levi stood a few feet away. He looked tired and annoyed. "Look, I'm sorry, all right?"

I narrowed my eyes at him. "You're going to have to do a heck of a lot better than that, Levi."

He took a deep breath, raked fingers through his hair and stepped closer. "I'm sorry." His voice had softened. "Now I know this must look," he paused, "bad."

I snorted.

"But I swear to you, nothing happened."

I hmphed, while subconsciously loving the fact that he was moving closer still.

Levi took another step until our feet were almost touching. "The whole night, I just wanted to get back to you. But Dom is so fucking picky about the equipment he uses. He took *ages* going through Katrina's gear and then there was the issue with her foot pedal." He broke away, rubbing fingers over fatigued eyes. "Anyway, by the time that got settled it was past one in the morning, my phone had died and Finn was already asleep on the couch. So we all just … crashed there."

He tucked some hair behind my ear and I let him. "I missed you," he breathed, "and I fucking hated seeing you with that piece of shit in there. He was all over you." Levi paused. "Why'd you let him?"

I didn't say anything. I just shut my eyes and basked in the feel of his touch.

"Look at me." My eyes popped open. "How'd you sleep?"

"Terribly."

Levi wrapped me in his arms, face buried in my hair, breathing deeply. "Fuck, you smell good."

Clinging to him, I listened to the rhythmic beat of his heart as it reassured me of the truth in his words. After a few minutes, I disentangled myself from his embrace. "This whole trust thing is still new for me. I wasn't exactly the product of a happy marriage and Dylan was... Well, to say he was a lying, cheating asshole doesn't seem to really cover it." I sighed. "Just be patient, okay?"

He cupped my face with his hands, running a thumb over my bottom lip. "I'm not Dylan, love." His face hardened. "And I meant what I said about that fucker, Aemon. I'll beat his conniving ass if he ever touches you again."

Gazing up at him, I murmured, "I know."

We kissed then. Like always, it started off innocent enough but soon our breathing grew erratic and clothes, or the fact we were still wearing them, suddenly became an issue. Levi broke away and looked down at me, a wicked glint lighting his eyes. "Can I make it up to you *now*?"

I glanced at the closed door and then back at the gorgeous man rubbing himself up against me. "What, here?"

Levi smiled broadly. It was sinfully hot.

"Someone might walk in on us."

"It's worth the risk though, right?"

I smiled devilishly up at him, unzipping his fly. "Hell yes."

****

I was still grinning like a loon by the time Riley

and I walked into The Ruby Room later that night. Makeup sex with Levi at the convention center had been just as mind-blowing as the good luck sex we'd had in the shower. Even the you-spoke-a-word-with-a-vowel-in-it sex was awesome. So after those out of body experiences, I finally got dressed. For once I took minor pains with my appearance, meaning I applied a touch of mascara and lip gloss. I still refused to tame my hair, it was so much easier on both of us if I just let it be.

Levi left for sound check a few hours before, so Riley and I were going to make our way in together. When I met her in the hotel lobby she looked me over and exclaimed far too loudly for the old couple standing behind her that orgasms suited me. I glanced at my complete outfit in one of the gilded mirrors. I took in the black heels, skinny black jeans and my naughty-but-nice red top. Just imagine a corset but with tiny lace-capped sleeves. Strangely, what appeared most striking was the light in my eyes. They shimmered a bright emerald green, for once not clouded with doubt, scorn or pithy anger. Not bad. However, never one to dwell on my own appearance for long, I then shrugged one shoulder, grabbed Riley by the hand and pulled her out front to catch a taxi.

After we arrived at The Ruby Room, we grabbed some drinks and moved to a quieter section on one side of the music venue. The place itself was an old two-story theater built back in the twenties. It had a Promethean-style stage, red velvet curtains on either side, lighting set up on exposed rigging overhead and the walls had all been painted black. There was a huge cavernous space in the center of the room for patrons to mingle, dance or mosh, depending on the genre of music played. I guessed this was where countless rows of seating must have once stood. Farther back and on either side of the room stood high, round tables with metallic bar stools. And as Riley and I took a seat at one of those, the first band started.

"Where are the guys?" she yelled over the thumping drumbeat.

I scanned the room quickly but couldn't see them anywhere, so looked back at her and shook my head. For the remainder of the first set we sat back and watched. The band was loud and easily managed to fill the space with sound. They also had a small, dedicated following who stood in solidarity, nodding their heads in time with the music just below the stage. It was too early in the night for the alcohol to have loosened people up enough to really start moving, so like us, most were content to hang back and observe.

Two drinks later, the first band finished and the boys from Mondez walked out on stage. Riley and I quickly downed what was left in our glasses and moved to stand at the front with at least fifty other curious onlookers. When the opening bars of their first song started, I stood still and shut my eyes, breathing in the wave of heavy sound that hit and then surrounded me, slowly seeping through my pores. I opened my eyes and glanced across at Riley. She was smiling stupidly, staring up at the stage. She then looked across at me and shook her head in genuine bewilderment.

I knew exactly what she meant.

The music those guys created was *phenomenal*. It was unapologetically fierce, passionate, and yet soulfully beautiful. It was everything I never knew I needed until it was right there in front of me.

Just like Levi.

Sweet Lord in heaven.

The way he shredded his electric guitar and alternated between crooning or screaming into the microphone made me want to throw away my pill packet and have his babies.

Seriously.

The other boys were awesome too. Dom looked like the reincarnation of what every mother around the world warned her teenage daughters about. He played his instrument with a masculine sensuality that left no doubt about how truly skillful he was with those fingers, both on and off the stage. Finn's heavily tattooed arms struck the drums with a force that quite literally shook me. His playing was tight, ruthless and the sheen of sweat on his skin served as a blatant reminder of how powerful those muscles underneath truly were. Tyler's bass playing was equally as intense. He swayed forward and back, head bent down while staring past his strings as he rocked out deep, arcane chords. They left me craving more. Much, much more.

Riley grabbed my arm, shaking me from my daze and we let loose. With each song Mondez played, the crowd around us grew larger and larger, as eager people joined the group of us at the front. By the end of their set, we were completely surrounded by a moving, heaving, sweaty crowd, all having the time of our lives. When the boys played their last song, waved to the crowd and moved off stage, we all screamed, cheered and stomped our feet in mad appreciation.

"Drink?" I yelled across to Riley, wiping the perspiration off my face with my hand.

"*Drink*," she agreed, lifting her blonde hair off the back of her neck and fanning it with her fingers.

We pushed our way through the throng of people excitedly talking about the hot new four piece from Geographe Bay and I couldn't help but swell with pride. Eventually, Riley and I reached the bar. We quickly downed some water and then slowly sipped on our drinks, savoring the refreshing liquid when it slid down our throats. As I gazed across the rim of the glass, my eyes widened. There, striding purposefully towards me and with people instinctively moving out of his way like he was Moses parting the fucking seas or something, was an impossibly tall, ridiculously handsome man. His eyes were trained on me and the blue in them was dark, sultry, and full of promise.

I finished my drink and placed the glass on the bar behind me just in time for Levi to lift me up by the waist. I crossed my ankles behind his hips and wrapped my arms around his neck, drawing him close.

"I saw you out there," he growled in my ear, "dancing away like a wild little thing. It took everything I had not to jump off stage and take you in the middle of that crowd."

"So, three orgasms since lunch aren't enough for you now?"

"When you look and move like that? No. They're really not."

I grinned before leaning in and kissing him passionately. No doubt we were drawing a crowd of our own by essentially mauling each other with our lips and tongue. I mean, there had been a queue for the bar four people deep just before. But I didn't care. It was awesome.

"Get a fucking room already."

Levi and I tore ourselves away from each another and looked over at Dom. He was standing next to Riley, his arm casually draped across her shoulders with a look of mock disgust on his face. She looked anything but comfortable. Whether it was from having to witness her best friend practically ravage a man in front of her or the proximity of Dom's sweaty armpit to her face, I wasn't entirely sure.

"People don't want to have to look at that shit.

We're trying to have a good time here."

I glanced at Levi and rolled my eyes. He grinned and gently put me back on my feet.

"Nice outfit." He leaned down and murmured in my ear, "I'm looking forward to peeling that off you later."

I flashed him a smile and subtly brushed my ass up against him. Levi's hold on my hips suddenly tightened which just made me smile even wider.

"Now that your dick's back in your pants, Casanova, let's go watch Adrift play, huh?" Dom retracted his arm from Riley and strode off towards the mass of people already facing the stage. Riley, Levi and I followed behind him and as we made our way through the dense crowd, a short man with dark hair raised his beer glass to Levi in salute. Levi nodded back but kept walking.

"Who's that?"

"Jimmy, Katrina's band manager."

The spot we finally found was far back from the stage. I mean, the set had already started, the venue was almost at full capacity and the majority of those people were hurling themselves at each other thanks to the mosh pit down front.

Katrina's band was unbelievable. Their overall sound was equally as merciless as the two bands before them. Her voice was powerful, wickedly husky and on stage it looked like she finally belonged somewhere. Gone was her awkwardness and embarrassment. In its place stood a confident, talented musician who, wearing ripped jeans, a tight black tank top and her brown hair loose, looked every bit a rock star in the making. Adrift was going to be massive. There was no doubt about it. And the way Katrina continuously pointed her microphone at the crowd so they could scream song lyrics back, meant that everyone had an incredible time.

When Adrift's set finally finished, everyone looked completely exhausted. Bedraggled mosh participants, entirely covered in sweat and smelling fucking awful, dragged their sorry asses past us on the way back to the bar. Shirts were ripped, mascara was smudged, hair was plastered to faces and necks. They all looked like a bunch of zombies caught up in an unexpected heat wave.

Riley and I gaped at each other. Not only were we completely awestruck by Adrift's ferocious performance but Katrina somehow looked even more stunningly beautiful up on stage than she did in real life. And we both freakin' hated her for it. I mean, if it hadn't been for Levi never letting go of my hand, I would have thrown my head back, cursed the gods and left. Katrina was that damn good.

Dom turned around, his eyes equally as spellbound. "Cold shower anyone?"

Riley and I glared at him while next to me, Levi chuckled.

****

I awoke the next morning to the sound of Levi talking softly on his phone. I checked the time, it was before seven. I was surprised he was even awake let alone lucid enough to actually speak to anyone. After finishing the call, he remained in the next room. Curious, I threw back the covers, stepped over last night's clothes that had been lovingly peeled off by the man in question and slipped on my Hitchcock t-shirt.

Levi was so lost in thought he didn't notice me padding towards him. It was only when I stepped in between his open legs and ran my fingers through his hair that he put his phone down on the coffee table. Before that he'd been absentmindedly running one finger over

273

the black screen, deep in thought.

"Hey," I murmured.

Levi slowly ran his hands up my legs and I shivered. "Hey yourself, kitten. What are you doing up so early?"

"I was going to ask you the same thing."

He pulled me down onto his lap, buried his head in my hair and breathed in deeply. "Katrina called."

I leaned back, staring at him.

"She said Jimmy wants to meet the Mondez boys over breakfast this morning."

"Why?"

Levi shook his head, but there was something in his eyes that bothered me.

"You're not telling me something." He looked away. "What is it?"

But he remained silent.

"Okay then, how long do you think the meeting will go for?"

"No idea."

"So you won't be at the conference this morning?"

"Probably not."

I stood, annoyed. "You're fucking impossible, Levi."

But he grabbed my fingers and pulled me back down. After pushing some hair out of my eyes and tucking it behind my ear, Levi murmured, "Look, I've got my suspicions but I don't want to say anything until I know for sure."

I glared at him.

His gaze softened. "When I find out what's going on, you'll be the first person I tell. Promise." He leaned forward and gently pressed his lips to mine. Using the effect he had on me to unfair advantage was seriously …

working.

"Fine," I sighed.

****

Levi didn't show up to the conference at all that day. It was official, he was a rubbish student teacher. And when Aemon tried to agree with me, I almost punched him in the face. Though, I didn't exactly hang around for the closing address either. A motivational speaker so wealthy he owned his own freakin' island was going to present. As far as I was concerned, someone who made a living off the insecurities of others was a complete asshole. I wasn't going to waste my time. So it was decided, Aemon and I were going to drink for the remainder of the afternoon. We were going to ingest so much alcohol that by the time Levi remembered my damn phone number, I would be too drunk to care.

As soon as we walked into Oblivion, I saw him. Levi was seated on one of the low couches. He was leaning forward, elbows resting on his knees, staring down at the beer in his hands. It looked like he was in the process of picking off the label and if the carnage on the bottle was anything to go by, he'd been at it a while.

I turned to Aemon. "Look, I'm really sorry—"

"But you don't want to drink with me because you're in love with someone else?"

"Yeah, something like that," I murmured.

Aemon gave a sad, wistful smile. "Can't blame a guy for trying. You're more than worth it, Grace."

"I'm really not."

He pulled me into a hug which I fervently hoped Levi didn't see. "You are, you just can't see it for yourself." Aemon pulled back and looked at me. "You're strong, loyal, intelligent. You know your own mind." He paused, his eyes roving over my face. "And you're so beautiful. If Levi ever forgets, you know where to find me."

I smiled.

"Let's keep in touch this time, huh?"

"I'd like that. Take care, Aemon."

"You too, Grace."

With that, he left.

I moved over to Patrick. As soon as he saw me, he poured a healthy shot of whiskey into a short glass.

"Thanks." I gestured to Levi. "How long has he been like this?"

Patrick shook his head, wiping the bar with a dishrag. "He came in just after twelve but has been doing *that*," he stopped and pointed to the mess Levi was making all over the table, "for at least an hour."

I nodded, grabbed my whiskey and strode over to Levi. After dumping my gear on the floor and clearing enough space amongst the tattered remains of the sticker label to put my own glass down, I sat next to him. Reaching across, I dug up Levi's phone and pushed the button at the base. His screen lit up.

"Well, would you look at that," I exclaimed, "it *does* work." I then swiveled around in my seat to face him and waited expectantly for a response.

And waited.

And waited.

After fifteen minutes of silence, I'd had enough. "Okay, what's going on?"

Levi's eyes briefly flicked to mine before shifting back to the bottle in his hands.

I grabbed it out his grasp and thumped it down on the table. "Well?"

But he still didn't say anything.

"So help me, Levi, if you don't say something soon I'm going to *really* lose my shit."

He took in a deep breath and then exhaled slowly.

"Jimmy likes our music. He reckons that with the right manager, we could do really well."

"Okay."

"He wants us to record a full-length album."

I shook my head. "Look, I'm struggling to find the negatives here. I mean, isn't that what you want? To record?"

Levi continued as though I hadn't spoken. "He's got exclusive access to Sunset Studios."

I nodded.

He stared at me. "It's here in Melbourne."

"Oh." I swallowed. "How long would recording take?"

"At best? About a month, but most likely six weeks."

"When would you start?" *Why am I even asking?*

"Next week."

I leaned back in the chair, suddenly glad for the extra support. "It's a great opportunity," I murmured.

We were both silent.

"But what's the rush? I mean, why do you have to start so soon?"

"Jimmy wants the album finished by the start of summer."

My blood stilled.

"He asked us to support Adrift on their east coast tour." Levi paused before continuing, "He says that a full-length album available for audiences would help keep the momentum going."

"Momentum?" I repeated faintly.

"After the tour, he reckons that more opportunities will come up. He says we need to be ready."

I could feel bile rising in my throat.

"And he thinks relocating to Melbourne is the best

way to do it."

Jesus fucking Christ.

Wrapping arms around my middle, I murmured, "What do the other guys think?"

He shook his head. "Well, Tyler and Finn grew up here, so they wanna come back."

"And Dom?"

"Dom is…" He paused. "I dunno, Dom's been a bit weird lately. But Mondez means everything to him and he's wanted to be a famous guitarist ever since he was a kid. So I don't think he'd pass up this chance."

"What about you?" I whispered.

Levi stared at his fingers. "If you'd asked me that question two weeks ago I wouldn't have given it a second thought. I mean, *fuck*, making a living playing music?" He shook his head. "That's a dream come true. But now," he looked at me, blue eyes anguished, "now I'm not so sure."

I shut my eyes. But instead of seeing black, flickering images like those on a movie screen appeared. They were of the only other time my heart had been ripped apart this badly.

I ran through the myriad of cream-colored corridors and finally, after what felt like hundreds of wrong turns and dead ends, found the correct nurses' station. Ever since I'd answered that dreaded phone call, I hadn't been able to move fast enough. Ironically, it felt like time had purposefully slowed down, sucking and dragging me backward while I desperately fought my way forward.

"Please," I gasped between ragged breaths, "I'm here to see Dad, I mean, Peter Thompson. Where is he?"

The nurse behind the desk looked up from her manila folder, brown eyes kind. "Has the doctor been in contact with you?"

I nodded my head, tears cascading down my cheeks.

"And do you have a support person coming?"

"My sister," I sniffed, "should be here soon."

"Good. Your father has just come back from ER and is now in room B15. Do you know where that is?"

I shook my head.

"Let me take you there, sweetheart." She stood and moved around the desk, gesturing for me to follow.

I needed Dad. I needed to see his loving smile, feel his comforting hug and hear his reassuring voice. I needed him to tell me that everything was going to be all right, that my world would continue spinning because he was still going to be a part of it.

When we finally stopped outside the closed door to his room, I stood as though frozen. I simply couldn't open it and go inside. If I did, then it meant all of this was real. I'd tried to ignore the doctor's words and even whispered a damn prayer to whoever was listening up above. But it was useless. As much as I wanted to pretend otherwise, deep down, I knew the truth. Dad had had a heart attack. He was in intensive care. He wasn't going to wake up.

Or come home.

I stared at the floor, my vision blurring the speckled patterns on the linoleum from yet another onslaught of tears.

The nurse put a gentle hand on my shoulder, rubbing me reassuringly. "Your dad's resting. He's been given some medication to make him more comfortable. Why don't you go in and talk to him? He can still hear you."

I looked up at her, completely lost. "What do I say?"

She smiled sorrowfully. "Goodbye."

Chapter Seventeen

Traded my heart, it's faded, my heart,
And I still hurt.
Traded my heart, it's faded, my heart,
And I'm still hurting.
-MONDEZ, "Hating the Silence"

Levi and I spent the rest of the evening in our hotel suite. We already knew the room service menu by heart so we ordered our favorite dishes. Not that I could taste anything. The only flavor my taste buds seemed to register was fear.

Genuine fear.

Clearly, I didn't have the stomach for it since most of my meal was left untouched. And by the look of Levi's full plate when he finally pushed it away, he wasn't much of a fan either. After we discarded our dishes, Levi moved the couch to face the window. He put on some of his heavy instrumental music and we lay there, nestled in each other's arms, staring up at the night sky.

Okay, so I was glaring at it more than anything else.

And berating the bejesus out of it.

Stupid twinkling stars in the stupid black sky, looking down at me like my life isn't about to be completely annihilated. Fuck you stars and sky. Fuck you all.

Needless to say, neither of us talked much. Well, not out loud anyway. To be honest, we both knew that words weren't going to make a difference. They weren't going to change the fact that I was getting on a flight to Perth tomorrow morning and Levi wasn't.

Dom called earlier, the other three bandmates had

decided to give the whole making-a-living-out-of-music thing a go. While listening on the other end, Levi had dejectedly nodded his head in agreement and I hated the fact that he appeared so underwhelmed with the incredible opportunity they just received. So I put on my happy face. Granted, it was dusty and virtually moth-eaten but despite those minor impediments, I talked incessantly. My ridiculous tirade was mostly about how the next six weeks were going to be the best of his life. Hell, I even tried to believe some of the bullshit that came out of my mouth.

It didn't work.

Neither Levi or I felt any better after my absurd pep talk. If anything, it solidified how difficult maintaining a long distance relationship was going to be. I mean, waiting six weeks to see him again was going to be tough, but after that he was only coming back so he could pack all his stuff and then move to fucking Melbourne.

How the heck are we going to survive that?

To be fair, I truly didn't blame the guys for their decision. If I were them, I would probably want to do the same thing myself. I just freakin' hated how this was going to be the last night Levi and I would be together in … almost forever. My heart ached.

Literally.

The incessant pounding pain made me hold on to him tighter and Levi kissed the top of my head, murmuring, "We're gonna make this work, kitten."

I didn't reply. Seriously, what was there to say?

He lifted my chin until our eyes met. "I'm not saying it'll be easy, but we're gonna do this. We'll be fine."

I smiled weakly.

"You don't believe me, do you?"

Shrugging one shoulder, I said, "Six weeks is a long time. I mean, look at what happened between us in just two."

Levi sat up, pushed me backward, and gripped both of my shoulders with his strong hands. "Don't you dare give up on us, Grace. I'm going to call every day to remind you that what we have is worth fighting for."

I searched his eyes, uncertain.

"Every fucking day. I mean it."

I couldn't help myself. At long last I whispered the nagging doubt that had been plaguing me ever since we left Oblivion two hours ago. "It could all fall apart. What if our love isn't strong enough?"

He cupped my face, blue eyes desperate. "It has to be. What other alternative do we have?"

I closed my eyes, not even wanting to entertain that terrifying possibility and felt a lone tear trickle down my cheek.

The remainder of the night was spent making love. On the couch, the floor, the bed, anywhere with a remotely flat surface really. I knew Levi was trying to show me how integral I'd become to his life and just like his music, his unrestrained passion surrounded me entirely, reverberated through me, completed me. I reciprocated his intensity with my own brand of declaration. With each movement, sound and utterance, I told him how much my world revolved around him. How he had become the most vital part of my life.

When dawn finally broke, we hadn't slept. Instead, we found ourselves with exhausted limbs entwined, internally pleading with time to stand still.

It wasn't fucking listening.

The seconds and minutes ticked by, each sounding like the death toll on any future happiness we might once have had. So I cuddled in closer and Levi caressed one side of my face as I pressed my ear directly above his heart. Its reassuring beat comforted my own fitful one and helped me think. My mind drifted back to two years ago.

"I still don't understand, Dad."

The sun had slowly slunk behind the horizon and darkness crept across the sky in its place. However, the evening was mild and the waves were calm. Dad stood and brushed the sand off his suit pants before rolling them back down to where they belonged. "What don't you understand, Grace?"

Like always, we'd talked about whatever was on our minds. Tonight it was Mum. It truly surprised me when Dad said they would've been married for thirty-one years had they still been together. And despite the fact that he seemed reconciled with it all, I sure as hell wasn't.

I stood, not bothering to wipe the sand away from my shorts, it would all fall off eventually. "Well, you say you loved Mum more than anything in this world, right?"

"Right."

"Despite everything she put you through."

"Yes."

I stopped, not sure how to proceed without sounding like the worst daughter of all time.

"Spit it out, Monkey."

I half-smiled, half-grimaced at his openly expectant face and then hastily blurted, "Then why didn't you fight harder? You know, to save your relationship. Why didn't you make her stay? Make her see reason?"

Dad smiled sadly down at me and I suddenly felt incredibly naïve despite not really knowing why. "But surely that's what love is, isn't it?"

I crinkled my forehead, confused. "What? Not

fighting for someone?"

He shook his head. "No, love is being able to set them free. And if they don't come back," he shrugged, "I guess they never belonged to you in the first place."

I sighed.

Somehow I had to get out of bed. Somehow, I had to function like a rational human being long enough to shower, dress and pack. Before leaving the man I'd fallen madly in love with. Surviving the next six weeks and beyond was going to be impossible if the mere thought of moving into the next room was enough to start me bawling. I scolded my overactive tear ducts and slowly sat up.

And then cursed fate.

She was an absolute bitch.

How was it that today of all days, the man in front of me looked so damn beautiful? The bed sheet pulled back with my movement and it dropped away from him, revealing an unbelievably muscular upper body. One arm was resting behind his head, the other possessively clasped my hip and his intricate tattoos stood out starkly against the white mattress. But what really forced me to stop and take notice was Levi's face. From the very start, those blue eyes had seen through my facade. They had dared me to stop hiding and in turn I'd told them my deepest, darkest secrets. That mouth had kissed every inch of my body, savoring its taste like a rare delicacy. It had shaped the three monumental words I never thought I would believe in ever again.

I leaned forward and gently brushed my lips against his. He buried his hands in my hair, drawing me closer and our kiss deepened. I stroked his face and he groaned, it was the growling one I loved. However, I pulled back, looking down at his heated gaze. "I need to get ready."

"No you don't."

I couldn't help but smile. "Yes I do. I've got a job to go home to, remember?"

"Quit."

I sat up, staring at him. The man was deadly serious.

"I mean it. Quit. Move here with me." His voice lowered. "I need you, kitten."

"I need you too," I whispered, "but I also need to work."

"I'm not asking you to stop working, I'd never do that." His eyes lit up. "What if you transferred here? There are heaps of high schools in Victoria to choose from. You could even ask dickhead Aemon if his school is hiring. That asshole would fucking jump at the chance to have you working with him."

I stayed silent, letting him talk, knowing that he had to get this off his chest.

"We could find our own place, make our own life together, you know? Make a real go of it."

Hearing him say this out loud was enough to make my heart break even further. But it was impossible.

"And what about Riley? Or when you go on tour? Think about it, Levi. You're asking me to move away from the only family I have, to a city I barely know, all the while knowing that you won't even be around for most of it."

He looked away.

My voice softened. "Honey, you know it's not fair to ask that of me."

He stayed silent.

"Though it doesn't change the fact that being apart from you is slowly going to kill me every fucking day. It just," I shrugged one shoulder, "has to be done."

Levi refused to speak any further, so I sluggishly got out of bed and dragged myself to the bathroom. At least the water from the shower would disguise my tears.

Half an hour later, I was fighting with the zipper of my suitcase. Cursing under my breath, I was about to pick it up and hurl the fucker into the next room when from behind me I heard a soft, "Kitten?"

I turned around and was momentarily taken aback by the seriousness of Levi's expression. He took a deep breath and then deliberately handed me his notebook. "These are my notes from the conference. I hope they help."

Smiling up at him, I murmured, "Thank you."

He tucked a stray strand of hair behind my ear. "You might want to get rid of a few pages before showing Serena though."

I flushed, remembering the diagram he'd drawn of us on Wednesday. I shook my head sadly. God, it seemed like a lifetime ago now. It had been just before Katrina arrived, before she officially turned my life to shit.

"When you get on that plane, or any other time you start questioning what we have and whether it's strong enough to survive living apart," he looked at me meaningfully, "for now at least. I want you to open up this notebook and read the first page."

"Why?"

"It's a song I wrote. It came to me just after we first met and I've been working on it ever since."

I nodded, gripping it tightly.

"I'll even fly home and sing you the lyrics if you ever forget."

I narrowed my eyes at him. "Do I look like the kind of girl who wants to be serenaded, Levi?"

He grinned. "Then don't fucking forget."

Smiling back, I tucked the notebook safely into

287

my handbag. No doubt I would be needing it soon.

Very soon.

Like, once I stepped into the elevator soon.

After checking the time on my phone, I sighed. "I've got to go. Riley's meeting me downstairs in five." I rolled my eyes. "She hates it when I'm late."

"Want me to walk you?"

Shaking my head, I murmured, "I'd rather you stay here. I wouldn't be able to leave if you came with me." I smiled. "Besides, the view's much better this way."

Levi quickly looked down and chuckled, realizing he'd managed to put on some jeans but had forgotten everything else. When he looked up at me again, his eyes instantly sobered. "I'm coming home for a few days before we go on tour. We're going to spend that time together, I promise."

"Can't wait."

Levi stepped closer, wrapping his arms around me before whispering in my ear, "I love you."

I held onto him, feeling like I was slowly being pulled under water and he was the only thing stopping me from drowning. "I love you too."

Riley took in my distraught expression as I entered the lobby. She immediately dumped her bags, ran straight over and hugged me, murmuring, "Thank God I changed my flight." Taking me by the hand, she led me back to her luggage and we walked through the hotel doors for the final time.

We hardly spoke a word after that. Mostly because the only sound that came out of my mouth whenever I opened it was a choked sob. So the taxi ride to the airport was insanely quiet.

The first class plane seats and glass of whiskey on board did little to numb the thumping pain originating from where my heart used to be. As a distraction, I pulled out Levi's notebook and surreptitiously breathed in the pages. I could smell him. That spicy scent of his pierced yet another gaping hole inside me. This time it stabbed my very core. It felt so overwhelmingly agonizing that I honestly thought I was going to split in two. Great, I was once again a hollow shell.

God, I missed him.

I glanced across at Riley. She was reclining in her seat, eyes closed, listening to her iPod. It sounded like Mondez was on her playlist and I briefly wondered how she'd managed to get a copy of their EP. Thankfully, she'd missed my notebook sniffing and consequent disintegration of inner body parts, so I finished my drink before carefully opening the first page.

There it was.

Levi's creative scrawl dominated the lined paper in that endearingly egotistical way of his. I took my time and traced with an index finger the loops and flourishes where his pen blatantly defied convention. A small smile reached my lips as I imagined the number of times he'd raked fingers through that disheveled hair of his as he wrote. I took a deep breath and began to read.

Retribution

I know a girl and her secret was told
The Devil came and it pleased him so
But you don't want me singing about this, do you?
Well listen close
I speak the truth, you gave your heart and it's living proof
Of a hurting soul demanding retribution
Retribution, retribution...

Well I know your fear but I'm built from hope
I saw you reading, so words I wrote
Your beauty in the darkness cut right through me
I dried your tears, your face, your hair
I held you close and I kept you there
And from my kiss I breathed your retribution

Retribution, retribution…

Kitten, it's been done before
We've felt this hurt and we've said, "No more"
I was also broken before I found you
And I've seen you screaming in the dark
And trust is not a scarring mark
This is love and it's a healing retribution

Retribution, retribution…

Now is the time that you need to know
What we reap is what we sow
Pair your faith with mine and I will prove you
Remember my eyes, they looked at you
Your own stared back and they felt it too
And every gaze we held was retribution

Retribution, retribution…

Maybe all this time apart
Will tell the truth that's in my heart
My life is only full when it is with you
So don't you cry when I'm not near
There's no darkness, just feel me here
This is love and it's a healing retribution

Retribution, retribution…

By the time I'd finished, I had to shove my fist in my mouth to quiet the racking cries. Riley's eyes popped open and she stared at me, shocked. She took out her headphones and rubbed my back, murmuring soothing words until I managed to get myself back under control. That girl was unbelievably empathetic at the best of times, it truly felt like she was living this agony along with me. I was so glad she was there and once the tears dried I rested my head against her shoulder. After all, without Levi next to me, she was all I had.

****

The remainder of the weekend proved uneventful. I moped around the apartment glaring at my phone, willing it to ring. It did. Each day Levi called, and we'd both try to cover up our obvious dejection with useless banter. Well, until it was time to hang up. That was when we'd fall silent. It was useless complaining though. I mean, sure we both hated what was going on, but I couldn't exactly quit my job and leave Riley, just like he couldn't quit the band and leave Melbourne. So we were stuck pretending to be fine for the other's benefit, all the while knowing it was a flimsy smokescreen.

Still, hearing his voice was like a balm and for a short while at least I felt peaceful. However, soon after I was back to battling that frayed temper of mine. Anything that moved or breathed seemed to feel the brunt of it. Except Riley, of course. Similar to hearing Levi's voice, being near her made my anger ease.

Slightly.

That old sense of disconnection came back too. The one where I felt like I was the only person glaringly out of place in Geographe Bay. It was beyond irritating, so by the time Monday morning rolled around, I was seriously questioning why the hell I'd even returned in the first place.

As I dragged my sorry ass into our office, Carli spun around on her chair exclaiming, *"Grace, I've missed you, babe.* How was—" But she broke off mid-sentence when I burst into tears. Jumping up, she draped an arm around my shoulders, concern written all over her freakishly healthy features. She walked me to my chair. "Oh my God, what happened?"

I collapsed onto the hard seat and carelessly dumped my gear on the floor, completely miserable. Okay, I might have been in serious melodrama mode by this stage but in my defense I was genuinely hurting. Shaking my head, I remained silent. There was no way I could even begin to voice what I was feeling, let alone do any justice to the magnitude of what I'd experienced the week before.

No words came close.

So after drying my eyes I half-smiled to Carli, pulled out my laptop and started reading some emails. She left me to it until I exclaimed, *"Fucking hell."*

Carli raised a questioning eyebrow and I scowled. When more words finally came, I verbalized every last expletive known to man. Well, that was before muttering, "Serena wants a damn meeting." I checked the time in the top right-hand corner of my laptop. "Now."

Carli's smile was sympathetic as I angrily collated the combined notes from last week's conference.

Half way across the quad, I stopped. It suddenly hit me. I didn't want the English coordinator role anymore. Hell, I didn't want any of this shit.

Honestly.

It all meant fucking nothing because the only person I wanted was in another freakin' state, desperately wanting me too.

What am I even doing here?

I groaned and then attempted to take in a deep, calming breath. It was uneven and far too shallow to do any real benefit but it was the best I could do under the circumstances. I just had to get through the next six weeks. After that, Levi and I would figure the whole mess out together and go from there.

I started walking again. Man, I really wasn't in the mood for an interrogation from Serena. Don't get me wrong, I resented her power trips most days, but today? I gritted my teeth. There was a very strong possibility that today's meeting could end in a homicide.

"Take a seat."

I shut the door to Serena's office with more force than necessary and strode forward, flouncing down onto a nearby chair.

Serena completely ignored my theatrics. She looked at me from behind her monstrous desk and began, "I received an email from Levi earlier this morning." She paused, expecting me to say something.

Only I didn't.

Couldn't.

The mere sound of his name was enough to constrict my chest. And it did. To the point where lack of airflow made my vision swim.

Unperturbed, she continued, "I understand he's deferring his studies until further notice due to," Serena looked down, reading off her laptop screen, "'a unique opportunity in the music industry.'" Looking up at me again she asked, "Is that correct?"

I nodded my head, still struggling to breathe.

"Levi then states," again, Serena read from her laptop, "'it is unfortunate that I will no longer be under the mentorship of Grace Thompson. She has been an absolute pleasure to work with.'" She raised an eyebrow but I stared back, blank faced. Serena continued, "'Grace has left a lasting impression on everything I think, say and do. She taught me that in order to live a fulfilled life, loyalty to one's dreams takes precedence.'"

I snorted. Yeah, because that's what we were both feeling right now—fucking fulfilled.

"'And I hope Geographe High School recognizes how truly remarkable she is. I do, and I am eternally grateful for being able to work closely with her while attending the National Independent Schools Conference in Melbourne.'"

My eyes welled up until I couldn't see, so I dropped my head.

Damn it, Levi.

Tears stained the crumpled pages of the conference notes in my lap.

"You two must have worked extremely well together."

My tear-filled gaze met her direct one.

"Well?"

"What are you really asking me, Serena?"

For the first time since I can remember, her face softened when she looked at me. "What happened?"

Taken off guard by her unexpected kindness, I spoke honestly. "Levi's in a band, a talented one. While we were in Melbourne an old friend of his asked Mondez to play a show as a favor." I narrowed my eyes at her. "This all happened outside of work hours, mind you."

A wry smile crossed Serena's face.

"Anyway, his friend's band manager liked their sound and asked them to support an upcoming tour over summer." I shrugged my shoulders. "They need to record a full-length album before then so…" My voice trailed away. "He stayed and I came home."

"I see."

"I doubt it."

Serena sighed. "I'm not completely blind, Grace. Your feelings for one another were glaringly obvious from the very beginning."

For some reason, Serena's last comment seriously pissed me off. So I stood, scowling down at her. "And what would you know about other people's feelings, *Mrs. Nebril?*"

"Grace—"

"Fucking nothing, that's what you know about them." I turned and stormed towards the door.

Just as my hand touched the cool metallic knob, Serena whispered, *"Monkey, I'm sorry."*

Her voice was barely audible over my self-righteous angst. But I heard her. And those words truly conflicted me because now I didn't know whether to leave or stay. She hadn't called me that in a long time and suddenly realization dawned. *Oh my God.* I stared at her over my shoulder, dumbfounded. "You planned the whole thing, didn't you?"

My sister had the decency to blush.

"The first class plane tickets, the limousine, the hotel room—" Letting go of the door handle I turned to face her squarely. "You organized it all."

"Yes."

I rubbed my forehead, trying to piece it all together in my mind. "Hang on, what about Sophie's illness? Surely you didn't have a hand in that too?"

"Ah. Well, that was a happy coincidence."

I stared at her, stunned. *"But why?"*

She looked at me for a moment, her green eyes impenetrable. "I already told you, because I'm sorry. I'm not proud of my actions, Grace. I threw away the only family I had. So when I saw you and Levi together, I wanted to help. I wanted to see you happy again even if you never knew I was behind it all."

I genuinely didn't know what to say to that, so turned my back and once again made to leave.

Just as I grasped the door handle she called out, "By the way, Dylan and I are getting a divorce. Thought you might like to know."

I stilled, completely shocked at what she'd just told me. I looked down at my hand, my knuckles were white.

It all came to nothing.

All the hurt and deception didn't even have a happy ending. There was nothing to help justify their selfish actions. Shaking my head, I murmured quietly, "Then I'm sorry too. Oh, and consider this my notice. I'm finishing up at the end of the term."

I walked out of her office, never once looking back.

Chapter Eighteen

You've left me waiting,
You've left me waiting,
Fading away.
-MONDEZ "Isn't it Obvious?"

I honestly tried to get my shit together. Over the next five and a half weeks, I truly did. I worked, drank, read, sat alone at the beach, hung out with Riley. I did everything I normally would have done had I never laid eyes on Levi Mondez. But it was impossible.

Misery followed me everywhere.

And a miserable Grace was a horrible housemate. Riley got so fed up with my moping that she even put together a health and fitness plan for me. One that didn't involve whiskey for breakfast on weekends. She printed it off and stuck it to the fridge. Apparently, day one involved yogurt with summer berries and a five-mile jog.

Day two could kiss my ass.

She gave up on me after that. Though I did attempt to mask my unhappiness and even went for a brisk walk with her. Once. While I staggered up what was surely the biggest fucking sand dune in all of Western Australia and she spouted encouraging catch phrases like, *"You've got this, G,"* I even bit back a scathing retort. It was my way of saying sorry.

Levi still called. Every day we found it harder and harder to pretend that our long distance relationship was enough for our malnourished hearts. It sure as hell wasn't enough for our rampant hormones. We even tried phone sex, only my phone died just as I was about to come. Didn't even bother finishing myself off after that. Just had a cold shower instead.

The only glimmer of hope that kept me from

completely losing my mind was Levi's promise. He was coming home. We would finally see each other on my first day of summer break/unemployment and I was so freakin' excited. Okay, so my excitement was somewhat mollified by the fact that we'd be together for a grand total of two days. Then he was going to be on tour for three months and after *that*…

I had to stop torturing myself.

Anyway, I was dealing as best I could with the whole situation. Well, until I received a phone call that changed everything.

"Hey, kitten."

"*Levi.*"

He gave a deep, throaty chuckle and I had to sit down on the couch before I collapsed in a swoon. "How's your day been?"

"Long. Boring. You?"

"Long. Frustrating."

"Why frustrating?"

Levi took in a deep breath and exhaled slowly.

I gripped the leather armrest. "Honey, what is it?"

"Recording hasn't gone well. Turns out, I can't concentrate. All I think about is how much I fucking miss you. Jimmy and the boys are pissed."

"Levi, I can't get in the way of this recording, I'd never forgive myself if I did. Please don't tell me I'm screwing it up for you."

He sighed. "It's just, the more I try to focus, the worse my music gets. I've got no patience, my timing's off, I'm playing like shit." He groaned. "I just wanna see you, hold you, bury myself inside you. This whole situation is fucking killing me."

"Me too," I murmured. "But at least we'll see each other this weekend. That's something, right?"

Silence.

"Levi?"

"Kitten, I'm so sorry."

Silence.

"We've still got three more tracks to go."

Silence.

"Grace?"

I hung up, threw my phone across the room and then burst into tears.

I didn't even bother going to work on the last day of school. To be fair, the kids had already left and it was just a staff lunch complete with farewell speeches for myself and other employees whose contracts had finished. I didn't even know the names of half the people I worked with, so I seriously didn't give a flying fuck if they were coming or going.

Riley was on an early shift at the hospital and had already left by the time I dragged my sorry ass out of bed. I wandered into the kitchen to make myself some coffee. A strong one. After that phone call from Levi, I'd switched my phone off. I refused to think about anything other than the bare essentials, like breathing. And drinking. It didn't work though. Sadly, my head refused to switch off quite as easily. So I hadn't slept all night because my father's words from two years ago kept circling my brain.

Over and over again.

"Love is being able to set them free. And if they don't come back, I guess they never belonged to you in the first place."

I was being selfish.

I had to set Levi free. I was trying to keep him all to myself and it was jeopardizing his future career. Music was something he was ridiculously good at. He was destined to do it. And by coveting Levi, I was also threatening the childhood dreams of the other guys too. I couldn't do that to them. Hell, I couldn't do that to Levi. I loved him too much.

Fuck, this is going to kill me.

After drinking my coffee and staring at the black screen of my phone for a good forty minutes, I finally plucked up the courage to call him. He didn't answer. There was no use even pretending I wasn't relieved. So instead, I read a chapter from *The Adventures of the Final Problem,* then took a deep breath and called again. Still no answer.

I scrubbed my face with my hand and sighed. He must have been recording, which meant his phone was on silent. So I did what I never thought I would do. Ever.

I messaged him.

Once I pushed the send button, I felt like such a fucking coward. Hiding behind a text message made me no better than Dylan, and that truly disgusted me. So I turned my phone off again, crawled into a ball on the couch and cried for the rest of the day.

Riley arrived home later than usual that night. Which was lucky because it meant I could shower, dress and pretend I wasn't the most chickenshit person of all time. When she stepped into my room, I was propped up against the headboard of my bed, freshly changed, eyes only slightly puffy and reading. I looked up. "*Wow*. Girl, you look sensational."

Riley patted her hair. "Really? You're not just saying that?"

"Hell no."

She'd had her long blonde hair cut into a short, wavy bob with a cute fringe. It looked freakin' awesome. Riley smiled and something glinted as it caught the light.

"Hang on." I stood up and moved closer. "Riley Sears is that a *nose ring*?"

She flushed, looked down and mumbled, "I've

always wanted one."

"Love it."

Her head shot up. "You do?"

"Absolutely. Do you?"

"Yeah." She smiled again.

"Not sure your mum will though."

Riley stuck her chin out defiantly. "Fuck her."

Grinning broadly, I clapped my hands. "Bravo, it's about time you took ownership of that sexy body."

Riley looked at me closely. "G, what's wrong?"

I moved away.

"You're doing that thing where you're upset but trying to hide it. I don't understand. For the last month and a half, you haven't bothered hiding your emotions at all."

I walked back over to the bed and sat. Staring at my hands, I mumbled, "I broke it off with Levi."

She gasped and moved to sit beside me. "What? Why?"

"It was never going to work. Had to admit it sooner or later." Riley looked at me, shocked, so I continued, "Levi told me their recording wasn't going well. They're running behind schedule and still have more tracks to lay down. Which means..." I sighed. "I won't be able to see him before he goes on tour."

Riley's short bangs swayed softly as she shook her head, blue eyes sympathetic.

I stood and began to pace. "I mean, for a relationship to work you actually have to catch up at some point, right?" I turned to face her, hands on my hips. "Six weeks has felt like a lifetime and now he's leaving for another three months." I threw my hands up. "Christ, and after *that* he's moving to goddamn Melbourne." I stopped, panting. "I was kidding myself. We were never going to work." My voice lowered. "I just wish it didn't hurt so much."

Riley was quiet for a minute, her manicured nails tapping against one leg. I looked at them warily. Just as she was about to say something, her phone rang.

I rolled my eyes. "Seriously, Riley? They're your ringtone now?" She smiled sheepishly and answered the call, walking out to the kitchen. By the animated chatter on the other end, I assumed it was Brea, so turned my attention back to the book I'd previously discarded.

A few pages later, Riley reentered. She stood in the doorway with a look on her face I didn't trust. Not one bit. "Well, you can either stay here in your bedroom and wallow in self-pity or you can take charge of your life and go live it."

"You've been reading motivational books again."

Riley's eyes narrowed. "What'll it be?"

"Self-pity."

They narrowed further.

I sighed. "We're going to The Hole, aren't we?"

"Yes, we are." She rummaged through a pile of clean laundry at the foot of my bed and threw me some clothes. "Now get dressed."

I smiled gently. "Love you, Riley."

She returned my smile. "Love you too. Now hurry up, we're leaving in twenty minutes."

When we entered The Hole two hours later, I screwed up my nose in disgust. "God, this place stinks."

Riley laughed, grabbed my arm and led me through the dense crowd of people standing between us and drunken salvation. "You'll forget all about the smell after a few drinks."

While waiting to be served, I tried to ignore the sense of déjà vu that washed over me. I mean, this very spot was where Levi and I first met. To my left was where I first heard Mondez play, and on my right was the booth where the whole world slipped away and it was just us … eye-fucking each other. Good times.

I sighed.

"Girls, so glad you made it. What can I get you?"

"Hey, Brea." Riley smiled. "Can I have a beer? And G here," her eyes slid to mine, "needs a double whiskey, neat."

I tried to smile back at her, though was pretty sure it came off as a grimace.

Noticing my pained expression, Brea popped the cap off Riley's beer, set it in front of her and then poured me a triple instead. She winked.

I smiled. A genuine one this time. "I owe you one."

"Try to enjoy yourselves, okay?"

We both nodded. "Will do."

Brea waved our cash away and moved on to the guy standing next to me. He showcased a decadent array of facial piercings. They were truly impressive. We then elbowed our way to an empty booth and sat. The first band was just finishing up and to be honest, I didn't mind their sound at all. This whole live rock music thing had grown on me.

Damn it.

We sat in silence. I stared down at my whiskey and Riley started picking at the label of her beer. *Shit. Not her too.* Her evident restlessness only added to my current sense of foreboding. In my peripheral vision I saw her eyes, they darted between me, her drink and the stage. After squaring her shoulders, she turned to me, cleared her throat and declared, "G, I need to tell you something."

I slowly unclasped the glass and placed my palms flat on the sticky wooden table. "Sounds serious."

But she didn't get a chance to respond, because

the opening chords of the next song began.

I froze.

My eyes widened.

My breath caught.

And I almost burst into tears.

I'd heard that melody before. Fuck, I even knew the lyrics. *It's my song.* The one Levi worked on in the hotel room after our first argument. I recognized the beautifully soulful cadence of his acoustic guitar and the anguished emotions it conjured. I knew what this meant. I'd hurt him. Again. And that's when I heard his voice.

I know a girl and her secret was told
The Devil came and it pleased him so
But you don't want me singing about this, do you?
Well listen close
I speak the truth, you gave your heart and it's living proof
Of a hurting soul demanding retribution

Retribution, retribution...

"Levi?" I stumbled out the booth, blindly pushing my way through the confused people crowded in front of the stage. They'd been expecting a song significantly heavier than this one and stood about awkwardly, staring at each other. If it had been under any other circumstance, I would have found their bafflement hilarious.

I roughly shouldered past the last person standing in my way and there he was.

Oh my God.

Levi was singing Retribution. Levi was *here* singing Retribution.

Holy fuck.

Dressed in dark ripped jeans, combat boots and a figure hugging faded green t-shirt was the love of my life. He sat perched on a bar stool, guitar resting on his lap as he sang. And he sang about me. Him. Us. I quickly looked heavenward, breathing out a heartfelt '*Thank you*' to Dad.

When the final echo of his vocals ceased and the last strum of his guitar faded, Levi looked up, blinded by the stage lights. The crowd erupted. I wasn't at all surprised. For some reason this man worked pure magic wherever he went. Audiences loved him if he played heavy music or something altogether sweet. Levi stood, stowed away his instrument, jumped off stage and purposely searched the crowd until he found what he was looking for.

Our eyes locked.

I forgot to breathe.

He slowly made his way towards me.

And he looked as angry as all hell.

Yikes.

At last, Levi towered over me. "A text message, Grace?" he ground out.

I gulped.

"You wanted to break up with me by fucking *text message*?" His jaw was working overtime and I couldn't remember ever seeing him this angry.

What the heck happened to the guy on stage a few minutes ago? I wanted that version of Levi back. He was much less … terrifying. I cautiously took a step away from him. When there was enough distance between the two of us, I yelled, "Well, I tried calling, but you didn't answer your damn phone."

He stepped closer, speaking dangerously low. "And do you wanna know why?"

"Not really."

His eyes narrowed.

I kept moving backward, not at all liking the fury blazing unchecked in his gaze, until I finally bumped against solid brick. Levi sauntered up to me then, an evil smile on his lips. He deliberately put one hand on either side of my head, leaning in so close I could smell the sweat on his skin.

I couldn't help it. Closing my eyes, I breathed him in.

Heaven.

"I didn't answer my phone, Grace, because *I was trying to record three fucking songs in two fucking days.*"

My eyes popped open. "You were?"

He nodded harshly. "A promise is a promise, I don't break them. And neither do you." He stepped closer again, until our bodies were flushed with one another. I looked up at him.

Shit.

"Levi—"

He grasped my face. "We're not over, Grace. We'll never be over. You know it and I know it." He leaned forward and I could feel his warm breath on my face. "Now admit it."

I stood frozen.

He bit my bottom lip. "Admit it."

I didn't move.

He licked my mouth. "Admit it."

Nothing.

His lips scorched mine. "Damn it, kitten. *Admit it.*"

I wavered, at last breathing. "We'll never be over, Levi."

"Thank fucking Christ." And with that ragged exhale, his lips crashed into mine. We were lost. Completely. I moaned, reaching up to tug his hair. He groaned, reaching down to grip my ass. Our tongues fought, our teeth clashed, our hearts realigned. It wasn't a pretty kiss, by any means. It was desperate, fierce and powerful.

Ours.

When we eventually broke apart, and mercifully with clothes still intact, Levi's breathing was heavy.

"You forgot, Grace. You forgot the meaning behind my lyrics. You said you wouldn't, but you did."

"I didn't forget," I murmured, placing my hands on Levi's chest, wholly aware of his erratic heartbeat. "For once in my life, I wanted to put other people's happiness before my own. That's all."

"That's all? *That's all?*" Levi moved away and started pacing in front of me. "Do you have any idea what you put me through?" He stopped, raking frustrated fingers through his hair and I couldn't help but smile. "Christ, woman. I left two guys, a producer, and one very pissed band manager in the middle of a fucking recording. All to fly back here and get it through that thick, beautiful head of yours—"

I grinned.

"What's so damn funny?"

"I should be the one who's pissed, not you."

He raised incredulous eyebrows. "You're not serious."

"Sure am."

Levi cursed under his breath, crossed arms over an obscenely broad chest and muttered, "Let's hear it then."

I narrowed my eyes at him, stepping in close. "You, Levi Mondez," I poked one of his pecs, "serenaded me."

His eyes grew wide.

I poked him again. "I told you *never* to serenade

307

me."

He stared in disbelief.

"Don't fucking do it again."

Levi flashed a lethal smile, growled, and then claimed my lips once more.

When we finally came up for air, he murmured, "Let's go somewhere quiet. We need to talk and then we need to fuck."

"So romantic," I muttered.

His eyes darkened. "Six weeks, kitten. I've been waiting six goddamn weeks to put my cock inside you and own that sweet pussy until you scream my name. And then you show up to a fucking bar wearing *this*." His fingers gripped the soft material of my short summer dress bunching it between his fingers. "You're not even wearing a bra," he groaned. "If we don't get out of here soon…" He swallowed. "Fuck it. I'm not waiting any longer."

I shivered. My female parts cheered wildly before emphatically waving a placard that read, *Sex in Public isn't a Crime, it's a Fucking Privilege*. Pretty sure they were onto something there.

"C'mon, let's go." He grabbed my hand and began leading me to the exit, but I stopped.

"Hang on, what about Riley? I'm not going to leave her here by herself."

"Do you trust me?"

"You know I do."

"Good, she's fine."

I raised an eyebrow at his abruptness but for once remained silent. He tugged my hand again and I grudgingly followed.

We left The Hole, crossed the main road and made our way down to the beach. As my feet sank in the cool sand, I broke free of Levi's grasp, bent to take off my strappy sandals and wiggled my toes. Straightening back up again, I then stared at the horizon. The night was clear and I could see the twinkling lights of fishing trawlers glimmering in the distance. Their brightness starkly contrasted against the inky black water, looking like floating stars in a rippling sky. I smiled.

At last, I felt centered. Calm. Sure. Not of the future, I had no idea what it would bring. And definitely not of the past, I wasn't at peace with that just yet. But I was sure of this moment. Oh boy, was I sure of the man standing beside me.

I breathed deeply.

Levi inhaled too before sitting and pulling me onto his lap. He kissed me again, it wasn't desperate like last time, it was lingering, sensual, full of promise. It made my toes curl and my heart skip a beat. It was everything I could ever want.

Sigh.

Levi pulled away, murmuring huskily, "Come on tour with me."

I blinked.

"I love you, kitten. The past month and a half has been … it's been completely fucked. Shit just doesn't make sense without you. I need you by my side, not just for three months—*always*. Say you'll come away with me. Please."

I looked down. More than anything in the world I wanted to say yes. Especially since I came to the same realization five and a half weeks ago.

Levi was right, life only made sense when it was spent with the person you loved. It just sucked I loved two people to distraction, though in two very different ways. I shook my head, bereft. "I'm sorry, Levi."

"But why?" His voice was desperate.

I remained silent, the black hole where my heart

309

used to be started imploding on itself.

"Is it because of Riley?"

I nodded. "I can't leave her. I just … please don't ask me to."

"You won't have to."

My head shot up. "What do you mean?"

He smiled. "She's coming too."

I stared at him, dumbfounded.

He tucked some hair behind my ear. "Think about it. If you and Riley are a package deal, then she has to come. It's simple."

I snorted. "Levi, this whole situation is anything but simple."

"Well, I've already run the idea past the boys and they're cool with it. Besides, Jimmy would bust my balls if I didn't bring you back since my music turns to crap without you." He grinned. It was that cajoling smile of his, the one which turned my brain to mush.

Focus, Grace.

"What about after the tour?"

Levi turned serious. "We'll sort it out, kitten. Either you move to Melbourne, or I'll stay here. I don't give a fuck. I just wanna be wherever you are, that's the only thing I care about."

All of a sudden, I felt the faint flicker of a heartbeat. "I want that too, Levi. So much it hurts."

He stared at me for a long moment. "So we're agreed. We're gonna make this work." He paused before asking, "Do you want us to stay in Geographe Bay?"

I considered his question carefully before answering, "No, not really." I held up my hand. "Just give me a second, I need to think this through in my head first."

Levi nodded and proceeded to pepper soft kisses along my jaw.

I'm sure I could find an equally satisfying teaching role somewhere else. After all, educators are needed around the globe.

His tongue followed the curve of my ear and I shut my eyes.

I'm not tied to Geographe High anymore. To be honest, some geographical and emotional distance from my sister would be awesome.

He moved to my neck and nibbled his way down.

Yes, I'd miss Carli, but she would understand. In fact, after my zombie-like state last term, she'd probably pack my bags and drive me to the airport. Hell, she might even get a speeding fine on the way.

His hands kneaded my breasts as he kissed the length of my collarbone.

Can't think. Oh. My. God.

I officially melted.

Okay, where was I? Oh right, the future. Well, I'd have to convince Riley to quit her job, move interstate and then start her life over. For me.

Shit.

I pulled away. "Levi, I can't. It's too much to ask Riley."

Levi's eyes slowly regained focus and his hands dropped to my waist. "So we're gonna live here, hating it, for her?"

I shrugged one shoulder. "Guess so."

He grinned wryly. "Man, you two are fucking stubborn." His hands slowly and deliberately slid up my arms.

I tingled but tried to disregard it. "What's that supposed to mean?"

But he ignored me as deft fingers slipped under the spaghetti straps of my dress. "It's a good thing she already said yes."

"Bullshit."

He pulled the flimsy material off my shoulders. "Well, on the condition that you relocate too." My dress fell away, pooling to my hips and I shivered at the touch of his calloused hands against my heated skin. "And you've already agreed to that."

I tried to stay focused as his fingers teased my hardening nipples. "But what about her work?" I breathed, back arched, eyes closed. "You think she's just going to give up nursing to come on tour and then move to Melbourne?"

I could feel Levi grinning as his mouth took over from the sweet torment of his hands. "Something tells me she's due for a career change," he murmured against my breasts.

"How the hell do you know more about my best friend than I do?"

He straightened up, gazing at me, his laughing eyes soft. "You're so adorable when you're angry."

I shot daggers at him. "I swear to God, Levi—"

"All right, all right." His fingers trailed across my cheek. "Dom told me."

"*Dom*? What the fuck does he have to do with it?"

Levi leaned forward and sucked on my bottom lip. My growing frustration immediately subsided and I moaned quietly, burying my hands in his hair.

"I love that smart mouth of yours, kitten," he purred, hands traveling down the length of my back. "Drove me fucking insane the first time I heard it. I love your fire, your heat, your goddamn everything." As we kissed his hands slipped around to cup my ass, quickly repositioning me until I sat astride him. "I'm gonna do sweet, dirty things to that mouth right here on this beach."

Shuffling forward, I felt the warning bulge in his

jeans as it rubbed tantalizingly against my soaked panties. I swore again. It echoed in the darkness.

"You ready for me, Grace?" His hands deliberately slid up my outer thighs, pushing my dress higher with each stroke. I could feel the sea breeze brush against my near naked body.

Sweet God. Tonight I'm actually gonna see the face of heaven.

Before I lost all sense of reason I tugged his hair, pulling his head back, demanding his eyes on me. "But what about Dom and Riley?"

Levi groaned from the pressure, kissed me deeply and I lost myself in the sensual rhythm of his lips and tongue for longer than I anticipated. Much longer. It was always going to be like this, I could tell.

As his hands moved to possessively clasp the curve of my hips, he breathed softly, "That's a story for another time, kitten."

And with a growl, he pushed me down onto the sand.

Completing me.

The End

www.leepiperauthor.com

LEE PIPER

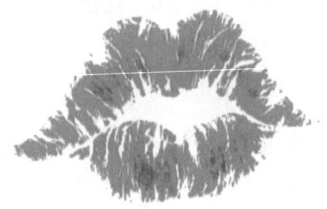

EVERNIGHT PUBLISHING ®

www.evernightpublishing.com